W9-ARG-981

CHANDLEFORT

Also by David Randall

Clovermead: In the Shadow of the Bear

Margaret K. McElderry Books

DAVID RANDALL

CHANDLEFORT

IN THE SHADOW OF THE BEAR

MARGARET K. MCELDERRY BOOKS

NEW YORK LONDON TORONTO SYDNEY

Margaret K. McElderry Books
An imprint of Simon & Schuster Children's Publishing Division
1230 Avenue of the Americas, New York, New York 10020

Book design by Greg Stadnyk
The text for this book is set in Cochin.
Manufactured in the United States of America
2 4 6 8 10 9 7 5 3 1
Library of Congress Cataloging-in-Publication Data
Randall, David, 1972–
Chandlefort / David Randall.—1st ed.
p. cm.—(In the shadow of the bear)
Summary: Now almost thirteen, Clovermead uses her shape-shifting powers to protect her family, friends, and herself against a figure from the past who tricks her by playing on her sympathy.
ISBN-13: 978-0-689-87870-1 ISBN-10: 0-689-87870-2 (hardcover)
[1. Fantasy.] I. Title. II. Series: Randall, David, 1972– . In the shadow of the bear.
PZ7.R15638Ch 2006
[Fic]—dc22 2005029558

To my uncle and aunt,

John Herman Randall III and

Lois McConnell Randall,

with all my love

Acknowledgments

As always, my editors, friends, and family have read, commented upon, and improved this novel; I am grateful to Kathryne Alfred, Emma Dryden, Simon Lipskar, David Rosen, Sarah Sevier, Christopher Welser, Ariane Randall, Francis Randall, Laura Randall, and, always and especially, my wife, Laura Congleton. This novel changed shape more often than I had at first anticipated, so a number of my readers took the time to comment on two very different manuscripts. To them I am particularly grateful.

CONTENTS

Note

The currency of Queensmart includes pennies, shillings, and sovereigns. There are twelve pennies to a shilling and twenty shillings to a sovereign. A penny is worth around $20, a shilling is worth $240, and a sovereign is worth $4,800. Pennies are sometimes sliced into halves and quarters, but most transactions below the penny level depend on barter or credit.

The Lands of Lady Moon

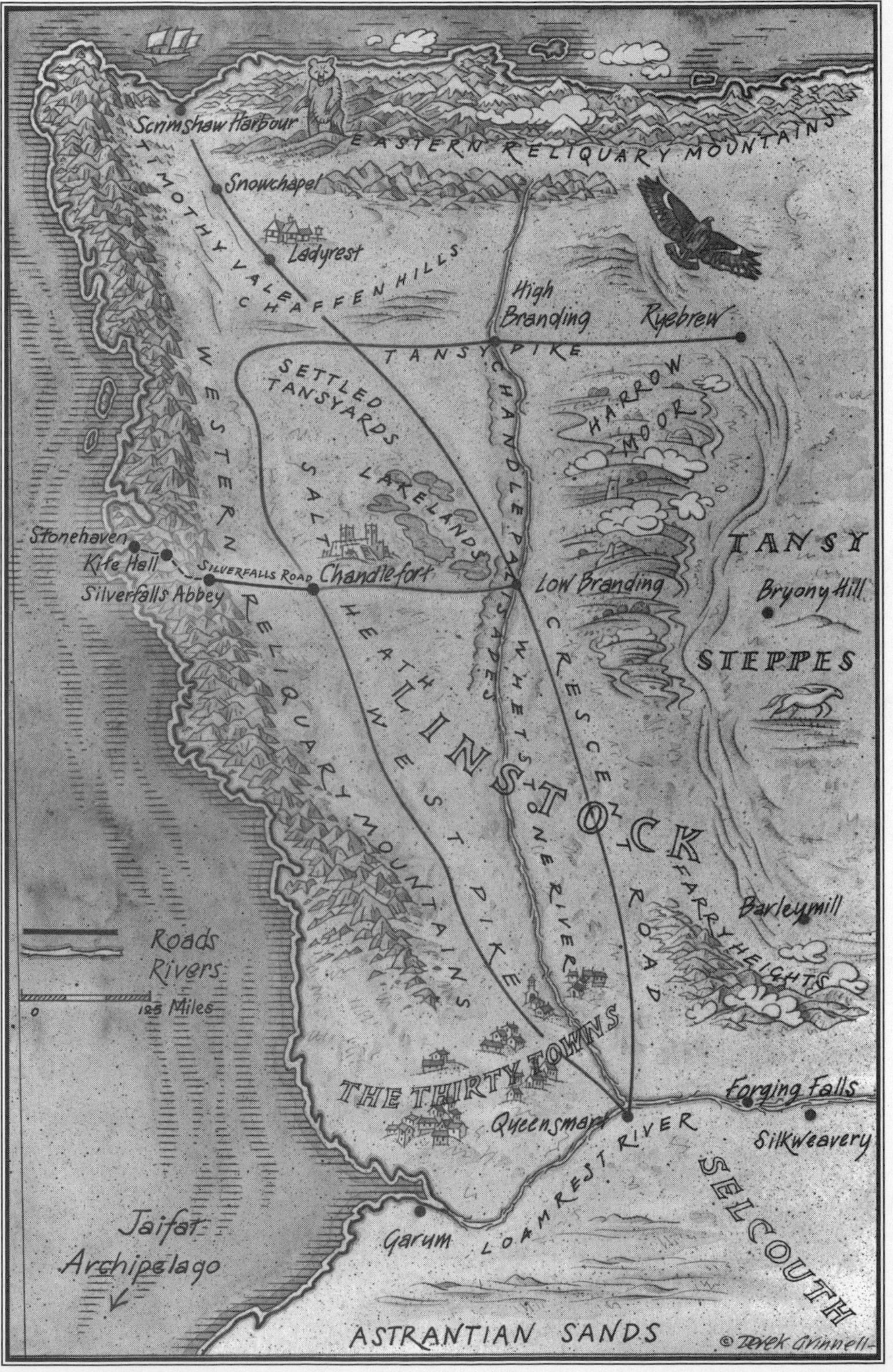

Chapter One

FIGHTING PRACTICE

"I AM GOING TO THUMP LADY SARABAND SCONCE," said Clovermead Wickward. Her hand swiped at the air as she paced back and forth along the wooden floor of her father's room. Her fingernails had turned into bear-claws, and small tufts of golden fur sprouted from the backs of her hands. "She is the most infuriating person I have ever met. In dance class today she said—oh, you have to hear the way she said it." Clovermead lifted her nose into the air and gave herself the cultivated drawl of a Chandlefort lady. "'Demoiselle, it is true that at a ball you will sometimes need to step on your partner's toes. Nevertheless, this should only happen as a deliberate choice. Please be more careful.'" Clovermead clawed the empty air. "She didn't lower her voice or anything. Everyone in class could hear her!"

"She is the image of cruelty, Clovermead," said Sorrel solemnly. "I would have words with her, if I did not remember how heavily you landed on my toes when I attempted to teach you that Tansyard dance last winter. My toes whisper to me that perhaps your dance teacher has a point."

Clovermead glared at Sorrel—but then Sorrel

slipped his feet from his boots and wiggled his toes accusingly at her, and she couldn't help giggling. Her claws shrank back into her hands. Her fur faded and left bare skin behind. "Your toes don't know what they're talking about. I didn't step on them that hard."

"My toes are quite attached to their opinion. It will be difficult to persuade them otherwise." A late-morning sunbeam lit up the windowsill where Sorrel had curled up. He yawned, stretched, and teetered on the edge. He was smartly dressed in a canary-yellow shirt with white sleeves, which proclaimed him a new-fledged cadet of the Yellowjacket Guards, and he had even tied a yellow ribbon around his long brown hair. Still, the crisscross blue tattoos on his cheeks were unmistakable signs that he had been raised with the Hordes that roamed the Tansy Steppes. He swallowed the end of his yawn and slipped his feet back into his boots. "Lord Wickward, do you also have sympathy for the Lady Saraband?"

Waxmelt Wickward flicked a stray speck of dust from his dresser. It was spotless already, but he cleaned it from nervous habit. "Stop making trouble, Tansyard. My sympathies are for my daughter alone." He smiled comfortingly at Clovermead—and shook his head bemusedly as he realized that her blue eyes were nearly even with his brown ones. "Why, you're almost as tall as me now, Clo," said Waxmelt. "I bet you'll be taller by the end of the summer." In the last six months Clovermead's cropped yellow hair had grown back to her shoulders, and she had shot up two inches. Her beige linen trousers were only a few months old, but they were short on her already. As for her short-sleeved sky-blue shirt—Clovermead's shirt exposed a faded rope of scar tissue that ran along the inside of her arm from her shoulder to the palm of her hand.

Last winter Clovermead had put one of Lord Ursus' bear-teeth into her arm and let it drink her blood and crumple her flesh. The scar remained. A little later she had put the bear-tooth in her mouth and it had ground away the upper left canine. When she laughed, anyone could see the gap. Clovermead could bend her elbow and move her shoulder without difficulty, and she could talk without a lisp, but there was no hiding the visible signs that she had once let Lord Ursus possess her. Not that Clovermead tried to hide them: She had worn short-sleeved shirts ever since the onset of the broiling Chandlefort summer, and she laughed as often as ever.

"I can't wait to finish growing. I'll wear boots with heels three inches thick, just to rub it in, and then I'll lean over, pat you on the head, and ruffle your bald spot," said Clovermead. She reached up to stroke Waxmelt's thinning hair. He shied away and anxiously felt at the back of his head. "Don't worry," said Clovermead. "You look handsome and hirsute. If you were a ram, all the ewes would sidle up to you and bleat that there wasn't a ram in Linstock with such curly wool."

"You aren't helping," Waxmelt grumbled. He looked sidelong at a mirror hung on the wall. Save for the thinning hair on the back of his head, his appearance was the same as ever—small and slender, graying and goateed, with lines of laughter and worry on his face. His clothes had changed more than his features: Lord Wickward of the Vale, ennobled by the curious kindness of Lady Cindertallow, dressed in far better style than he had as an innkeeper. Right then he wore a plain gray wool shirt and trousers, but the clothes were of a lordly cut and quality.

"I'm glad Father sympathizes with me," Clovermead continued. She directed a killing gaze at Sorrel, which he ignored with great aplomb. "Really, Saraband's dance class is awful. I hate learning how to dance Chandlefort-fashion with ten-year-olds who don't come up to my shoulder and snigger at me when they think I can't hear them. I hate that I never get better. And I especially hate the way Saraband plasters this kind look on her face when I make a mistake. She talks to me slowly and clearly, like I'm the village idiot, and then she shows me precisely what I should have done. She's always graceful and perfect, and she makes me want to—" She clawed at the air again.

She could picture Saraband vividly. She was some sort of cousin to Clovermead, but they didn't resemble each other at all. Pale, raven-haired Saraband was lovely; slender Saraband always dressed in the height of style; tall Saraband moved gracefully. Saraband's endless perfections would have been more tolerable if she were eighteen, or even seventeen—but she was just sixteen! It was the *just sixteen* that made her insufferable. Clovermead was almost thirteen already, with none of Saraband's graces.

Just once I'd like to see one hair on her head out of place, thought Clovermead. *Let me see that, Lady Moon,* she prayed, *and I wouldn't mind her half so much afterward.*

"Milady asked Saraband yesterday if I was ready to dance at the Midsummer Ball," Clovermead continued out loud. "I didn't want to give her a chance to say anything, so I said, 'I dance like a clumsy goat. I'm the laughingstock of the class and I'd just embarrass myself.' Then Saraband said, 'The Demoiselle exaggerates, Milady, but I believe she is correct to decline to dance.' Ugh! 'I believe she is correct to decline to dance!'" Clovermead swiped at a stray pillow, which Waxmelt hastily pulled out of the reach of her claws. "She was so polite, but she let Milady know just how awful I am. I don't much mind not being able to dance at the Ball—I knew anyway I shouldn't go—but she is such a *snob* about dancing! I've had enough dance classes with Saraband to last me a lifetime."

"Weary is the head that wears the crown," intoned Sorrel. "Furrowed is the brow of she who will one day rule all Chandlefort. Happy is the simple Tansyard who wanders where he will upon the Steppes, concerned only with purloining horseflesh from his neighbors." He winked at Clovermead. "Shall we ride together from Chandlefort and leave this torturous life behind us?" He turned to Waxmelt. "Do you wish to come with us, most noble Lord Wickward? When I was on guard outside Milady's chambers this morning, I heard you exchange some sharp words with her. You looked as peeved as Clovermead is with Lady Saraband when you emerged from Milady's room."

"Were you really angry with each other?" Clovermead asked Waxmelt anxiously. "I hope you didn't argue too much. I want you to get along with Moth—with Milady."

Clovermead still had trouble calling Lady Cindertallow her mother. She had only discovered half a year ago that she was not really Waxmelt's daughter, Clovermead, but Demoiselle Cerelune Cindertallow, daughter of Lady Melisande Cindertallow, the sovereign of Chandlefort. Clovermead's real father had been murdered before she was born. Waxmelt was in truth an embittered servant of Lady Cindertallow who had stolen Clovermead away as a baby and fled from Chandlefort to Timothy Vale. There he had started a new life as the master of Ladyrest Inn and raised Clovermead as his own child. When Clovermead had discovered who she truly was and realized that Waxmelt had deceived her all her life, she had been so overcome with anger that she had let Lord Ursus possess her. Yet eventually she had realized that she could not stop loving Waxmelt.

Lady Cindertallow detested the man who had stolen Clovermead from her, but she let Waxmelt stay in Chandlefort, so as not to alienate her newfound daughter. It was a strange life for Clovermead in Chandlefort, with a father who was no father and a mother who was still a stranger.

"I try to be civil to her," said Waxmelt. Now frustration crept into his voice. "But I just can't keep silent when I see how badly the servants are still treated here. I keep hoping I can convince Milady to improve their lot, but she just gives me a look of cold contempt when I speak to her, like I was an animal that had stood up on my hind legs. This morning she said, 'You presume too much on the safe-conduct I gave you for Clovermead's sake.' Then she left the room before I could say another word. Dear Lady, if she does that to me again, I will—"

"Challenge her to single combat, Father?" asked Clovermead. "I suggest sharpened skillets at thirty paces."

"Saucepans are better," said Sorrel. "In Yellowjacket training I have learned that they are particularly good for close-quarters fighting."

"One in each hand," said Clovermead. "I've been reading *The Astrantiad* in Milady's library—it's a wonderful book, all about the battles between Sir Tourmaline and the Reiver Prince, and their long rivalry for the heart of Queen Aurette—and in the sixth sally, Sir Tourmaline fights a sand dragon with a knife in either hand. You ought to do the same, Father. I'll bring sand and sprinkle it in the Throne Room."

"I sympathized with *you,* Clo," said Waxmelt reproachfully.

"On my part," said Sorrel, "it is disinterested mockery. I give it to any Wickward I find, father and daughter alike."

"I'm just teasing you a little, Father," said Clovermead. "Now that I'm here in Chandlefort, I see they do treat the servants as badly as you always said. I wish I knew what to do. Milady's very stubborn!" Quick panic suddenly flitted across her face as she looked out the window and realized how high the sun had risen in the sky. "Sorrel, we should have left for fighting practice half an hour ago."

Sorrel cursed in Tansyard and leaped from the

windowsill. "Please excuse us, Lord Wickward. I fear we have enjoyed your hospitality for too long. Oh dear, I shall receive another demerit. Somehow they accumulate on me like lint when I am in Clovermead's company."

"I don't get them except when I'm with you," said Clovermead indignantly. She kissed Waxmelt on the cheek and rushed to the door. "Bye, Father!" Then she and Sorrel were sprinting through Cindertallow Castle to the Training Grounds.

Cindertallow Castle consisted of five rectangular floors. The top floor was Lady Cindertallow's: Wide windows in her rooms gave her a panoramic view of the town, the fields, and the Salt Heath. The floor below was the Cindertallow Nursery, whose rooms had been built for the twelve daughters of the ninth Lady Cindertallow. Clovermead had one large room all to herself; most of the rest were used by the high nobles of Chandlefort when they were not at their own castles. Waxmelt's little room was by the staircase at the far end of the floor. It smelled of bleach, and Clovermead suspected that it had been a linen closet not so long ago.

Beneath the Nursery lay the State Floor, where the business of governing Chandlefort took place. Lady Cindertallow's Council Room and Hall of Justice were there, and so was the Chamber of Alms, where nuns in Chandlefort service dispensed relief to the poor. At ground level was the Ceremonial Floor, where the Ballroom and the Banquet Hall flanked Lady Cindertallow's enormous Throne Room. Lords, visitors, clerks, and supplicants entered the Castle through great bronze doors that led from the front courtyard to an atrium in front of the Banquet Hall.

The Servants' Floor was at the very bottom, half-buried underground and extending far beyond the perimeter of the Castle above. Its rough-plastered corridors were cut out of the rock, lit by torches even at midday, and provided with fresh air by thin shafts leading down from the surface. The Castle servants came to work through a stone ramp that descended from a back courtyard to the Servants' Floor, and the servants left by it when their work was done. Waxmelt had been among them twelve years ago, before he had stolen Clovermead from Lady Cindertallow and fled from Chandlefort. Scattered around the underground labyrinth were chilly wine cellars stacked ceiling-high with bottles, cabinets filled with earthenware and silver, laundry rooms filled with soapy clothes, and everything else needed to keep the Castle well fed, luxuriant, and clean.

It was only a hundred feet from the back door of the Servants' Floor to the Training Grounds gate. Once Clovermead and Sorrel had received two demerits from the duty officer, they scurried toward the sand-strewn quadrangle of open ground next to the Chandlefort stables, where the other cadets had already finished their exercises and begun to fight. Clovermead quickly donned a helmet, leather armor, and a blunted metal practice sword. She began to sweat, as the summer sun of Chandlefort beat down relentlessly upon her. Clovermead glanced up at the wall that ran alongside the Grounds, where lords and ladies idled along the parapet, and saw a slender figure in a white dress approaching them. It was Saraband. She lifted her parasol politely to Clovermead and drifted closer.

"Just what I need," Clovermead muttered to herself. "Now she can see Sorrel beat me at swordplay, and she'll know I can't dance *or* fight." Clovermead's swordsmanship had improved steadily during her training with the cadets, but so had Sorrel's. He still trounced her in most of their bouts together.

Sorrel and Clovermead hurried through their stretching exercises, saluted one another with their swords, and began to fight. Clovermead could feel Saraband's eye on her from above, and she just knew that Saraband was judging her as critically as she did in dance class. It was very difficult to concentrate. Sorrel's blade lunged toward her waist, and she barely parried it in time. Clovermead growled. She was very angry all of a sudden, and she wanted to lash out with claws and fangs.

Clovermead had torn Lord Ursus' bear-tooth from her mouth and crushed it, with the aid of Lady Moon herself, but she still could turn into a bear. Indeed, when she got upset, it was hard not to turn bearish. Clovermead didn't think her shape-shifting ability had anything to do with Lord Ursus, but she couldn't say exactly where it did come from. It was a mystery that perplexed and discomfited most Chandleforters. After all, Lord Ursus remained at war with Lady Cindertallow, and his army of enslaved bears and worshipful human bear-priests might march north from his capital in Garum to Chandlefort at any point: It was unnerving in those circumstances to realize that

Chandlefort's Heir Apparent could turn into a bear indistinguishable from Chandlefort's fearsome enemies. But Clovermead didn't worry too much. She knew how she had felt when she was possessed by Lord Ursus, and it was nothing like what she felt now when she became a bear.

I will stay human, Clovermead told herself. *I'm practicing sword-fighting, not paw-bashing. Control yourself.* She tried a particularly subtle feint against Sorrel that she had been practicing for the last week. He evaded it, even more subtly. Clovermead growled again. Sorrel was grinning now, and Saraband gasped with admiration at his skill, which was peculiarly annoying. *What's the use of being subtle and restrained?* Clovermead asked herself in frustration. *Sorrel will beat me, sooner or later, and Saraband will applaud him.* She didn't want to fight Sorrel anymore. She wanted to leap onto the parapet and snap her jaws at Saraband. *She'd be so startled, she wouldn't know what to do!* Clovermead thought gleefully. Then she smiled. *I'll bet I can startle you, too, Sorrel. I won't turn into a bear, but I'll fight like a bear, good and angry.*

It was easy to let the bear into her mind. *That's the prettiest girl in Chandlefort standing in front of me,* she told herself. *That's Saraband.* Then growling rage filled up her mind and she wasn't precisely thinking anymore. She leaped forward and smashed her blade against Sorrel's, then followed up with a shower of blows to bludgeon his arm into numbness. She didn't plan ahead, just let her arms and legs move by exhilarating instinct. Sorrel tried to counter her with the controlled and thoughtful blows he preferred, but this time they melted before

Clovermead's assault. Six months of endless drills had made lunges and parries an instinct in her muscles; her sword was as natural to her as her claws. Sorrel's blade shook in his hand, and he stumbled away from Clovermead. One by one his practiced stratagems failed him. He slammed into the back of the Training Grounds and desperately parried her assaults with his back to the wall.

Sorrel's eyes grew wide and wild, and he began to gasp a ragged chant in Tansyard. His sword shifted in his hand and it became a glittering snake that struck out against her like something alive. Now there was no control or thought in his fighting either, and he began to match Clovermead's blows. He forced her away from the wall and back to the sand-strewn center of the Training Grounds. His chant was a war cry, an ululation, a savage desire for blood and death. They fought as desperate animals, and his strength matched her strength, his speed her speed. Their swords clashed together one final time—and both blades spun to the ground. Sorrel and Clovermead stared at each other's empty hands. Then all at once their knees buckled and they collapsed to the sand.

The bear only slowly receded from Clovermead. When she could think once more, she found that she had a stitch in her side and her lungs were heaving. She swam with sweat underneath her leather armor; its cotton padding was drenched. Her limbs were limp. *But so are Sorrel's,* she thought with satisfaction. The Tansyard was just as exhausted as she was.

"So that is what it is like to fight a berserker," said

Sorrel at last. He sat up, his chest still heaving. "I had always been curious as to what that experience is like, much as I am curious about what it is like to be bitten by a snake. Will you be doing this often?"

"If it works," said Clovermead. "Being calm and collected doesn't work that well against you."

"Then I must consider how to defend myself against such an onslaught," said Sorrel thoughtfully. "I do *not* wish to become a berserker, but I think I must learn to be a little wilder in my swordplay. I must thank you for that lesson." He smiled suddenly, making the crosses on his cheeks flutter like flags. "You are a wildcat, Clovermead, a hellion, a spirit of flame. It is terrifying and wonderful to fight against you."

"Don't say such things," said Clovermead. She was sure her cheeks were glowing red with pleasure from his praise, and she was glad she had her helmet on. "I know you're still a better fighter than I am. I keep on thinking I'll get to the point where I can beat you in a fair fight, but then you learn some new trick and you wipe the floor with me."

"I do try to improve," said Sorrel. "I have made it my professional study to find new ways of defeating you in combat, so I may sing of my triumphs, and instill ever stronger in you the virtue of humility. I have concluded that a life spent whacking you on the ribs will be a life well spent."

"One of these days I'll get to the Steppes and I'll find out that 'Sorrel' is the Tansyard word for 'cock-a-hoop,'" said Clovermead. She tried to stand up, but her legs weren't yet in a mood to cooperate. "I don't think I'll be able to walk straight for a day. What was that you were singing? It sounded like a wolf howling."

"It is the *Dirge of Two Knives*. When Yarrow lay dying in the Farry Heights, after he had fought alone against ten warriors of the Gray Bar Horde and killed nine of them, Our Lady came and comforted him with the Dirge. In the Cyan Cross Horde we sing it in combat, as we commend our souls to Our Lady. It seemed appropriate as your sword glittered in my face, my shoulders scraped the bricks, and I began to wonder whether I would live to see a nineteenth winter."

"We didn't have songs about dying in battle in Timothy Vale," said Clovermead. "We sang drinking songs and wooing songs and songs about lost sheep. I tried singing *The Song of the Siege of the Silver Knight* out loud once, but Goody Weft told me to shush up because I had a voice like a rooster."

"That was an admirable bout, Demoiselle," said a gentle voice from above. Clovermead looked up and saw Saraband leaning over the parapet. She had tilted her parasol forward to shade her face, but its thin fabric let through enough light to show her features to proper advantage. She wore an intolerably fetching circlet of white daisies in her hair. "I see your talent is for fighting. I never saw you so quick in my class."

"That's because dance is torture and this is fun," said Clovermead softly. *Be polite, Clovermead,* she told herself. *Don't scowl at her too obviously.* "Teach me a sword dance, Lady Saraband, and I'll see what I can do," she said more loudly.

"A terrifying thought, Demoiselle," said Saraband

faintly. "But perhaps I will schedule one session, as an expression of my esteem for you." She glanced at Sorrel. "Tansyard—what is your name, Tansyard?"

"Sorrel, so please Your Ladyship." He staggered to his feet and bowed low to her.

"I have seen you around, Sorrel," said Saraband. "I recognize your tattoos."

"I know Your Ladyship by sight as well," said Sorrel. "Although most of what I know of you is by Clovermead's report."

Saraband laughed. "Don't believe a word she says." She unhooked a daisy from her crown and let it fall over the wall. Sorrel caught it in his fingers. "I esteem you also, Cadet. Please accept this token of my regard." She smiled at Sorrel, nodded respectfully to Clovermead, and ambled away from the parapet.

"She's such a show-off," said Clovermead disgustedly. "She always has to make herself the center of attention. Are you going to put that stupid flower away?"

"Hmm? Yes, I suppose I will." Absentmindedly Sorrel took off his helmet and stuck the flower behind his ear. Clovermead rolled her eyes. "I only have two hands, Clovermead. Can you think of a better place to keep her gift?"

"I have ideas, but they're not polite."

"Clovermead, I am shocked." Sorrel regaled her with an entirely unconvincing display of innocent horror. "In any case, a Yellowjacket cadet must always exhibit the utmost courtesy toward ladies. I believe it is in the rulebook somewhere."

"You can't read," said Clovermead. "You wouldn't

know." Groaning, she stood up, then lifted her sword. "Another bout?"

A whistle shrilled at the other end of the Training Grounds. "Our Lady has provided me a blessed excuse to avoid more buffeting for now," said Sorrel. They began to walk back to the Armory, to return their armor and practice swords to their cubbyholes. "Perhaps tomorrow?—no, the Midsummer Ball is tomorrow evening, and I do not wish to be too bruised to dance. The day after tomorrow, I think."

"You'll be dancing?"

"Of course." Sorrel's eyes sparkled. "I have been told just yesterday that it is a tradition for Yellowjacket cadets to steal dances at the Midsummer Ball with the prettiest young ladies and leave the lords fuming as we natural gentlemen show them that money and high blood do not always secure a lady's favor. This has become my favorite of all the traditions of Chandlefort. I will fight to the death to preserve it."

"Stop and say hello to me," said Clovermead. "Milady says I have to be there, even if I can't dance."

They had reached the Armory. "Until tomorrow evening." Sorrel waved farewell to Clovermead, then jogged into the changing rooms of the cadets, the flower firmly in place behind his ear.

Clovermead put away her sword and armor, then walked through the side courtyard toward the Castle's front entrance. There was a small room in the Armory where she could change clothes, but Clovermead wanted to go straight to her room, collapse into her bed, and sleep. "Every muscle in my body aches," she said to herself.

"Oof! Milady looks like she's made of solid muscle now, but I'll bet she was made of solid bruise first." She tried to lift her arms, but she couldn't. Then she saw that she had almost caught up to her languorously strolling dance teacher, and Clovermead pivoted abruptly and strode toward the courtyard's sidewall. She didn't want to give Saraband an excuse to talk with her again.

A tall man with curly red hair was leaning against the wall. His hands were manicured, his face was pale, and he was dressed in plain, faded clothes. He looked only a few years older than Sorrel. He stepped to one side as Clovermead approached the wall, and bowed courteously. As his head rose, he looked at her face. Then he frowned.

"Don't tell me I've offended you already!" said Clovermead. "I don't know you, I've never talked to you in my life, and you're scowling at me like I stole candy from your baby daughter just before I hurled a stone through your windows. What did I do wrong? Was I supposed to curtsy when you bowed?"

"Indeed you were, if etiquette hasn't changed since last I was in Chandlefort." The tall man's voice was a low rumble laced with teasing banter and a vein of acid melancholy. "But then, you wear trousers, and that wasn't usual among ladies either. Perhaps there has been a revolution in manners?"

"That's just me," said Clovermead. "Trousers are comfortable, so I wear them. Does that offend you too?" she asked defiantly.

The tall man laughed and shook his head. "I'm not offended, Miss, just curious. Your face is remarkably familiar." He scratched his head. "I can't have seen you before. You would have been a baby when last I was here. May I ask who your parents are?"

Clovermead fumbled a penny out of her trouser pocket and flicked it toward the tall man. Sunlight gleamed on Lady Cindertallow's portrait, engraved upon the coin's head. "I look a lot like Milady, my mother. Is that who you were thinking of, goodman?"

The tall man's eyes went wide. "Indeed, Demoiselle." He tossed the penny back. "I need no coin to tell me what your mother looks like. I knew her and your father well."

"You knew Ambrosius?" Clovermead's heart skipped. She had heard terribly little of her real father these last six months. Her mother never talked of him, and she answered Clovermead's questions with monosyllables. "Were you a friend of his?"

"I owe him my life," said the tall man. "He was an excellent friend to me." He shook his head. "I shouldn't say more. Pardon me, Demoiselle. I cannot stay." He turned to go.

"Wait!" cried Clovermead, and she caught at his hand. His fingers were cool in her grip. "I'm sorry if I was rude. Can't you stay another minute and tell me about him? Please don't go."

The tall man disengaged his hand from Clovermead's. "I'm sorry, Demoiselle. I shouldn't have come so near Milady's front door in the first place." He laughed harshly. "She wouldn't be happy to see me back in Chandlefort."

"Don't worry," said Clovermead. "If she gets upset

with you, I'll say I'm responsible. Just stay another minute."

"Your mother thinks I'm gone from Chandlefort forever," said the tall man fiercely. "Let her think that still." Clovermead gaped at him, and he grimaced. "I shouldn't have spoken to you at all," he muttered. Then he looked pleadingly in Clovermead's eyes. "I ask you in your father's name not to mention me to her."

Clovermead looked straight into his dark brown eyes. There was anger and good humor in them, malice and sadness, desperation and deception, and above all a loneliness that pled to Clovermead for pity.

"What would she do if I told her you had returned?" she asked at last.

"I think she'd try to kill me." The tall man smiled bitterly as he saw the shock in Clovermead's face. "She's an unscrupulous woman, Demoiselle. Other people pay the consequences for her desires. Don't you know that about her yet?"

"No," said Clovermead. Her throat was dry. "I hardly know her at all."

"You shall," said the tall man. He hesitated. "Will you tell her I was here?" Slowly Clovermead shook her head. "Thank you, Demoiselle," he said. "When next we meet, I'll tell you more about Ambrosius." He bowed to Clovermead, then strode toward the Castle gates. He ducked around a corner and in an instant he was gone.

Chapter Two

Hunting in the Heath

LADY CINDERTALLOW DIDN'T DINE WITH HER daughter that evening. "I have to talk with my spies," she said quickly as she strode to the dining table, took a soft roll from the bread basket, and bolted it down. "Don't imitate my manners. I've learned dreadful habits from my soldiers while on campaign. I'm sorry I can't stay. It sounds like good news, though. I gather Lord Ursus' infantry is marching toward Queensmart."

"That's *good* news?" asked Clovermead.

"They would have been marching against us otherwise," said her mother grimly. "It means we should be safe from him this year. Still, I wish I knew where his cavalry was." She swallowed another roll, then turned from the table.

Once again Clovermead was struck by how much she resembled her mother. Lady Cindertallow was still half a foot taller than Clovermead, regal and splendid as Clovermead could only dream of being, but she shared her daughter's fair skin and yellow hair, her freckles and the shape of her face. Yet her white gown decorated with golden bees was glorious, while Clovermead's clothes were only comfortable; and where Clovermead's face still fell naturally into smiles, her mother's face had grown set in the exercise of power. There was love and kindness in her face too, but sometimes they were difficult to see.

She is an unscrupulous woman, the tall man had said. One hundred thousand people lived in Queensmart, and Lady Cindertallow had called their doom "good news." Clovermead watched her mother stride away. *I ask you in your father's name not to mention me to her.* He had begged it of her with pleading, lonely eyes. *I think she would try to kill me.*

Clovermead opened her mouth, but the words stuck in her throat. *I don't think Milady would kill him,* she thought. *But I just don't know. I thought I knew Father, and he had been lying to me all his life. I've only known Milady six months. She's been kind to me so far, but she does like to have her way. Sometimes I contradict her, and the way she looks at me frightens me half to death. And I'm her daughter!* She shut her mouth. *I won't say anything yet.*

She dreamed that night that Lady Cindertallow was chasing after the tall man with a sword in her hand, swinging it wildly as he ran from her. He tripped into a grave, and her mother's sword became a spade. She shoveled the dirt onto him with furious speed. When only his struggling hand remained visible, Lady Cindertallow turned to Clovermead and handed her the spade. "You finish the job," she said. "You have to get dirt under your fingernails if you're going to be a proper Lady Cindertallow."

Clovermead woke gasping. Her muscles were tensed and her legs were ready to run. It was barely dawn and already it was sweltering hot. The desert sun throbbed on the eastern horizon and sent a glare of yellow light against her wall.

"She isn't like that," Clovermead told herself, her heart still hammering. "It's the heat, that's all. It gives me bad dreams." She poured herself a drink of cool water from an earthenware pitcher by her bedside, then splashed some water on her face. She felt better, but she could still see the tall man's hand thrash in the dirt. Clovermead grimaced. "I won't be getting back to sleep with that dream waiting for me!" She tossed the blankets off and began to get dressed.

Clovermead wandered idly through the Castle corridors and out into the back courtyards, where the breeze blew and it was a little cooler. After a few minutes she found herself in front of the Cindertallow graveyard. The gate was open. Inside, the grass was as verdant green as any meadow in Timothy Vale.

"I'd take stumbling across a cemetery just now as ominous, if it didn't look so peaceful inside," said Clovermead. "I don't think I'll see any open graves here." She smiled wryly. "Though, if I see a hand on the ground, I will run and scream without shame." With the slightest trepidation, she walked through the gates.

Irregularly scattered tombstones filled the graveyard. Twenty generations of Cindertallows were buried here—ladies and their consorts, infants dead in their cradles, and princes and princesses who had married among the nobility of Linstock. Simple slabs marked their resting places: Cindertallow splendor ended at the cemetery gates. Clovermead wandered past the orange trees that stood near the far end of the cemetery—and stopped abruptly. Lady Cindertallow stood in front of her, right by Ambrosius' gravestone. She held a vase of fresh lilies in her hands. Her mother touched the flowers gently, then kneeled and placed them before the grave.

How could I dream she was a killer? Clovermead stepped forward from the trees. "Hello, Ma'am," she said as she came to stand by her mother. Lady Cindertallow looked startled to see Clovermead, then moved to one side. They looked down at the gravestone together. The vase lay on a stretch of flattened grass before the grave and had been propped up with pebbles. "I didn't know you came here."

"It's the anniversary of his burial," said Lady Cindertallow. She gestured awkwardly at the vase. "I always bring flowers."

"You never told me he died in summertime," said Clovermead.

"I suppose I haven't." A tear trickled down Lady Cindertallow's cheek. Quickly she brushed it aside. "He rode out from Chandlefort at dawn, and already it was so hot that the air crackled in my lungs. He intended to hunt in the hills all day and return at dusk. The clouds rolled in from the Reliquary Mountains that morning, the land grew dark, and it rained for the first time in weeks. Burning raindrops spattered down, but soon the clouds passed by and it was as fresh and cool as spring. I went to the window to enjoy the breeze and I saw a distant horseman gallop down from the hills and ride toward Low Branding." Her mother turned from the gravestone to face the distant Heath. Her finger pointed out a spot in the western hills, then drew a line to the eastern horizon. "The hunting party came back while the sun was still high. I knew at once something was wrong. Ambrosius always rode ahead, to greet me as quickly as possible. I could not see him, and I ran to the gates. *It was an accident,* they said. *We shot a dozen shafts at a lioness, and an arrow went wild.* I remembered the fleeing horseman, and I knew it was no accident. I knew the Mayor of Low Branding had ordered him killed.

"We buried Ambrosius the next day at dawn. The graveyard was packed and the old Abbess of Silverfalls led the prayers. I never did know what she said—the words just floated by me. I had cried all the night before so I wouldn't cry in front of my subjects. I was dead to the world." Her mother smiled a little. "Except for you. I was seven months gone, and you were as heavy as a catapult stone. I leaned on a cane during the service, to keep from buckling. To top it all off, you kicked inside me the entire time. I didn't know if you were sad, or telling me there was a reason to keep living, or just uncomfortable because I stood for two solid hours. One time you kicked so hard, I almost cried out loud! Then I almost laughed out loud, but I couldn't do that at Ambrosius' funeral. I was grateful for the distraction you gave me."

"Happy to be of service, Ma'am," said Clovermead. Her throat was tight.

"I never dreamed I would spend so many years apart from him." Lady Cindertallow sighed, then looked curiously at Clovermead. "What are you doing here?"

"I couldn't sleep, so I took a walk." Clovermead

looked around her. "It's prettier here now there are orange blossoms over his grave."

"You've been here before?"

Clovermead shrugged uncomfortably. "I came here last month."

"I would have been glad to go with you."

"I wanted to go by myself." Clovermead looked away from her mother. "I saw fresh lilies laid by the stone then, too. Did you also put them there, Ma'am?" Lady Cindertallow nodded. "They covered up his last name. I moved them to one side so I could read it. Beechsplitter. Ambrosius Beechsplitter." Clovermead had never said his full name out loud before. She spoke it slowly; let the vowels fill her mouth, and savored the consonants. "I've never heard a name like that before. Where did he come from?"

"The Lakelands," said Lady Cindertallow. "The Beechsplitters are a family of furniture-makers from Elkhorn Lake. Ambrosius' father was an Alderman the year of my grandmother's diamond jubilee, so he came to the celebrations and brought Ambrosius with him. The way Ambrosius told it to me, he saw the Yellowjackets practicing their swordplay the first morning he was at Chandlefort, and he told himself then and there he would be a Yellowjacket too. It took him a year of kicking and screaming and building lopsided tables, but he finally convinced his family he was much better suited for soldiering than for carpentry. That summer he came to Chandlefort and was admitted into the Yellowjackets. The next winter I first saw him, and just the sight of him half-stole my heart away." Lady

Cindertallow looked at Clovermead's disgusted face and laughed. "I know that expression! I had it too when I was not quite thirteen."

Clovermead rolled her eyes. "I know, I know. Any day now my heart will start to twinge and boys will seem wonderful and this love business will make me groan like a lonely calf. The clocks are ticking, *Doom, doom, the day your mind will turn to porridge is soooon!* Goody Weft told me the same thing, and, heavens, I saw Sweetroot Miller getting porridgy just before I left Timothy Vale. I'm sure it will happen to me, too, but it hasn't yet, thank goodness! I'm still me."

"I'm glad. It would be terrible to get to know you only after you'd stopped being you." Lady Cindertallow reached out to Clovermead to caress her, hug her—Clovermead didn't know what—but she flinched from the touch. Her mother jerked her hand back and looked at Clovermead with pain in her eyes. "I'm sorry, Cerelune."

"Clovermead," Clovermead automatically corrected. Her stomach was clenched and she found it hard to breathe. "Please forgive me, Ma'am. I don't mind that you do that"—she left what *that* was unstated—"it's just that you startled me."

"I didn't intend to," said her mother. She was distant now, and that was a relief.

Clovermead looked down at Ambrosius' gravestone again. There were five stones on top of it. "What do those mean?" she asked, pointing them out to her mother.

"His friends put them there when he was buried,"

said Lady Cindertallow. "In Chandlefort that is a way for us to say that we pray to Our Lady to have mercy on the dead man's soul." She pointed at a dense scattering of stones fallen around the grave. "Dozens were put on the stone when he was buried. Wind and rain have knocked most to the ground."

He was an excellent friend to me, the tall man had said.

"Who were his friends, Ma'am?" Clovermead was nonchalance itself.

"A fair number of Yellowjackets. He got on less well with the lords. They didn't fancy a commoner jumped up to be Lord Cindertallow."

"Are any of them still around? I'd love to talk with them about Ambrosius." Clovermead couldn't call him *Father. Father* was Waxmelt.

"Most of them died during the war with Low Branding," said Lady Cindertallow. She frowned. "None remain in Chandlefort. I sent his old friends to garrisons far away and told them never to return. The sight of them reminded me too much of him. I don't want them back."

"But, Ma'am," Clovermead began, "I just want to talk with them."

"It still hurts too much," said Lady Cindertallow brusquely. "I won't let them in my sight, Clovermead. That is final."

Other people pay the consequences for her desires, the tall man had said. *Don't you know that about her yet?*

Poor man! thought Clovermead indignantly. *He must be one of the Yellowjackets that Milady exiled. I was right to keep silent about him.* Outrage filled her—until she saw old grief furrow Lady Cindertallow's face as she gazed at Ambrosius' gravestone. For a moment Clovermead wanted to squeeze her mother's hand, to hug her, to comfort her any way she could.

But she stayed still, suspended between anger and pity.

"What did you like about Ambrosius?" she asked after a minute.

"Everything," said Lady Cindertallow. "The shimmer of his hair in the sun. The love in his eyes when he looked at me. The mischief in his smile and his unthinking bravery." She thought for a moment. "He never let injuries rankle him or fester. I never learned that art. I tried to, but it wasn't in me to forgive the way he did. I miss that most of all."

"I wish I had known him, Ma'am," said Clovermead. It was the first time she had let herself say that. "Are his parents still alive?"

"Dead some years ago," said Lady Cindertallow. "Of nothing worse than ripe old age: He was their youngest child. I suppose his brothers and sisters are still in the Lakelands. I'm sorry, Clovermead. There isn't much of him left behind." Then she suddenly smiled. "I know! It's just the thing. Now, do we have time? I believe we were supposed to go hunting in the Heath this morning."

"Yes, Ma'am, same as always." Clovermead tried to keep the boredom and distaste out of her voice. The two of them went hunting in the cool of the morning once a week, like clockwork. Her mother loved hunting, and she delighted in sharing her enjoyment with Clovermead. Clovermead had learned how to hunt in Timothy Vale, but she had never found it much fun. She liked hunting even less after a long spring slaughtering small animals. Still, she didn't complain. Her mother was terribly busy as Lady Cindertallow, and Clovermead welcomed any chance to spend time with her.

Besides, Clovermead reflected. *It could be worse. She could have liked counting her jewels with me or knitting sweaters together or boring me with stories about all the battles she should have won against the Mayor. I ought to be grateful it isn't anything worse than hunting.*

Lady Cindertallow looked at the sun. "We have an hour. Come with me to my rooms, Clovermead." She strode off, confident that Clovermead would follow.

"One day you'll turn around and I won't be there," said Clovermead irritatedly. She frowned and ran after her mother.

When they reached her rooms, Lady Cindertallow went straight to her wardrobe. From the top drawer she took out an old sword in a serviceable, plain leather scabbard. "This was Ambrosius' sword," she said. She hesitated a moment, looked it over lingeringly, then thrust the hilt toward Clovermead. "Take it."

"Ma'am!" Clovermead felt tears springing to her eyes. "Are you sure?"

"I have other things to remember him by," said Lady Cindertallow. "He'd want you to have this." She put it firmly into Clovermead's hands. "Now, this isn't a royal blade, Clovermead. It's just the sword and scabbard he got when he became a Yellowjacket. We don't give our soldiers shoddy blades, but it isn't anything out of the ordinary." Clovermead drew the sword and swung it experimentally in midair. It had a good balance, though it was still a bit long and heavy for her. "The wood plaques are his. Take a look at them."

Clovermead brought the sword closer to her. Where the hilt met the blade, two wooden oval medallions carved from pale birchwood were set in silver bands. On one side of the hilt, the first plaque showed a bear with her paw caught in a trap. A boy knelt by the bear's side and opened the trap's jaws. On the other side the second plaque depicted a young man who held a sword upraised to the moon.

"What do they mean?" asked Clovermead as her fingers traced the figures on the medallions. They were finely done, with spirit and compassion.

"He never told me." Lady Cindertallow shrugged. "What matters is that Ambrosius carved them. He wasn't a good man for furniture, but he had a talent for that sort of artistry. Look at them, touch them—there's a good deal of him in those carvings." Lady Cindertallow touched the plaque of the trapped bear one last time, then drew back her fingers.

"I'm awfully glad to have something of his, Ma'am," said Clovermead. She sheathed the sword, ran her hand over the medallions once more, and smiled joyfully at her mother. "And his sword!—that's the best thing of all."

"I thought it might be. I'm told you're rather pugnacious at fighting practice." Lady Cindertallow returned her daughter's smile. Then her eyes strayed toward the window and her smile grew wider. "It occurs to me that we could go hunting now and have breakfast later."

Clovermead rolled her eyes. "Now I know how

Father felt when I would drag him out of bed in the morning to go watch fawns in the meadows. I'll come now, Ma'am—just let me get a muffin first." She carefully placed Ambrosius' sword at her waist. Its tip brushed against her calves. She held herself up straight. *I don't care if it's the wrong size,* thought Clovermead. *I'll wear it until it fits!* "What do we hunt today?" she asked absently.

"Coyotes," said Lady Cindertallow. "Not the noblest game, but a pack of them stole a calf the other day. The farmers will be glad if we thin their numbers."

They went down to the stables and quickly attired themselves for the hunt. Lady Cindertallow picked up her own enormous yew bow from the bench where it lay. It was old and battered, but well-oiled and supple. Clovermead slung her own lighter bow and quiver onto her back. Then Lady Cindertallow and Clovermead saddled their horses, put on cotton caps to protect themselves from the fierce sun of the open Heath, and rode out from the stables. Ambrosius' sword jounced against Clovermead's leg, and she adjusted the way it hung. They rode out the Castle gates, through the surrounding town, and between the open town gates into the encircling fields.

From Chandlefort's enormous spring, eight great pipes cut through the rose walls to carry water into the canals lacing the fields. Now that the war with Low Branding was over, Lady Cindertallow had opened the pipes; for the first time in years the thirsty land drank. Each canal was elevated above the fields. Every hundred yards, on each side, water flowed down into earthen ditches from outlets chopped into the canal walls. The ditches belonged to the individual farmers to carve as they would, and each farmer had engraved his land with a unique skein of glittering water, olive trees, and fields of pale wheat. Clovermead saw a gang of laborers clearing a sand-strewn road. Farther off, a dozen children gleefully uprooted the thorn bushes that had encroached on their parents' land.

Happily Clovermead kicked her pony to a gallop. She reveled in the speed and the wind and the sudden distance that separated her from Chandlefort. Clovermead was away from the lords and ladies, away from the Castle walls, away from the baking heat of the sun on Chandlefort stone. The breeze blew, the fields were a lovely green, and the path underneath her pony's hooves was honest dirt. Joy bubbled out of her and she could not help laughing.

Then they came to the Heath, and Clovermead's joy fled from her. The boundary between the Salt Heath and the green land was as sharp as if a great knife had cut through the earth: Where the canals ended, so too ended the fields. Ahead of them smoldering red earth turned into a slope of gravel that descended toward thorny bushes huddling in the shade of a boulder. Beyond was a dun plain, where patches of yellow grass alternated with cracks in the earth that exposed layers of burned red soil, and rocky chimneys heaved up to the sky. Eastward the Heath was bounded by the shady green trees of the Chandle Palisades, and westward the distant Reliquary Mountains promised cool relief from the baking heat, but straight ahead the sere, terrible Heath went on to the horizon.

Clovermead shuddered as the Heath surrounded them. *I'll never like this awful place,* she thought gloomily. *Dear Lady, I miss the cool green of Timothy Vale.*

"I think I see coyote spoor," said Lady Cindertallow, intent on the ground ahead of them. The desolate landscape did not bother her at all. "Let's go this way."

They rode farther into the Heath. While her mother wasn't watching, Clovermead let her snout grow and her furry ears poke up. It was a relief to turn a little bearish. Lady Cindertallow didn't let her turn into a bear when they were inside Chandlefort, and they only went outside the town walls when Lady Cindertallow took her hunting.

I suppose Milady's right, thought Clovermead sadly. *It does make Chandleforters nervous when I turn bearish, and I really shouldn't do it where they can see me.* Then laughter rumbled in her. *I guess that first time I should have given some warning and not just turned into a bear right in the middle of the Throne Room. I wanted to surprise everyone, but I didn't think they'd be that shocked! How was I to know that sourpuss Lady Turnbolt was going to faint?* She sighed. *Poor Milady, she spent days calming everybody. I won't ever live down the reputation that gave me.*

Now she could hear and smell all sorts of animals creeping about the Heath. There was a squirrel hiding behind a cactus, a long snake slithering along the bottom of a gulch, and two coyotes creeping behind a ridge to the left. It would be easy enough to find them and kill them. Not many animals could escape Clovermead, now that she could use both a bear's sharp senses and a human's even sharper weapons.

It would be cruel, she told herself disgustedly. *They wouldn't have a chance.* She let her ears and nose go back to human. *Milady can track them down by herself.*

"Why do you like hunting?" she asked her mother abruptly.

"Good training," said Lady Cindertallow. Her eyes were darting here and there over the landscape. "It exercises the body and makes it fit for fighting. It exercises the mind, too—you learn how to kill swiftly when you hunt. A Lady Cindertallow needs to know how to do that. You can't hesitate when you're fighting a real battle, or you'll be dead, and your soldiers, too. Practice on the coyotes, Clovermead. You'll need the experience when you become Lady Cindertallow.

"There," breathed Lady Cindertallow, and Clovermead saw the two coyotes come out from behind the ridge and pad by the base of a light yellow bluff, eighty yards away. They walked slowly in the brilliant sun, their tan coats barely visible against the creamy rocks. "Shoot with me," said her mother. "You don't want to give the other one warning." Her mother took her yew bow from behind her back and easily strung it, while Clovermead struggled to bend her own small bow. Then Lady Cindertallow notched an arrow and drew back the string. "Aim for the one on the right; I'll take the one on the left." The muscles of her mother's arms bunched as she aimed at the coyotes.

Clovermead thought of sending the arrow at them, and it made her sick. *I know how to order soldiers to fight, Milady,* she said silently. *Don't you remember? The snow lay on the Salt Heath, and I ordered the bears and bear-priests to attack the Yellowjackets and the Mayor's men. They screamed, the snow turned red, and Lord Ursus and I laughed with pleasure. I have more than enough experience killing.*

Still she drew her bow, notched her arrow, and squinted through the bright sun at the distant coyotes. She didn't want to disappoint her mother. Besides, she had just been reading in *The Astrantiad* how Sir Tourmaline enjoyed hunting sand foxes with the Reiver Prince, and it *was* exciting to feel her muscles tense as they held the bow steady, to calculate distance and altitude and wind as she guessed which way the distant coyote would move. She could see why her mother loved hunting so much.

"Now!" cried Lady Cindertallow. She released her arrow, and Clovermead—

Clovermead jerked her bow up half an inch, while her mother's arrow went straight into the side of the left coyote, who howled once, then slumped over dead. Clovermead's arrow went whistling over the right coyote to splinter into the rock above him. He whined with fear and scampered off in an instant. Within seconds he was hidden behind a hill. Clovermead heard him howl in anguished loneliness.

"You must do better," said Lady Cindertallow harshly. "It's kill or nothing when you hunt. That was nothing." They cantered over to the dead coyote, and Lady Cindertallow swung down from her horse and nudged its body with her foot. It lay limp and still. "I'll bring him to that last homestead we passed. Farmers like meat for their stewpots." She hoisted up the coyote, carried it back, and began to tie its body to the back of her horse. "It was a good shot," she added gruffly, not looking at her daughter. "If you keep on practicing, I'm sure you'll hit the mark the next time."

Clovermead nodded curtly, but didn't reply. She hopped down from her pony and walked slowly to join her mother. She held the coyote's paws while Lady Cindertallow knotted them together.

She looked up at her mother. *Kill or nothing,* she repeated to herself, and she shuddered. *I think you would try to kill that tall man if I told you about him. Maybe you'd be sorry later, but that would be too late, because you've gotten used to killing swiftly. I don't think you're a villain like Lord Ursus or Lucifer Snuff, but you're awfully dangerous.* She remembered the berserker rage she had let sweep over her as she fought Sorrel, and she shuddered. *That wasn't the bear in me, Ma'am. That was you.*

Over the hill she heard the mournful howl of the coyote her arrow had missed.

Chapter Three

The Midsummer Ball

Clovermead impatiently watched the swirling dancers from the side of the Ballroom that evening. "Do I have to stay here much longer, Ma'am?" she muttered to her mother. "This isn't much fun when you don't know how to dance properly and have to just stand and watch."

"You are one of the attractions of the Midsummer Ball," said Lady Cindertallow. She nodded politely to a passing couple, and Clovermead made a hasty curtsy. Her mother raised her hand, and a servant came hurrying to her with a cup of water. She drank, gave the empty cup back to the servant, and waved him away. "Let the lords and ladies see their new Demoiselle in her fetching new dress, so they will think fondly of you hereafter. Someday one of these young men will be an old man you have outraged with a new tax, but he will shrug and say, 'She was so pretty in that yellow gown! Why make a fuss?' But I think another half hour will do. Our guests will have drunk enough wine by then that I doubt they will remember anything from that point on."

"I'll just twiddle my thumbs," said Clovermead dolefully. Then she looked down happily at her gown. It was simple and decorous, light yellow to match her hair, with long sleeves that covered the scar on her arm. *It does look nice on me,* she thought complacently. *Not that I like dresses or anything, but I'm glad it's this one if I have to wear one at all.* She stole a glance at her mother. Lady Cindertallow was dressed in a far more elegant scarlet gown. Clovermead wondered if she would ever be able to get away with wearing clothing so magnificent.

Her eyes strayed to the dance. Eighty couples in four long lines filled the Ballroom. Lords peacocked in silvery tunics and jet-black trousers, and ladies swirled down the hall in gowns of lace and silk—blue, pink, and violet. Most of the dancers had disguised themselves in colored wigs and domino masks that covered the top halves of their faces. The windows were open wide to cool the hall, but the summer night was baking hot. The crowd of bodies exuded sweat, perfume, and dank heat; the dancers' cheerful, laughing din filled the room; and the music rang out louder still. The floorboards had been polished till they gleamed, and torches roared from every sconce. Four musicians sat on a dais at the end of the hall, playing flute, harp, bagpipe, and fiddle, and the dancers leaped and whirled to the prompting of their furious, joyful tune. Clovermead's foot tapped the floor restlessly, and she wished that she had tried harder in Saraband's class, so she could join this giddy crowd. The crude farm dances she had learned in Timothy Vale were no preparation for these dances' complexity, elegance, and sensuous charm.

Now the music drowned out the stamp of the dancers' feet. Clovermead peered at the musicians on the dais. The bagpiper's face was red, and all of the musicians gleamed with sweat. The harpist looked wan and tired. They stood at the far end of the Ballroom from the windows; what breeze blew in failed to reach them. Servants scurried around the edges of the room with glasses of ice water on trays, but none stopped at the dais.

"Will you excuse me a moment, Ma'am?" asked Clovermead. "I want to get the musicians some water. They look thirsty."

"Go if you wish," said her mother. She looked idly at the musicians, shrugged, then looked away again.

"They could faint in this sweatbox," Clovermead said angrily. "Don't you care?"

"Not particularly," said Lady Cindertallow. "Musicians are just servants who can carry a tune." She frowned at Clovermead. "Are you going to start singing to Lord Wickward's tune? Every time I meet him, he gives me the same lecture. Give your pot-boys more pennies to waste on drink! Give your scullery-girls an hour to snore in the afternoon! Feed them plum jam and tuck them in at night! I'm tired of that nonsense. Do what you will, but don't pester me about servants."

"As you say, Ma'am," said Clovermead. She curtsied, turned quickly from Lady Cindertallow, and shuffled along the edge of the Ballroom. There were a great many things she wanted to say to her mother, but all that came out of her was a muffled growl.

When she came near to the musicians' dais, Clovermead plucked a pitcher of water from a tray held by a balding servant. "I'm taking this for the musicians," she said.

The servant blinked at her with startled goggle eyes. "The water is for Lady Turnbolt, Demoiselle. She particularly asked—"

"Bother Lady Turnbolt," said Clovermead. "She can't be as hot as the musicians. If Lady Turnbolt has words for you, tell her to say them to me."

A slight smile sneaked across the servant's face. "It will be my pleasure to serve you in this, Demoiselle," he said softly. He bowed quickly to Clovermead and scuttled away for more water.

Clovermead looked at the dais. It was three feet high, and she didn't think she could jump up there without spilling the water. There were steps to the dais twenty feet down, but it was impossible to get there past the whirling feet of dancers. "Now how do I get up?" she asked herself.

"With help," said Sorrel. He was by her side, resplendent in a domino mask and full-dress uniform. He hopped up onto the stage in an instant and held out his hands. Clovermead gave him the pitcher and he ran swiftly to the musicians' side. He left the water with them and in another instant had hopped down to rejoin Clovermead. The musicians couldn't stop playing to thank them, but they added a joyful, grateful tune to the dance. The fiddler winked at the two of them.

"Thank you," said Clovermead. She inspected his uniform critically—and suddenly fell backward against the dais. She moaned.

"What is wrong with you, Clovermead?" asked Sorrel. Anxiously he put his hand to her forehead. "Are you too hot? I can take you out of here."

"He looked so handsome in his yellow coat," said Clovermead dreamily. "My knees wobbled and I couldn't stay on my feet. Oh, those Tansyards!" She bounced upright and shook her head in amused disgust. "How long did you polish your buttons? They'll blind me."

Sorrel looked relieved and stung. "I wish to look presentable, little imp who does not scruple to trifle with my cares for her health. We do not suffer from vanity on the Steppes. I am motivated solely by respect for the occasion."

"You've put something in your hair, haven't you? It shines," said Clovermead. Sorrel glared at her, and Clovermead giggled. "I don't mind if you preen. I just want a chance to have a dig at you."

"*You* accuse *me* of preening? You, who has put on a dress for the first time ever? You, who looks—" Sorrel examined Clovermead's dress closely, then held his tongue until Clovermead couldn't stand it anymore, and she punched him in the arm. "You must get out of that habit, Clovermead, before I am bruised from head to toe. You look quite the lovely young miss. You should wear such confections more often."

"Don't be silly. I can hardly move in this." But Clovermead was blushing happily. It *was* the first time she'd worn a gown at Chandlefort, and she'd been afraid that she'd look ridiculous.

"Where have you been?" she asked. "I've been looking for you all evening. Milady said I'll be able to leave the Ball in a few minutes, and I've found a marvelous new passageway behind the wine cellars for us to explore. It's full of spiderwebs and old wooden crates that don't look like they've been opened for a hundred years. I think they're full of forgotten gold."

"I think they are full of moldy apple cider," said Sorrel. "Still, I will be glad to explore them with you tomorrow evening."

"Not tonight?" asked Clovermead. She pouted.

"Alas, no. We cadets must stay at the Ball and dance. But I will meet you tomorrow at the guard post." He fiddled with his lapel, and Clovermead saw that he had pinned Saraband's daisy to it. His eyes caught something in the room, he smiled, and he bowed hastily to Clovermead. "I must be going. Until tomorrow." He dashed away.

"Bother being a cadet!" said Clovermead to herself. "Bother dancing! And why does he still have Saraband's wretched flower?" She began to sidle back to her mother. Lady Cindertallow was talking with Waxmelt—Clovermead's eyes widened. *What's Father doing here?* She hastened toward the two of them. *Please don't be arguing.*

"No need to frown, Clo," Waxmelt said as she came close. He gave her a reassuring smile. "I was wandering by and I saw Milady alone for the moment. I thought I would seize the opportunity to apologize to her for my shortness with her yesterday."

"Which he has done more politely than half my noblemen could manage," said Lady Cindertallow. She made herself look directly at Waxmelt for a moment, then glanced away. "As I recollect, I provoked your shortness. Do you think I should apologize to you, too, Lord Wickward?"

"I don't ask for any apology, Milady," said Waxmelt. "All I ask is that you listen to me about the servants."

"Dear Lady! Between you and Clovermead I'll never hear the end about these servants." Lady Cindertallow's eyes flicked around the room. Everywhere there were servants in livery bowing, fawning, sweating, and jumping out of the way of the dancing lords and ladies. Some were anxious, some uncomfortable, some simply looked hungry as they stared at the food the lords devoured. One or two surreptitiously lifted sandwiches from the tables of food by the windows and popped them into their mouths.

"The way they are treated is not just," said Lady Cindertallow in a low voice. Her eyes fell from the scene. "I know that, Lord Wickward. I just wish that Our Lady had chosen some other man to tell me so." The dance ended, and Clovermead turned to look at the dais. The musicians took gulps of water with great relish, mopped their faces with their handkerchiefs, then started playing a fresh tune with renewed energy. "Tell me, Clovermead, were the musicians grateful?"

"Yes, Ma'am," said Clovermead. "They had gotten awfully hot and dry."

"I'm glad to hear it." Her mother studied the dais, then made herself look back at Waxmelt. "You raised her to be kindly."

Waxmelt smiled fondly at Clovermead. "I raised her to be quick with cups of ale in the dining room and never to let our guests get thirsty. She was born kind."

"Ambrosius must have given that to her," said Lady Cindertallow. "I lost my kindness when he died." Her fists clenched for a moment and only slowly loosened. "Come to me again some other day, Lord Wickward. I'll try to listen more temperately about the condition of my servants." She smiled wryly. "We should go somewhere private. I'm sure I'll yell at you at some point, and I'd rather do that without letting the whole Castle know."

Waxmelt chuckled. "I've been told that our last argument is common knowledge. Where would you like to meet, Milady?"

An idea struck Clovermead. *A brilliant idea!* she told herself modestly. "How about a picnic? We could all go out and sit under a tree and eat cold chicken, and the two of you could hash things out afterward while I nap or climb a tree or something. Maybe you wouldn't yell at each other so much if I were around. Wouldn't that be nice, Ma'am?"

Lady Cindertallow's face lit up. "That is a lovely idea, Clovermead. I haven't been on a picnic since, gracious, before you were born. Dear Lady, it's been a while. Lord Wickward, shall we go picnicking the day after tomorrow? There's a hayfield in the western fields that will make a delightful spot."

"With pleasure, Milady," said Waxmelt. "Though I warn you that Clovermead will eat more than her fair share of drumsticks if you don't keep an eye on her."

"I'll watch her like a hawk," said Lady Cindertallow. Then she sighed. "Here comes that fearful bore Lord Tamarisk. I have to talk with him, but there's no need either of you should. Stay here while I go intercept him. Clovermead, you may leave the Ball now if you like. Good night the both of you, if I don't see you again." She swept forward with a practiced smile to meet Lord Tamarisk.

"I once served at a ball like this," said Waxmelt. "I never expected to attend one as a lord of Chandlefort." He looked at the scurrying servitors in livery, then at his own noble clothes, and plucked bemusedly at his silk sleeves. "Milady's generosity is whimsical. I'm no better a lord than I was a servant."

"You could open an inn in Chandlefort town," said Clovermead. "Would you like that?"

For a moment Waxmelt looked tempted. Then he shook his head. "If Our Lady intended for me to stay an innkeeper, she would never have let Lucifer Snuff come to Timothy Vale and make us flee from Ladyrest. I think she means me to do something to help the servants here. I may be a second-rate agitator, but there's no one better available." Waxmelt's eyes widened as he recognized a fat man standing behind a table by the window, who was clearing away a pile of dirty glasses. "Lady's mercy, that's Charfennel Comb! I didn't know Char had become an indoors servant. Look, his hair's gone white!"

"You have aged better than he has," Clovermead said thoughtfully. "You're not nearly as pudgy, and I do think balding is better than white-haired."

Waxmelt clutched his head. "His white hair means he has three daughters. Will you excuse me, Clo? We were friends once, and I haven't talked with him in twelve years."

"Shoo," said Clovermead, and Waxmelt hurried away to greet his old comrade. "Now, where were those sandwiches?" Clovermead asked herself. "Ah, over there in the corner. Fortunately, I'm still a growing girl. I think I can indulge without danger to my waistline." She started to sidle toward the refreshments.

Clovermead saw Saraband coming down the nearest line of dancers. She wore an impossibly lovely gown of white lace, slender cut and beaded with pearls, that was demure and fetching, and left her feet free to move with giddy abandon. Her domino mask was made of cloth-of-gold, and she had sprinkled glinting gold dust into her raven hair. Her body moved in perfect time to the music, her feet were tireless, and her face was full of a joy that went out to everyone she danced with, inspiring them to dance with renewed vigor and skill. She was more beautiful than ever, and she left a trail of admiring men behind her. Her gauzy sleeves showed all her arms, up to the shoulders. Clovermead's stomach knotted as she looked at the translucent fabric on Saraband's unscarred flesh. The music was ending, and a new dance was about to begin. Some lords approached Saraband.

Sorrel stepped out onto the dance floor, slipped his way past the lords, and stood in front of Saraband. He took the daisy from his lapel, bowed low to Saraband in her domino, and proffered it to her. "May I present you with a token of my esteem, Lady Saraband?" he asked.

Saraband smiled demurely. "Certainly, Cadet." She took the daisy and tucked it into an eyelet on the fringe of her sleeve. She raised an eyebrow. "Do you have any other business with me?"

"I would be honored if I could have this dance," said Sorrel. He held out his arm.

"How presumptuous you are!" said Saraband. She

took his hand in hers. "I'm glad you asked." They smiled at each other and they began to dance.

They were a wonderful sight. Sorrel didn't have Saraband's grace, but he danced with a supple strength that matched her dancing well. Their white and yellow clothes shone like jewels in the torchlight; their smiles and their enjoyment of the dance caught the eye even more. They could not keep from gazing at each other, and their distance and formality lessened by the minute. They whispered to one another and laughed in delight.

"Hello, Demoiselle," said a voice behind her. Clovermead recognized it, and she looked back and saw the tall man. He wore a domino mask over his eyes and a green wig to cover his red hair. "I told you we'd meet again."

"What are you doing here?" hissed Clovermead in alarm. She looked to see where her mother was. Lady Cindertallow was talking with Lord Tamarisk at the other side of the room. "You're one of Ambrosius' Yellowjacket friends, aren't you?" The tall man nodded quickly and Clovermead hurried on. "Milady told me she'd sent them all away from Chandlefort, and I think she just might kill you if she knew you'd come back. You have to get out of here!"

"Don't worry, Demoiselle. I'm well enough disguised for the evening." The tall man gestured at his mask and wig. "I haven't been to a Chandlefort ball in many years. Give me a little time to enjoy it."

"Please," said Clovermead. Her dream was suddenly as vivid as ever, and she could see her mother shoveling earth over the tall man. "I don't want to take the risk. I don't want you to die."

"Life away from Chandlefort is no life at all," said the tall man. "Let the risk be what it may, I'd like to enjoy myself now that I've returned."

"You're mad as a hatter," Clovermead informed him. "Also you're completely barmy and you've spent too much time in the sun. You're leaving now." She tugged at the tall man's arm and determinedly pulled him toward the door. The tall man laughed, then shrugged and let Clovermead take him from the Ball.

At the Ballroom doors the tall man stopped and looked wonderingly at Clovermead. "How curious. You care whether a stranger lives or dies."

"Of course I do," said Clovermead crossly. "Anyway, how could I let one of Ambrosius' friends get killed?" She let go of the tall man, then glanced nervously toward her mother. She and Lord Tamarisk were still deep in conversation, and Clovermead relaxed a little. "Really, what on earth possessed you to come here?"

"I was never happier than when I danced in this room," the tall man said quietly. "Perhaps it is madness, as you say, but I wished to see it again." He looked around the glittering torch-lit room once more, then turned toward the front doors of the Castle. "Do not fear, Demoiselle; I have had my fill of Castle entertainment. Good evening."

"Wait!" cried Clovermead. "You said you would tell me something about Ambrosius." She gulped. "About my true father."

"So I did." The tall man looked at Clovermead and his lips twisted into a bitter, humorless smile. "I never dreamed that I would be the one to tell his daughter about him. What can I say? He was handsome and brave, modest and good-humored. He made friends easily and kept them tenaciously. He was the kindest man I knew."

"How did you become friends?"

"He saved me from my sister's wrath. I had somehow forgotten her birthday was approaching, and I realized half an hour before her party was supposed to begin that I had no present for her. I was in the Yellowjackets' barracks, and I started to despair very loudly. I hardly knew Ambrosius then—we had spoken occasionally, sometimes fought with each other on the Training Grounds, but ours was a very casual friendliness. Yet as soon as he heard my laments, Ambrosius took a stick of wood and started to whittle it. In five minutes he had carved the wood into the jolliest clown's head you ever set eyes on. 'Give this to your sister,' he said, and he put it into my hands. I knew at once it would be perfect for her. 'I'm in your debt forever,' I said, and I rushed out of the barracks." The tall man laughed, and now there was no bitterness in him. "Sister did love it. I'll warrant you she still keeps it on her bookshelf."

"Thank you for telling me that story." Clovermead couldn't help but jump up and kiss the tall man on his cool cheek. "You really must go now, but will we meet again? I want to hear more about Ambrosius."

"I don't think we will," said the tall man. His fingers trailed over his cheek, where Clovermead had kissed him. Then he glided out the front doors, into the Castle courtyard, and out of sight.

"I hope you're wrong," said Clovermead to the

empty night. "Though I suppose that means I should spend more time away from Milady, since you can't let her see you." She turned back toward the Ballroom, to see if her mother was still talking to Lord Tamarisk.

Clovermead saw that Sorrel and Saraband were still dancing, and suddenly she was cold and empty inside. She turned from the dancing couple and stole away from the Ballroom as fast as she could, through the nearly deserted corridors of the Castle, back to her bedroom. It was dark, save for the moonlight that shone in through the window and glittered off the full-length mirror by her bedside.

Clovermead stopped to look at her reflection and saw a stranger. Her image had begun to stretch like pulled taffy the last few months. She was taller, she had lost some baby fat, and she was widening in the chest and hips. She looked more closely at her face. Her hair was unruly, she was sunburned, and her cheeks were remarkably full of freckles. Back in Timothy Vale, Card Merrin had once thought she was pretty, but then he had decided that Sweetroot Miller was prettier. Clovermead hadn't much minded back then.

She smiled at the image in the mirror. Her lips drew up, and now there was no hiding the gap where her upper left canine had been before the bear-tooth ground it away. *Every time you feel joy, the world will know you once were mine,* Ursus whispered in her from far away. *Laugh, and you will remember me.* The old bear roared his own malignant laughter as Clovermead's smile faded and the missing tooth disappeared behind concealing lips.

Clovermead stretched out her left arm, drew up the

sleeve of her yellow dress, and exposed the long scar that ran from her palm to her shoulder. It didn't hurt. Nothing was wrong with her arm except the way it looked. She tried to imagine her arm in gauzy sleeves, and bitter laughter almost choked her. "Wouldn't *you* be the belle of the ball?" Clovermead told her image quietly. "Think of all the cadets lined up to dance with you." No matter how well she learned to dance, her arm would still be scarred.

Clovermead could still see Sorrel and Saraband dancing in her mind's eye.

She wanted to howl, she wanted to cry, and she lashed out with an arm grown huge and furred. Her claws crunched into the mirror, and silvered shards crashed to the floor. Only the top third of the mirror remained. In the reflection she saw the huge head and snapping jaws of a raging golden bear.

Chapter Four

The Picnic

CLOVERMEAD WAS IN BETTER SPIRITS BY THE TIME she rode out of Chandlefort with Lady Cindertallow and Waxmelt for the picnic. She'd persuaded a servant the day before to replace the shattered mirror and not mention anything to her mother, which was a great relief. She hadn't relished explaining how it had come to be broken. Then she and Sorrel had gone exploring in the cellars in the evening, and she had found an actual secret passage! It only led from the wine cellar to the laundry room, but even a short secret passage was nothing to be sneezed at. They had also found a great many empty wine bottles in the laundry hamper that covered the passageway. Sorrel suspected the laundrywomen had been pilfering good Queensmart vintages from her mother for quite some time. Sorrel hadn't mentioned Saraband once that evening, and the world was a better place. Even the oppressive summer heat had broken as a north wind blew in from the Chaffen Hills, and now it was pleasantly warm as Clovermead, Lady Cindertallow, and Waxmelt rode through the fields on a path that curved between two lines of lush olive trees. The olives' gray-green leaves shimmered in the sun, and their branches extended in a canopy over the path, like a vaulted chamber in a green temple. One Yellowjacket rode ahead of them and one behind, each carrying a sword, tablecloths, and hampers of food and drink.

They had their picnic in a hayfield that belonged to Lady Cindertallow herself, who kept it for winter fodder for the Yellowjackets' horses. Within its border of ditches and olive trees the tall grass fraternized with daisies and buttercups, while bees and butterflies flitted from petal to petal. The Yellowjackets spread the tablecloths on the grass and scattered pillows, baskets of food, and bottles on top of them while Clovermead and her mother took the picnickers' horses and tied their reins to a tree. The picnic began with cucumber salad and ginger beer, went on to freshly baked white bread and roast chicken, and finished with fresh strawberries and sorbets packed in ice. Clovermead talked with Lady Cindertallow about horses, *The Astrantiad,* fighting practice, and the fine art of chewing hayseeds, of which Clovermead had much lore to share. Waxmelt listened quietly and took only a few bites from each course. The hot sun shone down, and by the end of the meal Clovermead was stuffed and drowsy.

"And how are your handwriting classes going?" her mother asked.

"Wretchedly. I've gone cross-eyed learning to write beautiful, flowing, insanely difficult script. It's very pretty, but it's not worth the bother."

Her mother laughed. "You would understand at once why a good, clear hand is an essential skill if I made you read the latest letter from the Mayor of Low Branding.

The man has an especially crabbed hand. I fear he will drive me to spectacles." She wiped her mouth with a soft linen napkin. "But enough of handwriting." She turned to Waxmelt. "Lord Wickward, we came here to discuss the servants. Tell me what you propose I do about them."

Waxmelt took a moment to gather his thoughts, then spoke with precision. "I have told you often enough, Milady. Pay them more and work them less. Show them a little respect." His voice was as calm as ever, but now his eyes blazed. "We are as dear to Our Lady as you, but you lords and ladies treat us as beasts of burden. Do you know how much it rankles in our hearts to see nothing but contempt on your faces, when you deign to notice us at all? We have our dignity too."

"Bootblacks? Chambermaids?" Lady Cindertallow laughed incredulously.

"I polished any number of pilgrims' boots when I was at Ladyrest Inn, Ma'am," said Clovermead. "I cleaned their rooms, too—well, I didn't always sweep under the beds, but that's not the point. I did all the work the servants do here. I'm not ashamed!"

"That is an interesting point." Lady Cindertallow smiled. "And it comes back to me that I didn't care tuppence that Ambrosius was a tradesman's son when I fell in love with him." She turned back to Waxmelt. "I will grant that I should treat my servants with some respect, Lord Wickward. But it seems to me that I do already. I give them justice. I protect them from Chandlefort's enemies. Isn't that enough?"

"You protect your cows," said Waxmelt. "You give

your pigs equal amounts of food from the trough. Are we more to you than beasts?"

"Honestly?" Lady Cindertallow looked at Waxmelt steadily. "Lord Wickward, when I was a little older than Clovermead, I saw a mob in Lackey Lane burn down a bakery. Food was scarce and dear that year, and half a dozen stable-boys insisted the baker sell them cheaper bread. He refused and locked the door on them when they would not go away. The street was full of hungry servants. The stable-boys whipped up the other servants until they started throwing stones at the bakery windows. Then they threw a torch. They would not let water be brought from the well to douse the flames. I came with a squad of Yellowjackets as soon as I heard what was going on. Bootblacks and cooks and chambermaids threw bricks at us to keep us away. They dumped vegetable carts into Lackey Lane to keep us from charging them. By the time we had fought through to the bakery, it had nearly burned to the ground. We barely got the baker's family out in time. Their clothes were black rags, and half their skin was blistered. The servants didn't spare a second glance for the people they had meant to kill. They were too busy stealing loaves of bread from the charred timbers. I confess I have found it difficult to regard the servants as entirely human since then." She smiled grimly. "What would such wild beasts do with money and free time, Lord Wickward?"

"I once saw a lord beat his servant half to death," said Waxmelt quietly. "He had money and leisure, he was not maddened by hunger, and he was a wild beast too."

"I think both of you should be politer about wild

beasts," said Clovermead. "The two of you make it sound like us bears are much nicer than any of you Chandleforters. Be angry at each other, but leave us out of it."

Lady Cindertallow laughed abruptly. "All right, Clo," said Waxmelt. "I won't say a word against anything with four legs." He turned back to Lady Cindertallow. "Milady, I'm sure we both have many bitter memories. Can we set them aside? What can I do now to convince you to treat the servants better?"

"Nothing comes to mind," said Lady Cindertallow.

A distant trumpet blasted a long, rising blare. The Yellowjackets scrambled to their feet and Lady Cindertallow followed them the next instant. It took Clovermead another second to remember what the signal meant: *Strange riders, danger.*

"It can't be," said Lady Cindertallow. Her face was pale. "There shouldn't be bear-priests within two hundred miles of here. They're attacking Queensmart." The trumpets blasted again, and Lady Cindertallow cursed. "Where are they? By Our Lady's girdle, give me the direction!" She fumbled at the reins of her horse. She had tied them tightly around the tree and was muzzy and clumsy from her full lunch. The trumpet blared two double beats. "From the west. Dear Lady, they're coming here." She grabbed the carving knife from the chicken's carcass. Clovermead looked for another knife, but her mother had taken the only one. She was weaponless.

"How did they get past the south forts?" asked Lady Cindertallow. "Why wasn't a warning sent?" Her eyes blazed with murderous fury. "I would never have let you beyond the walls if I'd thought—" She could not finish her sentence but growled as deeply and raging as any bear. "If you're harmed, I'll flay my border guards alive," she concluded. Lady Cindertallow looked over the peaceful linens spread on the grass, then turned angrily away. "No time to waste. Back to Chandlefort, as quick as we can."

"You'll be safer if you ride with me, Father," said Clovermead. "I've practiced some cavalry maneuvers with the Yellowjackets." Waxmelt nodded, and he stumbled after Clovermead as she ran to her pony and untied him. Clovermead helped her father up onto her pony, then untied Waxmelt's horse and gave him a whack. He whinnied and began to canter back to the Castle. Clovermead scrambled up in front of her father, and they began to ride.

The Yellowjackets had their swords out. Lady Cindertallow and one Yellowjacket rode ahead of Clovermead and Waxmelt; the other Yellowjacket brought up the rear. Clovermead listened for hoofbeats, but all she heard was the blaring trumpet. Beyond the meadow the olive trees blocked their sight. They rode into the groves, and the curving path, so attractive before, now slowed them down to an agonizing trot. Far to either side she could hear the shouts of farmers running to their houses. The land looked at peace, but the trumpet blasted its warning of danger. *Fear and terror,* it repeated; *terror and fear.*

They came out of the olive groves and into a cornfield that bordered a canal. All Clovermead could see around her were the corn's chest-high stalks, waving in the slight breeze, and the olive trees encircling the corn. A scarecrow stood awkwardly in the center of the field.

The scarecrow *moved*. He put a horn to his lips, blew a baying cry, and charged through the corn. He drew his scimitar: The handle was made of carved bone and the blade shone with a liquid gleam. The scarecrow wore a helmet over his face, he rode a dark horse, and all around Clovermead three more riders wavered into sight. Bear-priests. The furs they wore were gray blotches, and their bronzed, jagged teeth were snarling and open and shone in the sun. The three bear-priests and the scarecrow came from all directions with unsheathed scimitars in their hands. The bear-priests answered the baying horn with ululating howls.

The Yellowjackets and Lady Cindertallow drew their blades and formed a triangle around Clovermead and Waxmelt. Then the bear-priests were on them, scimitars slashing. Both Yellowjackets were fighting bear-priests, her mother was fighting the howling scarecrow, and the fourth bear-priest had gotten past them and had raised up his scimitar in front of Clovermead. Clovermead swung an arm grown large and furred and clawed at the bear-priest. His scimitar curved under her swinging arm and cut toward her eyes, and then Clovermead ducked as the scimitar whistled over her head, past Waxmelt, and sliced a stalk of corn. The head of corn sighed and fell, and the bear-priest rode away.

Clovermead turned and saw the helmeted scarecrow disarm her mother with one blow of his sword. "No!"

Clovermead cried (or did she only roar her dismay?), and she kicked her pony's flanks and galloped desperately hard toward her mother while Waxmelt clung to her waist. The scarecrow struck down at Lady Cindertallow with his sword, she stumbled backward, and Clovermead lashed out with her long paw to knock the bear-priest's wrist to one side. His scimitar sliced down her mother's forearm and through her wrist. Clovermead roared in anguish and struck him backhanded with all her might. The scarecrow flew through the air and crunched against a tree at the edge of the cornfield. His helmet flew off his head.

It was the tall man. A stray sunbeam gleamed through the leaves above him and lit up his pale face and his curly red hair.

"Mallow Kite," said Lady Cindertallow from her horse. Her face had gone pale. "No. It can't be."

"But it is," said Mallow Kite. "Lord Ursus has raised me up from where you left me. I am revenged on you at last." He turned from Lady Cindertallow to where Clovermead gaped at him, and he shrugged at her apologetically. Then he twisted himself around the tree, Clovermead heard him running, and he was gone. His dark horse neighed, stomped on the earth with a crack that shivered in Clovermead's bones, and ran after his master.

Birds cheeped in the trees. A mouse scampered through the green stalks of the field. Clovermead could hear the water flowing in the canal and felt Waxmelt shaking with relief in the saddle behind her. Somewhere trumpets blared, *danger,* and two dead men lay among the trampled corn. A bear-priest and a Yellowjacket had slain each other and fallen side by side.

"I've been a fool," Clovermead whispered in numb horror as she stared after Mallow Kite. *I ask you in your father's name not to mention me to her,* he had said. *I think she would try to kill me.* Clovermead had listened to Mallow, she had said nothing, she had even dragged him from the Ballroom to save his life, but he was the killer, not Lady Cindertallow. A tear trickled down Clovermead's cheek. "Mother, what have I done to you?"

She turned and saw Lady Cindertallow staring at the trees. "Mallow," her mother whispered. Her teeth were chattering, and she made the crescent sign. Blood dripped steadily from her hand and forearm—and she swayed in her saddle.

"Milady!" Waxmelt cried, and Clovermead swung off her pony and ran to Lady Cindertallow. Her mother half-fell from her horse, and her unwounded hand fell on Clovermead's shoulder for support.

"I feel faint," said Lady Cindertallow. "And my arm itches. Clovermead, help me down." She tried to remove her feet from her stirrups, tottered, and fell heavily into Clovermead. Clovermead staggered beneath her mother's weight, barely held her, and laid her flat on the ground. She looked at her mother's cut flesh and saw yellow venom ooze in the blood. Lady Cindertallow looked at her arm and groaned. "A poisoned weapon," she said. "I should have expected Mallow would use that against me." She turned to one side, vomited, and fainted.

Waxmelt came up by Clovermead and knelt over Lady Cindertallow. "Let me look, Clo," he said urgently.

Clovermead moved to give him room, and he tore off her mother's sleeve at the shoulder. Then he gently pulled the cloth away and made sure to draw every thread out of Lady Cindertallow's gashed arm. Clovermead gasped when she saw her mother's wounds. The flesh around them had bloated and turned black.

"Fetch water from the canal," Waxmelt snapped to the remaining Yellowjacket. "We have to clean her wounds." The Yellowjacket nodded and scampered away. Then Waxmelt bent over Lady Cindertallow's arm, put his mouth to the ragged cut, and sucked out the oozing venom. He spat the yellow liquid into the grass, then sucked more from her hand. The Yellowjacket came back with a flask of water, and Waxmelt sloshed some onto Lady Cindertallow's wounds and some into his mouth. He spat out more watery venom. The touch of the poison had swollen his lips.

Lady Cindertallow's wounds still bled. Clovermead saw glints of yellow venom sinking ever deeper into her mother's blackened flesh. "Will she live?" asked Clovermead. *Don't let my folly kill her, Lady,* she prayed frantically.

"If we get her back to Chandlefort in time," said Waxmelt. "I've gotten rid of what venom I can, but some's gotten into her blood. She needs a doctor." He tore a strip of cloth from his shirt and bound it lightly around Lady Cindertallow's wounds. Then he beckoned to the Yellowjacket. "Help me carry her to her horse." The Yellowjacket ran to help him lift Lady Cindertallow from the ground.

Lady Cindertallow opened her eyes as they pulled

her up. "Stop," she said. "I can walk." They let her go, and carefully Lady Cindertallow took a step. She looked at her bandaged arm and at the dripping blood visible through the cloth. "Do you hate me that much, Mallow?" she asked in horror and in anger.

"Who is he?" asked Clovermead. She growled with shame and fury. "I'll kill him! I swear it, by Our Lady."

Lady Cindertallow laughed, with rising hysteria. "Kill Mallow Kite? You can't."

"Let me try," said Clovermead. Her claws scrabbled at the air.

"He's dead already," said Lady Cindertallow. "Long in his grave."

Chapter Five

Under Siege

A dead man, **thought Clovermead as they rode** through the wooded lanes toward Chandlefort. Her head was swimming. *His flesh was cool. I kissed his cheek.* Behind her, Waxmelt held the dead Yellowjacket's sword. Lady Cindertallow, pale and bleeding, rode beside her and wielded the dead bear-priest's scimitar in her left hand. The surviving Yellowjacket rode in the lead. All around them were distant cries, the crackle of flames, and the soft clamor of hoofbeats. From Chandlefort itself she heard the trumpets of the Yellowjackets riding out from the walls, but nearer were the hoarse cries of bear-priests and the screams of farmers. Beyond the peaceful olive trees and thick hedges that lined the road, smoke rose from a dozen places. *I should have told her about him,* thought Clovermead numbly. *Milady, I'm so sorry.*

The woods ended five hundred yards from the town gates: The remainder of the way lay through open ground. Yellowjackets on the walls watched for an attack, while more Yellowjackets rode from the gates toward the blossoming fires in the fields. Cadets rode out with them, pale with anticipation and fear at the thought of their first battle. A trickle of wounded Yellowjackets had already begun to return to Chandlefort. They brought with them riderless horses, and horses with dead bodies lashed to their backs.

"My poor Chandlefort," said Lady Cindertallow. "I thought you would have a year of peace." She wiped away a tear, then spurred her horse. "Quickly, now." They burst into the open ground and galloped toward the gates.

A roar erupted to their right. Two hundred yards away three bears charged out from the woods to intercept them. Clovermead spurred her pony to go even faster, but he was panting and tired from the distance he had already run. Some far-off Yellowjackets checked their horses and turned to gallop toward them, but the bears would reach them long before the Yellowjackets could arrive.

"They won't get to you, Milady," Clovermead said with grim determination. "I won't fail you again." She turned to Waxmelt and asked him, "Can you keep control of my pony?" He nodded, and Clovermead handed him the reins. She gave her father a fleeting kiss on the cheek, jumped up from her stirrups to crouch lightly on her pony's back, and leaped into midair.

Her clothes melted into her fur—she didn't quite know how that happened, but during the winter she had learned to think *this* way instead of *that* way when she changed into a bear, and then her clothes had started transforming with her and reappearing when she became human again. She landed on the ground on all four paws and pounded forward. She was a golden bear seven feet long and three feet thick, her arms and legs were a foot across, and her claws were huge as they scrabbled against the dirt. She was still missing a tooth, and her scar stretched from her neck all the way down her left foreleg to her paw. No fur grew on the scar tissue, but the luxuriant tufts to either side obscured the welt. Her sight was dim, but her hearing was keen and her smell keener. She growled with satisfaction as she barreled nearer to the oncoming bears.

Clovermead blinked, and now she could see pale and shining tendrils of light hooked into each bear's skull. They were like the red web of the blood-net Lord Ursus used to enslave the bears who served him, but no human blood pulsed in these coils. They shone with the phosphorescence of rotting flesh. The tendrils vibrated to the sound of clanking bones, Mallow Kite's acid laughter rasped through them, and the coils moved the bears like marionettes.

Clovermead blinked again, the vision of the glowing tendrils was gone, and the nearest bear was ten feet away and swinging to face her. She leaped on him—but could not strike. Mallow's laughter echoed in every movement the bear made. Clovermead looked into his helpless eyes, and she knew that he did not control his own body. She buffeted him with her paws, but not to kill.

Foolish girl, said the bear, and Mallow Kite's voice rustled in his growl. He leaped at Clovermead, and his claws raked down her side, while his jaws tore fur and skin from her shoulder. Clovermead shrieked and flailed at the bear with her own sharp claws; she bit and she held nothing back. She grabbed his front leg between her jaws and twisted, oh, Lady, twisted, and she felt his bones crack. He howled and fell to the earth. He could not move, and the pale tendrils flickered out of his skull and abandoned him. He was just a bear again.

Forgive me, said Clovermead. The world whirled around her, and there were tears in her eyes and the bear's blood in her mouth. *I didn't have a choice.*

You're the changeling, said the bear curiously. *Boulderbash said the changeling freed her for a little while. Free me, too, forever.*

I don't know how, said Clovermead miserably.

Then sooner or later you will have to kill me, said the bear. *If my leg heals, I'll be enslaved again, and I'll come to hunt you once more.* Slowly he got onto three legs and gave Clovermead a pleading look. *I don't want to serve Lord Ursus or Lord Kite. I want to run free in the Reliquaries. Save me, changeling.*

I can't, said Clovermead. *I wish I could.*

The bear growled in despair and began to hobble toward the trees. *It would have been kinder to kill me,* he said.

I'm sorry, said Clovermead, but she didn't know if she was sorry for striking him or for not striking him hard enough. She turned to face the other two bears—and saw that the Yellowjacket was fighting one and Waxmelt was fighting the other. Clovermead gaped to see her father wield a sword. He held it like a kitchen knife and swung it with clumsy, vigorous strokes. He fended off a grizzled brown she-bear and gave her a whack across the nose. She yipped, then whined and fled as

Clovermead pounced at her tail. The last bear took a look at the odds, ducked under the Yellowjacket's sword, and joined the other bear in flight.

Lady Cindertallow watched the bears flee, then looked at Waxmelt with surprise. "You display unexpected talents, Lord Wickward! We'll make a soldier of you yet."

"Dear Lady, I hope not." Waxmelt's sword shook in his hand as he slid it back into its scabbard. He looked at Clovermead and his eyes widened. "Clo!"

Clovermead turned human. Her clothes had been rent up and down her side, she bled from four runnels across her ribs, and her bitten shoulder ached. "Don't worry, Father. It looks worse than it feels." She felt a wave of dizziness. "Although I could use some help getting up." She reached out her hand, and Waxmelt pulled her back onto her pony. Then Waxmelt kicked it in the sides, and they galloped the last yards through the gates and into Chandlefort town.

Hundreds of farmers seeking refuge milled in the square just within the town gates. Some had only their clothes; others had brought spades and rakes, chickens and goats. A few had hitched oxen to their wagons and carted all of their possessions with them. Yellowjackets with drawn swords shouted at the farmers to move on quickly and leave room for the soldiers to ride in and out of the gates. The farmers sullenly obeyed, but every now and then a panicky surge sent a farmer stumbling toward a Yellowjacket, to recoil at a waggle of the soldier's blade.

"Praise Our Lady," said the Commander of the

Yellowjackets. He rode up to Lady Cindertallow with a haggard look on his face. "I heard you were dead, Milady."

"Not yet," said Lady Cindertallow. She lifted up her bleeding hand and grimaced. "Give it time, Commander. How many bear-priests are out there?"

"Hundreds," said the Commander. "Lord Ursus must have sent all his cavalry. I haven't seen more than a few dozen of his bears, but that's bad enough. The bear-priests are burning farms everywhere and killing any farmers they can catch. Milady, we're still short of men from that mauling Ursus gave us last winter. I don't have enough Yellowjackets to bring the rest of the farmers back to Chandlefort."

Lady Cindertallow cursed. "How many farmers are still out there?"

The Commander looked around the crowded square and counted quickly. "Two thousand at a guess."

Lady Cindertallow looked at the walls. "And those Yellowjackets up there?"

"I need them to guard the walls, Milady. If the bear-priests attack—"

"I understand." Lady Cindertallow turned abruptly to Waxmelt. "Lord Wickward, if I put swords in the servants' hands, which way will they point them?"

Waxmelt's eyes went large, then he forced himself to answer evenly. "They will be loyal, Milady."

"I trust they will," said Lady Cindertallow grimly. For a moment her face went dead white and she clenched her teeth to keep from screaming. She could not speak again for several long moments. "Lord

Wickward," she continued at last, her voice still ragged with pain, "I am about to provide you a rare opportunity to convince me that you menials are worthy of better treatment. I need another regiment for as long as this siege lasts, and I need them on the walls within the hour. Raise me that many servants, and they'll have my gratitude and my respect."

"They won't disappoint you, Milady," said Waxmelt. His face was pale. "Thank you for giving us a chance to prove ourselves."

"Thank Lord Ursus," said Lady Cindertallow. "I wouldn't do this if I had a choice. Hurry. Two thousand lives depend on your precious servants."

"We'll be there," said Waxmelt. He swung down off Clovermead's pony, bowed quickly to Lady Cindertallow, then set off at a dead run toward the Castle.

"There's a silver lining in every cloud. How delighted that little man is!" Lady Cindertallow shivered, beads of fever-sweat trickling down her face, then turned to the Commander. "Open up the Armory. Give out swords, bows, and armor to everyone Lord Wickward brings to you, and send them to guard the walls. When they get there, take away a regiment of Yellowjackets and send them into the fields. Tell them to save as many farmers as they can."

Clovermead wobbled on her saddle. "Excuse me, Milady," she interrupted, "but I think those scratches are getting to me. I feel light-headed." She could feel blood dripping down her side. "Can we go to the doctor now?"

"At once," said Lady Cindertallow. "Do you understand your orders?" she asked the Commander. He nodded, and Lady Cindertallow gave him a golden ring set with a ruby bee. "You have command of the battle today. If anyone disobeys you, show them this. If you need me, the Demoiselle and I will be getting our wounds treated in my rooms." She wheeled around, then galloped with Clovermead to the Castle stables.

A pair of servants supported them from the stables to Lady Cindertallow's rooms, where Clovermead and Lady Cindertallow collapsed into two chairs near the door. "Fetch Lady Saraband," her mother said to the first servant. "Bring medicines, medical instruments, boiling water, and bandages," she said to the second. They nodded and dashed out the door.

"What do you want Saraband for?" Clovermead's shoulder ached and she wanted to scream.

"Your cousin learned medicine from the Abbess at Silverfalls. She's not half the healer the Abbess is, but she's the best doctor in Chandlefort," said Lady Cindertallow impatiently. "Didn't you know that?"

"I should have expected it. She's the best at everything." Clovermead had more sour comments on the tip of her tongue, but she was too weak to say them. She leaned back in her chair and waited for Saraband.

Saraband rushed in a few minutes later, and the servant with the medical supplies stumbled in after her. Saraband went quickly to the two of them—then hesitated. "Who should I treat first, Milady?"

"I've just got flesh wounds," said Clovermead quickly. "Milady's poisoned."

Saraband knelt by Lady Cindertallow, unwrapped the rough bandage from her arm, and hissed in horror when she saw the wounds. "I'll see what I can do," she said uncertainly, and she started to treat Lady Cindertallow.

Clovermead reached out a hand for her mother to grip, but her stomach flip-flopped and she couldn't look. *I'm not a coward,* she told herself tremulously. *Really I'm not. But I don't want to look at surgery.* She heard Lady Cindertallow gasp, again and again, and once she heard her mother scream. She caught a glimpse of Saraband's silk dress out of the corner of her eye, and she shook her head in wonder. *Who'd have dreamed a dainty thing like her was a doctor? I'd have thought she'd scream at the sight of blood.*

Saraband finished with Lady Cindertallow, then quickly cleaned and bandaged Clovermead's wounds. Now it was Clovermead's turn to gasp and Lady Cindertallow's turn to give her daughter her hand. Clovermead felt tears coming to her eyes. Her cuts were shallow and clean, but Saraband's ministrations still hurt an awful lot. Clovermead felt weak as a kitten by the time Saraband finished bandaging her up.

"How is she?" asked Lady Cindertallow.

"She'll heal, Milady," said Saraband. She sat back wearily in her chair, while her arms hung by her sides. She had rolled up her sleeves, but there were flecks of blood up and down her dress. "She should rest for a few days, while the scars set."

"I promise not to jump on the bed," said Clovermead. "I don't even want to walk to bed. I'll just fall asleep here."

Lady Cindertallow chuckled. Then her fingers fumbled over the cloth of her new bandages. A red trickle had already seeped through them. "I can feel it itch," she said to Saraband. "Can you cure the poison?"

"I don't even know what it is. The medicines I've given you will slow its spread through your body, but I have no antidote." Saraband hesitated a moment, then leaned forward in her chair. "Milady, you should ride to Silverfalls Abbey. The Abbess knows far more about poisons than I do."

"Meadowlark? No, not her. It was Mallow Kite who wounded me."

Saraband frowned uneasily. "Milady, Mallow Kite died eleven years ago."

"I know he did," said Lady Cindertallow. Her teeth chattered. "I saw his corpse myself, run through a dozen times. He's dead and buried, but I saw him not two hours ago. He drove the sword into my arm. He would have driven it into my heart if Clovermead hadn't prevented him. Do you think Meadowlark gave him the poison? Do you think she raised her dead brother from the grave?"

"Milady, you're unwell," said Saraband. "Perhaps he only resembled Lord Kite."

"I know him," said Lady Cindertallow violently. She rose from her chair and glared at Saraband. "I know his face as well as my own. He's not one day older than the day he died."

"He had cool flesh," said Clovermead. She looked up at her mother. "I've seen him before. I touched him. The day was broiling hot, but he was cool." Tears came to her eyes. "I'm so sorry, Ma'am. I didn't know who he was, and he said not to tell you about him. He said you'd kill him. I thought he was one of Ambrosius' friends whom you exiled, and you made it sound like you *would* kill one of them if he came back to Chandlefort, so I kept quiet. Ma'am, please forgive me."

"Dear Lady," Saraband whispered. The blood slowly drained from her face.

Lady Cindertallow fell back in her chair. "Is that why you were asking me those questions the other day? Our Lady is just. I would have killed any of Ambrosius' friends who broke their exile, and I am well paid for my cruelty. Oh, Clovermead, I can't blame you for being merciful. Who could imagine a dead man walked the earth?"

"I still don't know who he is," said Clovermead. "Who he was, I guess I should say. Ma'am, why does he want to kill you?" *He rose from his coffin to get revenge on you. What did you do to him?*

"I once made certain choices. He died as a result of them." Lady Cindertallow glanced at Saraband. "Ask me some other time, Clovermead."

"I will not intrude on your privacy any longer than I have to," Saraband said stiffly. "But, Milady, if it truly is Mallow Kite, you must ride to the Abbess. A poison out of the grave—"

"Meadowlark will not touch me," snapped Lady Cindertallow. "Will I be fool enough to let the sister complete her brother's work? Which other doctors in Linstock can cure me?"

"None that I know of, Milady."

Lady Cindertallow swore. "Then I'll send to the Thirty Towns."

"You might not last that long, Milady," said Saraband. "The medicines I gave you can't slow the poison much beyond the waning of the moon." Clovermead looked out the window at the full moon rising in the late afternoon sky. Her mother had only two weeks. "Milady, your suspicions of the Abbess are unjust. Lady knows she doesn't care for you, but she's not a poisoner. And to raise the dead?—she's no magician, either. Please go to her."

"She calls me a murderer, Saraband." Lady Cindertallow lifted her bleeding arm and tried to clench her fist. She could not, and she whimpered in pain. "She'll have me apologize for what is not my fault. She'll make me abase myself."

"Not if you are dying," Saraband said quietly. "She's not that cruel."

"She will!" Lady Cindertallow's cheeks were red and flushed. "I won't humble myself before her. I'd rather die."

"No!" cried out Clovermead. She jerked to her feet. "You can't! Not when I've just started to get to know you."

Lady Cindertallow looked in anguish at her daughter, but wrapped her pride more closely around her. "I'm sorry, Clovermead. I won't go."

"Then I'll go," Clovermead blurted out. "Send me to Silverfalls. I'll be as humble as can be to this Abbess of yours, I'll apologize for everything in the world, and I'll ask her on my knees to come back with me to Chandlefort to cure you. Won't it mean something to her if the Demoiselle comes to her? I'll say you were too ill to come yourself, and that's true enough, Ma'am, you shouldn't be going anywhere. But I won't just let you die." She wiped more tears from her eyes. "Please, Ma'am, don't let my mistake kill you."

"Perhaps you could go," Lady Cindertallow began—but then she shook her head. "It's too dangerous for you to leave while the bear-priests besiege the city."

"I'll run away," said Clovermead. "I'll slip out the gates and run through the Salt Heath to Silverfalls, wherever that is, and I'll apologize for you and fetch back your blessed Abbess. You can't keep me here!"

Lady Cindertallow chuckled. "Actually, I can. There are a number of very secure dungeon cells I could order you to right now. I think that would keep you out of mischief! I wonder I didn't think of that before now." She smiled sadly. "It's a kind offer, Clovermead, but I won't let you risk being killed."

"If Chandlefort is under siege, perhaps it is too dangerous for the Demoiselle to stay here," said Saraband slowly. "We may fall to the bear-priests, Milady." There was a long silence as Lady Cindertallow took in that thought. "Outside of Chandlefort there's no safer place in Linstock than Silverfalls Abbey. Even if she doesn't agree to help you, I'm sure she'd agree to keep the Demoiselle safe behind the Abbey walls."

"And once she lets me in, I'll try my hardest to convince her to come here and cure you," said Clovermead eagerly. "Please, Ma'am. Let me at least try."

Lady Cindertallow looked at her arm, then at her daughter, then sighed. "Very well. I'll send you to

Meadowlark for safekeeping. If you can soften her heart, well and good." Her eyes unfocused as she calculated what to do. "You'll go tomorrow morning, before any more bear-priests arrive. I'll send an escort of Yellowjackets with you to Silverfalls."

"Can Sorrel come with me? I'd like to have a friend along."

"Granted," said Lady Cindertallow. "He's done some errands for me in that direction, and he'll make a good guide for you. And since you want a friend, he may stay with you when the other Yellowjackets return. Send him to me as a courier in case of need. As I remember, he's a fast rider." Her eyes fell on Saraband. "Lady Saraband, I want you to accompany my daughter as well."

Saraband turned pale again. "You know how the Abbess and I parted. I have no wish to return to Silverfalls. Please allow me to decline your offer, Milady."

"Lady Saraband doesn't have to come," said Clovermead. "If she's at loggerheads with the Abbess, I don't see that it'll help to have her along. Anyway, she should stay here to tend to you." She tried to sound thoughtful and considerate, but all she could think about was the way Sorrel and Saraband had smiled at each other as they danced. *Don't let her come, Lady,* she prayed. *She'll spend all her time making eyes at Sorrel. I don't want to have to look at the two of them together.* A dot of cold bile was jittering in her stomach.

"You will go, Lady Saraband," said Lady Cindertallow firmly. "You say you can't do anything more for me, and Clovermead is about to have a hard journey across the Heath. I want you with her in case the ride reopens her wounds. You can tell the Abbess that you're following my orders."

"That will not mollify her," said Saraband. "But I suppose I have no choice. May I be excused, Milady? I'll need to pack for the morning." Lady Cindertallow nodded, and Saraband curtsied, gave Clovermead a bitter look, and left the room.

It's not what I want either, Clovermead thought angrily. *I don't want you along, and I hope you twist an ankle tonight. That'll keep you in Chandlefort!*

Clovermead heard a faint clamor. She walked to the window, wincing and slow, and saw the first two-score servants arriving at the town walls. They ran heavily and awkwardly in their just-donned chain mail and kept on tripping over their swords and spears. The Yellowjackets they replaced began to run toward their waiting horses in the town square. Clovermead saw a little man who had to be her father hurry another hundred servants through the streets. She smiled to see him herd the straggling mob like a sheep dog.

Lady Cindertallow staggered to her bed and fell down. "There's wine in the cupboard," she said to Clovermead. "Bring it to me." Clovermead opened up the oak drawers, took out a half-empty bottle and a glass, and brought them to her mother. Lady Cindertallow tried to uncork the bottle but could not. Clovermead loosened the cork for her mother, then poured some wine into the glass. Lady Cindertallow took it in a shaky hand, brought it to her lips, and gulped. "At least I can still do this by myself," she muttered. She gulped again, and now half the wine in the glass was gone. Her face began to flush. "Wine puts me to sleep," she explained. She closed her eyes. "Thank you, Clovermead."

"I'm glad to help, Ma'am," said Clovermead awkwardly. She paused a moment. "Ma'am, who is Mallow Kite? Can you tell me now?" His lonely eyes still called out to her for pity. His bitter laugh of dead bones, which moved bears like puppets on a string, echoed in her still.

"The man I almost married," said Lady Cindertallow. She shivered. "Lady, Lady, I thought our sorrows ended at death. How can he hate me still?"

"What happened?" asked Clovermead.

Lady Cindertallow took another, smaller drink. "I was hunting," she began.

Chapter Six

The Huntress

It was winter in the Lakelands, and we were hunting wolves. My cousin Athanor came with me. He loved the hunt as much as I did, though he had excused himself from hunting the winter before, in order to dote on his newborn babe with his wife, Meadowlark. Lord Mallow Kite came hunting too. Mallow was Meadowlark's brother and Athanor's best friend. He was a handsome man with hair like copper rings, he was high-spirited and daring, tall and strong. I liked him very much. I thought perhaps I more than liked him; certainly I had let him fall in love with me. We had been so for some months. It was cruel of me to leave him in suspense so long—but, truly, I was undecided.

Ambrosius Beechsplitter came with the Yellowjackets who accompanied me. I pretended it was because he was from the Lakelands and knew the woods as a native, but there was more to it than that. He had half-stolen my heart the first time I saw him, and it had never come back to me entirely. He had lovely light-brown hair that turned to gold when the sun shone on it, a downy beard, and eyes as blue as the summer sky. He was a slender man, almost dainty, but he could joust as well as any Yellowjacket in Chandlefort, and he had won his fair share of prizes in their races and games. We had spoken to each other often enough over the years that I knew the sound of his voice and the shape of his smile. I told myself that it was only the pleasure of admiring his features that led me to keep him in my guard.

Bugles blared and dogs howled as we chased a pack of wolves over the ridge between Elkhorn Lake and Marten Lake. The land was clear enough for horses to ride but broken enough that we had to part from one another to make our way through the snow-clad forest. I galloped alone over fallen trees with a wolf-spear in my hand. My companions had fallen away when my horse leaped a frozen stream in one bound. I heard the howling of wolves, and my blood quickened. I hoped I would be first to reach the pack.

I heard hoofbeats come up behind me, and I turned to see Athanor. I was disappointed but not surprised. My cousin had always been an excellent horseman. Indeed, I had learned to ride from him. The trees thinned out at the ridgetop, and we rode side by side for a while. "Hello, cousin," I said, "where have you been?"

"Off to Chandlefort and back again," he said with a smile. Athanor was a pale man with black hair, pockmarked skin, and a long nose. "I've kissed Meadowlark, petted the little one, and now I'm back for the hunt. Where is the rest of our merry band?"

"Far behind," I said. "Only Cindertallow blood can ride this fast." I laughed, but I meant it. No one ever rode faster than we two cousins. I was better in sprints, but Athanor surpassed me in long-distance riding. I enjoyed competing with him.

"You must take pity on your men, Melisande," said Athanor. "Let them catch up. How will they ever reach you otherwise?"

I looked sideways at Athanor and wondered if there was a double meaning in what he said. The wind whipped at his black hair, and he grinned at me. There was a moral there, all right. I'd heard it often enough, and would again until I was married. Chandleforters are anxious when the Lady Cindertallow has no husband and no heir.

"The Lady Cindertallow should never condescend," I said fiercely. "I will not shackle myself to soothe their pride. If any of them are able, they will reach me without help. If not, I'll kill the whole pack of wolves myself and leave the men to skin them."

"Tush, you're selfish," said Athanor. "You must learn to share."

"Only with a man who's earned his portion," I said.

There was a sudden howling ahead, and two wolves broke from the underbrush. They ran forward and to the right, seeking to slip behind a ridge of rock. I turned one way to check their advance while Athanor whirled behind them to close the trap. The wolves screeched to a halt, saw no escape—and leaped! The first wolf flew straight toward my face. My horse reared, my spear was already up, and I skewered him in midair. He slid down the shaft, his jaws snapped at me as he died, and his body slammed into mine and almost jolted me from my saddle. I turned to look for the second wolf, but Athanor had already chopped her down.

We left their bodies for the huntsmen behind us to

find and skin, and continued riding. Now Mallow Kite had caught up with us. He saw that my cousin and I had already killed, and chagrin crossed his face—petulance, almost. It made him less handsome. But it was gone quickly as he heard more howling ahead, and he spurred his horse the harder. Athanor and I slowed down. Now that we had slain, we were required in due courtesy to leave the other huntsmen a chance for glory.

The three of us came to a stretch of flat, bare rock at the top of the ridge, and I watched Mallow as he sped after a wolf. He was bareheaded—vanity, perhaps, but it showed his ringlets off beautifully. He strove with all his might to catch the wolf, kicked hard into his horse's flanks, but the wolf was too fleet of foot. It had nearly disappeared over the ridge into the far forest when Mallow threw his spear. He was marvelously strong; the spear flew fifty feet and struck the wolf through the heart. The creature whimpered, fell, and died. Mallow turned to me and smiled. I confess I smiled back at him. It was a pretty feat and he was a pretty man.

Just then we heard yelping growing louder from the trees ahead, and we turned to see what caused the sound. Suddenly half a dozen wolves burst out of the forest toward us—and behind them was Ambrosius. He was—oh, it was the funniest thing. He *herded* them, spanked them with his wolf-spear so that they yipped with terror, and made sure none escaped as he drove them back toward us. I laughed with delight, Athanor guffawed, and I realized Ambrosius had outridden us all, outsped the wolves, galloped so fast that he could play with the wolves like a cat with mice.

"Insolent rogue," said Athanor, but he said so admiringly.

"Excellent rogue," I said, and I could not help smiling at Ambrosius. He saw my smile and returned it in a way that was friendly, deferential, and something more. He bowed as best he could as he passed us, then rode on and out of sight, still herding the wolves toward the oncoming huntsmen. Some of them had just come into view and seen what Ambrosius had done. Word of it spread quickly among the hunting party.

And Mallow, whose moment of triumph had been completely undone, who had seen me turn my smiles from him to Ambrosius—Mallow scowled, and he looked at Ambrosius with envy and hatred.

That evening we stayed at Aurhelia Hall on Marten Lake. The Hall had been built for Queen Aurhelia to rest in between campaigns during her wars against the Tansyards. It is a palace of pink marble and buttery limestone, an airy edifice suited for the warm clime of Queensmart in all save the high-pitched roof tacked on to ward off Linstock snow. Queen Aurlinde had pawned it to my grandmother in return for enough gold to wage war against her sister for a summer. The gold was never repaid, and my grandmother kept Aurhelia Hall as her hunting lodge. She had hung furs and antlers over the frescoed walls and made the palace's southern splendor more homey and familiar.

That night, as Athanor and I read the latest letters of news from Queensmart in a second-story room, I heard raised voices. Curious, I turned to the door. "What is that noise?" I asked.

Athanor went to the hallway and peered down. After a moment he returned and shut the door again, shaking his head. "Mallow's drunk and picking a quarrel with your rogue. It promises to be a vulgar scene. Pay no attention, Melisande."

My heart pounded oddly. "A quarrel?" I asked, more lightly than I felt. "I don't think I've seen one of those before. I'd like to watch."

Athanor gave me a queer look. "You should not be seen at such an event."

"Then I will watch secretly," I said. I was giddy and smiling and no longer thinking of anything beyond the Hall. "Come along, Athanor. This is too good to miss." Athanor gave me another look, shrugged his shoulders, and stepped out of my way.

I crept into the hall. The balcony on the second floor was wide and dark with shadow, and Athanor and I were invisible from the floor below as we peeped out from behind a pair of marble busts. Mallow faced Ambrosius in the open space between the wooden tables laden with food, drink, and snoring lords. Behind Mallow sprawled some of his lordly friends in fine hunting clothes; behind Ambrosius sat a pair of Yellowjackets. Mallow's cheeks were flushed with wine.

"Tell me about making furniture," said Mallow. "What's it like to work for a living?" He had a cup in his hand and downed another gulp.

"I was a very bad furniture-maker, Lord Kite," said Ambrosius amiably. "The legs fell off my stools, and the varnish peeled. I'm sure if I'd gone into business for myself, I'd have starved to death."

"But you worked," said Mallow. "You put your hands to wood so you could sell the stuff. I can't imagine being so degraded." He flung the last word at Ambrosius, and his hand twitched toward the knife at his belt.

"My Lord, these last few months I have come to think of you as a friend," Ambrosius said more quietly. "I have enjoyed sparring with you on the Training Grounds. Must you say such things?"

"I have no choice now." Mallow laughed with desperate, loud bitterness. He swayed forward as he stood, so that he almost touched Ambrosius. Ambrosius took a step backward. "Dishonorable. That's what it is. There isn't a speck of honor in woodworking. Do you hear me, Beechsplitter?"

"I hear you, My Lord," said Ambrosius. His smile had drained from his face. "Your Lordship is most nobly stationed," he said after a moment. "I cannot claim to be your equal in honor. Still, Your Lordship is unjust to my former profession. It is a most reputable and worthy calling, however much I have fallen short of giving it its due. I could wish Your Lordship to condescend to speak more charitably of it."

A hush fell across the Hall, because Ambrosius had disagreed with Mallow. He had done so very respectfully, he had done so under great provocation, but he had disagreed. Mallow could choose to make a quarrel of it.

Mallow did. "Speak well of your trade, Ambrosius? I cannot, little Yellowjacket. It's filthy and degrading work, no better than cleaning sties. I say that you and your father and your whole family all did filthy work."

"I say you're a drunken, lovesick fool," said one of the Yellowjackets as he stepped up to Ambrosius' side. "Quarrel with me if you've lost Milady's favor."

"Hold your tongue, Hob," Ambrosius hissed. Hob looked surprised and hurt, and Ambrosius' look was suddenly gentle again. "We must not sully Milady's name by saying we quarrel over her. We are disputing my family's honor. Do you understand?" Hob reluctantly nodded and so did the other Yellowjacket.

Ambrosius turned back to Mallow, and there was a flash of real anger in him now. "I must differ with Your Lordship. My father loves his craft, and he is a master of it. He has tramped all through the Lakelands to find timber suitable for proper furniture. He has spent days smoothing the surface of a chair leg, passed more days mixing varnish properly, and he sells to men who have no conception of what effort he makes for them. Only old men understand, who come to him and say, 'You made me a chair forty years ago, and it's as sturdy and handsome today as the day you sold it to me.'

"My father is a reputable merchant. He can come into any town in the Lakelands with empty pockets and buy cartloads of wood. He does not even need to swear to Our Lady that he will pay in due course. The timber merchants know that his word is a surety worth gold. He has been elected an Alderman of Elkhorn Lake seven times because his fellows know that he is an upright man. He has been the town's treasurer ten years, and he renders accounts accurate to the last penny. His honesty is unimpeachable.

"My father is an honorable man, Lord Kite. He may

not be the equal of a lord of Chandlefort, but he is an honorable man. On that I must insist."

Mallow was still angry, still bitter and drunken, but now there was regret on his face. I think at that point he would rather not have quarreled with Ambrosius, but it was too late. I stole a glance at Athanor. There was terrible sadness on his face. "You poor fool," he whispered to Mallow. He looked at me with tear-bright eyes. "Please, Melisande, go back into the room. You know what will happen."

"I will stay," I whispered back. My stomach coiled oddly, and I was short of breath and terribly excited. I knew indeed what would happen to Mallow, but I felt no pity for him. All my affections were elsewhere.

"You lie," said Mallow wearily. He drew his knife from his belt, drank the dregs of his wine, and let the cup fall to the floor. It clanged and rolled under a table. "You lie as vilely as your father lives. Deny it!" He jabbed his knife toward Ambrosius.

"I cannot agree with you, Lord Kite," said Ambrosius. He drew his knife, and the fight began.

They were more evenly matched than I had expected. Mallow was drunk, but he was a strong man with a long reach, and he had fought many knife-duels. In the first seconds Ambrosius barely avoided having his stomach sliced open. Mallow struck and struck, so powerfully that any blow would have killed Ambrosius had it hit home. As it was, his blade twice grazed Ambrosius and left him bleeding from his left arm and right leg. Ambrosius retreated steadily from his hammer-blows.

Then Mallow swung so hard that his knife lodged into a table. In the second it took him to wrench the blade free, Ambrosius attacked. Now Mallow had to jump back from Ambrosius' knife, and the fight was evenly balanced. Both jabbed and feinted, sidestepped and ducked. Their limbs were flecked with blood. It was nothing like the swordplay of the Yellowjackets, where armor and shield can defend you, but a dreadful, naked violence, with their soft flesh perpetually vulnerable to each other's knives.

Mallow struck with all his might, and Ambrosius cracked down with the hilt of his knife on Mallow's wrist. Mallow cried out as his knife skittered across the marble floor. Ambrosius slammed his knife toward Mallow—and stopped, with the knife tip touching Mallow's chest. "My father is an honorable man," he said quietly, in a silent room. He let the knife stay long enough for Mallow to know what could have happened, then wiped his blade on his sleeve and returned it to its scabbard.

"Why don't you kill me?" asked Mallow. His tongue was thick with shock and drink. "You won. What is there left for me?"

"You are mistaken, Lord Kite," said Ambrosius. "We have never fought. I quarreled with you, but then I was afraid to fight. I fled into the night, to Chandlefort, to resign my commission in the Yellowjackets out of shame."

"I don't understand," said Mallow. "Your knife touched my chest."

"Of course it did," said Hob. "What are you blathering about, Ambrosius?"

Ambrosius lifted great blazing eyes to Hob, to

Mallow, to all the huntsmen in the room. "Lord Kite, I regret that I forgot my place at the hunt this afternoon. I should not have provoked you. I daydreamed, hoped for the impossible, and I made myself conspicuous to gain her smile. A furniture-maker's son should never do such things. It is folly to seek her smile when her hand is destined to be yours. And since it is destined to be yours, I think my duty to Chandlefort requires that I relieve Milady's future consort of all embarrassment. The world must be told that you were the victor in our fight, and I must be gone before I am tempted to further folly." He turned to Hob. "Hob, accompany Lord Kite until he returns to Chandlefort. If anyone should ask him about tonight, relieve Lord Kite of the necessity of telling the story himself. Speak for him and say how I fled."

I could not stay still any longer. He was discretion itself, as gentlemanly as he was strong and beautiful, and I was in love with him to the full of my heart. I could not let him exile himself from me. There was more love in the way he said the word *folly* than in any sonnet I had ever heard. I began to rise—and Athanor's hand caught me.

"If you speak, you must marry him," he whispered to me. His grip was like iron. "As he says, he is only a furniture-maker's son. The lords of Chandlefort will not be pleased to bow to him."

"What do I care for the lords of Chandlefort?" I asked. "Let me go, Athanor."

"You will kill Mallow," said Athanor. "He is a fragile man and he will break. When he breaks, Meadowlark will too. She loves her brother dearly, and her soul is bound up in his. I can see it already, Melisande. In Our Lady's name, I beg you not to do this."

"I will not lose him," I said in a passion. "I will not let him go." I tore my wrist from Athanor's grip, and I stood up at the balcony. "Ambrosius Beechsplitter," I called out, and my voice rang through the Hall. He was at the door, and he turned slowly. His face was white and he scarcely dared meet my eyes. "You do not have my permission to go," I said. Then I smiled at him as I had never let myself smile before, and I sparked an answering smile in him, so full of love that my skin was warmed by it from where I stood. I wanted to see him smile at me forever.

Athanor looked at me with sorrow and reproach. Mallow stood slack and ashen, his heart and his pride hollowed out in one blow. Later I would regret what I had done to Mallow, to Athanor, to Meadowlark, but then I had no eyes for anyone but Ambrosius. Joy swept me up and I could think of no one else.

"What happened afterward?" asked Clovermead.

"Mallow had no will to live after that day," said Lady Cindertallow. "He courted death in every battle after the war started, and he died at the Battle of the Cliffs two years later in a mad charge against the soldiers of Low Branding. Athanor died with him, trying to save him from the Mayor's men. I sent their bodies back to Meadowlark to be buried. Meadowlark entered the Silverfalls Abbey soon after. She has never forgiven me for their deaths."

She looked at her arm. "And neither, it seems, has Mallow."

Chapter Seven

ACROSS THE SALT HEATH

CLOVERMEAD ATE BREAKFAST WITH LADY Cindertallow at dawn. Her mother awkwardly spooned up oatmeal with her left hand. Her eyes drifted to Clovermead every few seconds. "I won't come with you to the town gates," she said at last. "I don't like long good-byes." She looked away from Clovermead. "Get to the Heath as quickly as you can, before the bear-priests realize you're outside the walls. The rest of Lord Ursus' army may be here soon. Don't come back until we've fought them off."

"I'll come back with a cure for you, and I don't care if it's safe or not." Clovermead stalked around the table and seized her mother in her arms. Her side and shoulder hurt, but she didn't care. Lady Cindertallow shrank back a moment, then let her unwounded arm go around Clovermead's shoulders. Clovermead's heart beat loudly: They had never hugged each other so tightly before. She kissed her mother lightly on the cheek, then let her go. "You can't get rid of me that easily, Ma'am."

"I don't want to get rid of you at all." Now Lady Cindertallow looked at her daughter with anguish and longing. "I've had you so short a time."

"I promise I'll be back safe and sound," said Clovermead. She made the crescent sign. "I've really liked our six months together. I never dreamed I would have a mother. I'm glad it's you."

Lady Cindertallow's eyes were moist, and they hugged each other again. This time it was easier for them.

"Don't strain your side," her mother said briskly as they parted. "I want you to get well soon." Her eyes skimmed over Clovermead's comfortable traveling clothes and lit up as they saw Ambrosius' sword buckled around her waist. "That will serve you well. Take good care of it. Clovermead, if there's any trouble, listen to the Yellowjackets and do what they tell you to do."

"Don't you worry, Ma'am," said Clovermead as she walked to the door. "I'll be just as dutiful and proper as I've been here in Chandlefort."

"Why am I not reassured?" Lady Cindertallow smiled a last time at her daughter.

Clovermead looked back quickly from the dining room door. *She looks thinner already,* she thought, and a new tremor of fear throbbed in her. *Maybe I won't come back in time to save her, no matter how hard I try. Maybe I won't see her again.* She did her best to memorize her mother's face before she let the door shut.

Waxmelt walked with her from the Castle to the town gates. He had donned a too-large helmet and a too-small shirt of chain mail and exchanged the dead Yellowjacket's broadsword for a light rapier. Clovermead couldn't help but laugh when she saw him.

"It wasn't my idea to play soldier," he grumbled. "That dratted Commander said somebody had to lead the servants' regiment, and there wasn't anybody else who would."

"First a lord, now a general! You're moving up in the world, Father. Next thing you know, you'll be commanding the Yellowjackets."

"Don't listen to her, Lady," said Waxmelt, his eyes turned up to the sky. "I'd rather spend my life dipping sheep. Clo, I want to take off this ridiculous garb as soon as I can."

"You know, you don't look nearly so bald in that helmet," said Clovermead thoughtfully. "It's actually rather becoming on you."

"Do you think so?" asked Waxmelt—then glared at his daughter as she started giggling. "Clearly Our Lady intended you to preserve me from vanity."

They passed a stoop where a family of farmers had curled up to sleep for the night. Clovermead looked ahead and saw more farmers lining the sidewalks down toward the town gates. Some had woken already: They looked with hollow eyes toward the walls and their abandoned farms beyond. A few bowed their heads to Clovermead as she walked by them.

"How many farmers did the Yellowjackets rescue?" Clovermead asked quietly.

"Another thousand came inside the walls by sundown and some hundreds during the night. Most of them are safe." Waxmelt looked at the farmers on the sidewalks, and he smiled with bemused pride. "The farmers cheered when they saw the servants on the walls."

"You deserve it," said Clovermead. "You're all awfully brave."

"We're all awfully raw, Clo. We'll have a Yellowjacket sergeant start to drill us today, but I'm not sure if we'll be proper soldiers by the time Ursus' main army arrives."

"I'm sure you'll be fine, Father," said Clovermead stoutly.

"I wish I were so sure," said Waxmelt. "All we've ever been is lackeys. I hope Milady has not put too much faith in us." He smiled wryly and clanked his ringleted sleeve against his side. "Come what may, at least I know what it's like to wear armor! I dreamed of that when I was a boy watching the Yellowjackets ride by Lackey Lane. I feel a fool, but a part of me feels gleeful, too."

Clovermead laughed, and by then they had arrived at the square in front of the town gates, where Sorrel, Saraband, and a dozen Yellowjackets waited. Sleepy servants and yawning Yellowjackets lined the walls on either side of the gates. Sorrel sat on his horse, Brown Barley. The Tansyard had Clovermead's pony by his side, and he sent him trotting over to his mistress. Clovermead gave Waxmelt a kiss and a good-bye hug as fierce as the one she had given her mother, though this time her aching ribs told her that she had given quite enough hugs for one day. Then she swung onto her pony's back and waved farewell to her father, and the party galloped through the town gates and into the fields.

In the strangely quiet countryside all Clovermead could hear was the pounding of horses' hooves. There should have been farmers in every field, but Clovermead saw nothing but a few crows flapping above the corn rows. Most of the fires set the day before had burned out; only a few soggy plumes of smoke remained to mark the bear-priests' arson.

Clovermead heard a sudden crackling to her right. A new jet of fire rose into the air. In the distance bear-priests began to yell with savage joy.

"Let's go a little faster, Demoiselle," said the Sergeant leading the Yellowjackets. He kicked his heels into his horse's flanks, the party began to gallop along the western road, and the greenery of Chandlefort's fields dwindled quickly behind them. In half an hour they passed into the Heath.

They traveled on a road of gray flagstones straight west over a flat plain toward the distant line of the Reliquary Mountains. The land here was brick-hard ochre earth, pockmarked with knee-high spiky bushes and covered with a thick blanket of fine red dust that whipped back and forth in the breeze. The sun beat down hard, and the horses gasped with pleasure whenever a roadside thorn tree provided a bit of shade. Sorrel trickled water from his flask onto Brown Barley's face and rubbed the water from his ears to his nostrils while he whinnied with pleasure; Clovermead did the same for her pony. She wiped dust from her face five times before she gave up and let it cake on her. She felt cooler beneath the red grime, if unpleasantly filthy.

Clovermead had expected Saraband to blister and burn as she rode in the desert sun, but her cousin wore a sensible cap to ward off the glare, a high-necked blouse tied tightly around her throat, comfortable riding trousers, and a stout flask of water by her side. She wore no weapon, but otherwise she seemed as well prepared for the rigors of the Heath as Clovermead was. She looked slighter and daintier than ever as she rode among the burly Yellowjackets, but she was as fit a rider as any of them.

They rode alone through a land empty of humans, of animals, of everything but the occasional straggling bush. The emptiness was oppressive, but at the same time comforting. It would be difficult for bear-priests to sneak up on them in this desolation.

Clovermead looked back toward the green fields and saw more fires rise.

What good will it do to cure Milady? Clovermead wondered bleakly. *Lord Ursus' army will still be there and there still won't be enough soldiers to drive them away.* She cast about in her mind for some solution, but none came to her.

Two more fires flared up on either side of Chandlefort.

The party stopped for a lunch of hard cheese and oat bread at a cluster of teardrop-shaped pillars inscribed with the burning bee, duplicates of the pillars east of Chandlefort that Clovermead had seen the last winter while she marched with the army of Low Branding. The flat Heath stretched out around them. The Sergeant laid out a cloth for Saraband and Clovermead to sit on, but didn't join them. Sorrel ate with the other Yellowjackets. Clovermead gulped down her food, while Saraband ate hers with delicate care.

"Is it far to Silverfalls?" asked Clovermead after a while. She didn't look at Saraband and tried to speak in a nonchalant monotone. She didn't want Saraband to think it mattered to her if she received an answer.

"It's three days hard riding from Chandlefort, Demoiselle." Saraband's voice was flat and unhappy.

"Is it like this all the way?" Clovermead gestured at the blasted land around them.

"The Heath gets gentler as we get farther from Chandlefort," said Saraband. "You should see grass tomorrow." She took a bite of bread while Clovermead took a swallow from her water-flask. Clovermead turned to see Sorrel gazing at Saraband with a revoltingly admiring expression on his face. When Clovermead looked back at Saraband, the unhappiness had faded from her face. She wasn't exactly smiling, but there was a certain sparkle in her eyes. Saraband adjusted herself on the cloth so as to present her profile to Sorrel.

"You don't look so unhappy about going to Silverfalls now," said Clovermead. She tried to keep her voice even.

"I would rather be in Chandlefort, Demoiselle. Yet if I must make this journey, there are certain compensations." She glanced at Sorrel, smiled, and finished her lunch with demure little bites.

She looks like a cat about to make mincemeat of a canary, thought Clovermead disgustedly. *And the canary likes the cat! Ugh.*

The dot of bile squirmed in her again, but it had grown larger. Now it was a long string coiling in her guts.

They rode through more thorny scrub in the afternoon, and by the end of the day the crest of the Reliquaries was perceptibly larger. Clovermead saw clouds nestle on their peaks, and she felt a breath more moisture in the air. Birds flew among the updrafts, and small animals scurried through the scrub. At evening the party came to a small oasis surrounded by a tumbledown brick wall. Inside, a score of ragtag farmer families tended to straggling fields of rye and vegetables. Near the wall stood a low fort garrisoned by a dozen slouching soldiers in rusting chain mail, who slunk away from the scornful gaze of the Yellowjackets. Their Commander bowed low to Clovermead when he heard who she was, and arranged for beds for the party.

After dinner, in the deep twilight, Clovermead walked very slowly from the fort through a vegetable garden and to the eastern wall. Her ribs had been jostled all day as she rode, and now she ached very badly. She yawned. *Oof, Lady, I need my rest!* In the last glimmer of light she tried to see Chandlefort, but not even the fires were visible anymore.

"Hello, Clovermead." Sorrel stepped up to her side and peered eastward with her. "Do you wish company while you stare?"

Clovermead nodded. "I wonder if I'll ever see Father or Milady again," she said in a low voice. "Half of me wants to turn back to Chandlefort now."

"I will not say that you should not be afraid. I have lost father and mother, brother and sister, and all my Horde to the jaws of bears and the swords of bear-priests. I cannot tell you that it will not happen again. But do not lose hope too soon. Do not anticipate sorrows."

"I try not to," said Clovermead, "but my imagination's awfully morbid. And Mallow—" Her eyes went wide. "You don't know yet what's happened, do you?"

"I have heard rumors," Sorrel said cautiously. "Some people said Milady was injured, others said it was you. One cadet said you had both been ambushed by bears outside the town walls and eaten up by the furry monsters—but soon afterward my Sergeant told me that Milady had ordered me to escort you to Silverfalls Abbey and remain there as your companion, so that tale did not frighten me for long. I would be glad to know what occurred yesterday, especially now that you inquire of my ignorance with tones of great forbidding. What exactly *has* happened, Clovermead?"

"Milady's terribly hurt." Clovermead quickly told Sorrel about Mallow Kite's attack on her mother, who Mallow was, and how Saraband had suggested going to the Abbess of Silverfalls for a cure.

"A dead man?" Sorrel's voice squeaked. "Do you know any particular reason how he comes to be up and walking? Or if any other of Milady's deceased acquaintances will be joining him in this peculiar revival?" Clovermead shook her head, and Sorrel groaned. "These sorts of things did not happen in the Tansy Steppes. There were no bear-teeth trying to eat people and no dead men rising out of their graves. We led a quiet everyday life of raiding and thievery, with nothing stranger than the odd four-leafed clover to disturb our routines. I disapprove of these goings-on."

"It's not like *I* raised Mallow Kite up from the dead. You needn't give me that reproachful look as if it's all my fault."

"I assure you that the look I give Mallow Kite when I meet him will be far more dire." Sorrel shivered. "What exactly does this ambulating corpse look like?"

"He looks like anybody else. He's just a little pale, and his flesh is cool." She looked at Sorrel's own remarkably pale face, and she asked him uncertainly, "You won't leave me alone if he comes after me?"

Sorrel swallowed hard. "No, no. I will face him at your side completely terrified, and together we will sing the *Dirge of Two Knives* at him."

"Thank you," said Clovermead. "That makes going on easier." She heard a sound behind her and saw Saraband stroll into the vegetable garden, to walk idly between rows of tomatoes. Sorrel would have to pass her by to get back to the fort. "She sure must have liked that dance," Clovermead muttered.

"I flatter myself that I am not unskillful at dancing," said Sorrel, and Clovermead blushed to realize that she had spoken loud enough to be heard. He smiled. "She is much more pleasant than you told me, Clovermead. How ever did you come to have so poor an opinion of such a sweet lady?"

"Sweet lady, fiddlesticks," said Clovermead. "She could eat babies for breakfast and you'd still say she was a nice young girl. I'm not fooled by the way she looks."

"By the moon's sweet light! Do you mean that I have been ensorceled by a pair of pretty eyes?"

"Yes," said Clovermead concisely. "And you'd better watch out. She has her claws out for you."

"Such pretty claws," said Sorrel dreamily. "I think you are too late, Clovermead. I am enchanted beyond hope of salvation."

"Do you really like her?" Clovermead's stomach felt

queasy. "I know she's pretty and all, but she's hoity-toity and sugary and refined and how can you stand to talk with her?"

"I am no enemy to refinement, Clovermead. I admire Lady Saraband's manners greatly." Sorrel looked at Clovermead seriously. "I have only spent the one evening of the Ball talking with her, but I like her very much. She is reserved about many matters, which some might take for stiffness, but I would not care for a lady who spills her heart to every gallant she meets. And it is something we have in common. On many matters I am reserved too."

Clovermead laughed. "I'm sure that's because everyone's reserved in the Cyan Cross Horde and no one ever knows anything about anyone else. Days go by without anyone exchanging a word, and when they do say something, it's to say, 'Pass the salt, the horse steak's a bit dull today.'"

"Actually, we were quite talkative in the Cyan Cross Horde," said Sorrel. "If I were still among them, I would sing a loud song of admiration to the Lady Saraband, so publicly that she would blush a most-furious-and-yet-becoming red." He paused a moment. "I have not talked much of matters of the heart since the Horde was destroyed, Clovermead. I prefer to say little of what I feel and to make jokes. You are my only companion to whom I would speak of my admiration for the Lady Saraband." He glanced at Clovermead. "I ask you as my cherished friend to think more kindly of her."

His cherished friend, thought Clovermead. *I should be so happy to hear him call me that, but I'm not. It means he already likes Saraband more than he likes me.* Her face was hot and her eyes felt like they were being rubbed by rough wool.

"I'll try," said Clovermead, but she knew she didn't sound very eager. She made herself smile and say briskly, "Anyway, don't ever step on Saraband's toes when you dance with her. She got very cross with me when I did that, and she wasn't the least bit reserved about it."

"Thank you for your warning." Sorrel turned toward the vegetable garden, where Saraband was waiting. "Shall we go in?"

"You first," said Clovermead. "I'll stay out here a bit. I like the breeze."

"As you wish." Sorrel walked away, and soon Clovermead heard Saraband say, "Cadet, I am curious. What are the words in Tansyard for these vegetables?"

"I would be glad to tell you, Lady," said Sorrel, and then their voices dwindled as they wandered farther from the fort and into the garden's darkness.

Clovermead shuffled slowly toward the barracks when they were safely out of the way. "Go and tell her the Tansyard word for *carrot,*" she muttered. "And *lettuce* and *celery,* too! Now I know you don't need to make clever conversation with someone you like. You can just talk about garden greens." Her stomach clenched, and she told herself furiously, "I don't care what Sorrel says. I don't like Saraband, and I won't like her. She's awful and she's stealing Sorrel away from me so he can moon over her. Cherished friend? Ha! That doesn't mean a thing."

Clovermead's claws were long inside her clenched fists.

• • •

A thin grass sprang up on the Heath the next day, just as Saraband had predicted, and the horses neighed with pleasure as they left the naked dust of the inner Heath behind. The flat plain began to crumple into a series of low hills and valleys. Sorrel's eyes sparkled avariciously as a family of mustangs pounded by in the distance; with a sigh he kept himself to his duties as escort. The sun was less harsh here than in Chandlefort, and Clovermead luxuriated in its warmth. Toward noon a flock of pigeons flapped overhead, flying from the south. Clovermead marveled as they passed by in their thousands.

"It's lovely here," Clovermead said to Sorrel. She felt much better after a good night's sleep. This morning she had been able to walk at almost normal speed, despite the ache in her ribs and shoulder. "I wish I could have been here in spring to see the meadow flowers bloom."

"You should come to the Steppes in springtime! The bluebells and the daffodils cover the land, and you cannot see an end to them. The grass is still short, and it is as if a rainbow had come to Earth to paint the land with all its loveliness. We call the flower-fields the Sky's Tattoo—" Sorrel stopped speaking abruptly and cocked his head. Then he whistled and the Yellowjackets came to a halt. In the silence Clovermead could hear distant hoofbeats coming after them from the east.

Bear-priests, thought Clovermead fearfully. The hoofbeats grew louder.

"I would advise us to leave the road, sir," Sorrel said to the Yellowjacket Sergeant. He pointed to a copse of linden trees profuse with leaves that lined the banks of a nearby stream. "I believe we can hide there."

The Sergeant looked around the open grassland, then nodded agreement. He spoke soft orders, and the Yellowjackets brought their horses hoof-deep into the shallow water of the stream. The lindens obscured the view of the road. Clovermead kept a tight rein on her pony. He didn't like water underneath his hooves, and he was nervous.

"There's a good pony," Clovermead whispered, stroking his nose. "I'll keep you safe. Don't you worry." He nickered uneasily.

The hoofbeats came ever nearer. Then Clovermead heard neighing and savage yelling, a horse screamed, and ten, fifteen, twenty bear-priests galloped past the screen of leaves that hid them from the road. They wore scimitars and rode white Phoenixian horses. Dust billowed from the road, the bear-priests were ghosts in the haze, and only their bronzed teeth gleamed as bright as ever. Then they were gone, dwindling into the distance ahead of Clovermead and her companions.

"Will they come back this way?" Clovermead's heart was beating double-time.

"I wouldn't risk the road anymore," said the Sergeant. He glanced at Sorrel. "You've been to Silverfalls before, Tansyard. Do you know any other paths?"

Sorrel scratched his head, looked around, then pointed to a muddy track on the other side of the stream. "That cow-path follows the stream, and the stream departs from the road in another mile. Both stream and cow-path will eventually curve to Silverfalls. We will go more slowly than on the road, but we will get there soon enough. Also, since the path sticks to the valley bottom, I do not think we will be visible from far away."

"Sounds good to me," said the Sergeant. "Demoiselle?"

"Just so we watch out for cowpats." Clovermead saw Saraband still staring after the bear-priests, her beautiful face pale with fear, and somehow her fear made her look more irritatingly delicate than ever. "Wear a sword if you're so scared of them," Clovermead called out.

Saraband's face went cold. "I would rather die," she said.

They rode on through the grasslands of the valley bottom. Galloping made Clovermead's shoulder and ribs hurt more again, but not as badly as the day before. The Heath began to slope upward toward the Reliquaries, and Clovermead could make out bare mountaintops and dark green forests ahead of her. The mountains west of them were lower than their brethren to the north and south, and clouds from the ocean beyond lazed through the gap. Now the Heath was thick with gangs of herdsmen and lowing throngs of cattle, long-haired, shaggy, and red like the soil of the Heath underneath the grass.

The Yellowjackets camped for the night in a shanty set up for traveling herdsmen. Before going to bed Saraband removed Clovermead's bandages, cleaned her wounds, and tied new swaths of cloth around them. "Thank you," said Clovermead unwillingly.

"Milady wouldn't want you to bleed all over the

Heath. It would be untidy." Saraband drew the last bandage tight. "You heal astonishingly quickly. Is it something bears do?"

"I wouldn't know," said Clovermead. "Next time I fight one, I'll ask."

Saraband looked at Clovermead with a hint of impatience. "I know you didn't enjoy my class, Demoiselle, and I'm reasonably sure you didn't care for me as a teacher, but can you set that aside? We're not in dance class anymore."

"I don't know what you're talking about." Clovermead buttoned up her shirt and stalked away from Saraband. "Minx," she muttered as she stepped outside the shanty. "Conniving vixen! You're stealing my friend, and I won't set it aside. I'll be rude and I'll be nasty and I'll—" She growled in anger and despair. "What's the use? It doesn't matter if I'm sweet or horrid. He'll still want you."

Clovermead fell into an uncomfortable sleep that night. She dreamed she was a Tansyard girl out on the Steppes, chasing on horseback after Sorrel. He kicked his horse to a gallop and raced away from her into the plains, faster than she could ride. He was catching up with another Tansyard, who was Saraband, and they were riding into the distance together. Clovermead growled her sorrow, and her claws pierced the flesh of her steed. He neighed with sudden pain. Then there were more growls all around her and she was sleeping in a tent of the Cyan Cross Horde. The bear-priests were coming to kill her, to set their tents afire, just as Sorrel had told her. She heard a scream—

She was awake and she heard screaming still.

A sentry cried out "Bear-priests," swords clashed, hoofbeats hammered, and bear-priests howled all around her. A great scimitar cracked open the top of the shanty, and Clovermead saw a Phoenixian with a bear-priest rear up in the starlight. His sword came down, and Clovermead ducked under it, out the shanty door.

"Sorrel!" Clovermead yelled, but she couldn't see him. "Where are you?" Her heart ached with fear, but there was no reply in the clamoring night.

Yellowjackets and bear-priests fought in the darkness in confused knots. The bear-priests had the advantage of surprise, but the Yellowjackets had gone to sleep fully armed, and they hewed with abandon at every horseman they saw. Clovermead drew her sword, parried the ferocious slash of a bear-priest, then thrust after him as he rode past. She felt a pulse of joy to be using Ambrosius' sword for the first time. She sliced air, and another bear-priest was riding toward her, swinging his sword wildly in hopes of hitting something. Clovermead cut into his ankle, and he yowled. His Phoenixian was nearly on top of her, and Clovermead tumbled to one side.

She found herself in back of the shanty, where Saraband stood panting in the darkness, frozen in terror as soldiers fought all around them.

"I have a sword," said Clovermead. She had reopened one of the slashes down her ribs; she could feel her blood dripping down her side in the dark. She strode over to Saraband and held out her father's blade. "Here, take it."

Saraband reached out a trembling hand—then

jerked it back. "I don't fight," she said. Determination kept her fear in check.

"Lady's curse on you," said Clovermead, and she was about to say a great deal more when a bear-priest came charging into the alcove behind the shanty. His sword was swinging toward Saraband's neck, and Clovermead barely had time to think *I have to save her* before she was leaping forward with her sword. The birchwood medallions shone, the blade glittered, and the bear-priest cursed as moonlight reflected from the sword into his eyes. Blinded, the bear-priest stumbled, and Clovermead brought her sword down on his sword-arm. The glistening edge crunched through a steel gauntlet and halfway through the bear-priest's wrist, and he howled in pain as his sword spun into darkness. Clovermead slapped him backhanded with an arm suddenly grown into a bear's foreleg, and he flew unconscious to the ground as his Phoenixian bolted away.

"We have to get out of here now," said Clovermead, turning her foreleg back into an arm. The yelling had grown even louder, and she saw flames rising around them. She sheathed her sword and walked over to the still-frozen Saraband. "I don't know where our horses are. Can you ride on my back if I turn into a bear?" Saraband looked at her vacantly. "Are you deaf as well as useless? Answer me!" Saraband still said nothing, and a shanty timber collapsed in flames. Clovermead growled with exasperation and fury, and she slapped Saraband on the cheek.

Saraband reeled from Clovermead's slap, and suddenly her eyes focused. "How dare you!" Saraband began furiously, but then there was another scream on the other side of the shanty. "Change, farm-girl," she spat out.

"Hold tight," said Clovermead. "I won't go slow to make Your Ladyship feel comfortable." Then she was changing, growing, thickening. She was a golden bear again, and she stood before Saraband in the darkness. *Hurry,* she growled, though Saraband couldn't understand her. Saraband jumped onto her back, and her hands twisted hard into Clovermead's fur.

Clovermead ran. She couldn't quite go at top speed, slowed by her wounds and Saraband's extra weight, but she barreled through the fight. There were Yellowjackets and bear-priests everywhere, and it looked like the bear-priests were winning. She looked for Sorrel, but she couldn't see him, couldn't hear him, couldn't smell him. A bear-priest brought his scimitar down toward her, but Clovermead swerved, jumped over the still-lit cooking fire, and was beyond the bear-priests. Clovermead raced away into the open Heath.

She stopped at the top of the hill. Behind them was darkness and the distant clash of swords. She looked a last time for Sorrel, for anybody, then turned and roared her grief as she fled into the Heath. After a while she heard sobbing, and Saraband buried her face in Clovermead's fur. Clovermead's fur grew damp as they raced away.

Chapter Eight

THE BARGAIN

CLOVERMEAD FOUND A PLACE TO REST IN A CUP OF earth at the top of a distant ridge. They could see for miles from there but were hidden by the crumbling lip around them. Without blankets the Heath at night was chilly, so Clovermead stayed in bear-form while she slept. Saraband began the night at the opposite side of their resting place, but her cousin had curled up next to her warm fur when Clovermead woke at dawn.

Saraband woke a few minutes later, yawned and sat up, and looked around the empty plains. Rain clouds swept over the Heath for the first time in weeks. Lightning flickered among the storms already pounding the Reliquaries, while the curtain of rain blew eastward toward them. There were no bear-priests visible—but neither were there cattle or herdsmen. Not even birds flew.

"Turn human, farm-girl," said Saraband. "I should look at your wounds, and I'm not a bear-doctor." Clovermead changed back and shivered as the damp wind cut into her skin. She touched the reopened wound on her ribs and winced: It was no longer bleeding, but it was far more tender than it had been.

Saraband undid Clovermead's bandages, ran her fingers along the scar tissue, and whistled low. "You twisted that wound terribly when you were running. I'd have sworn the strain would break a rib, but your bones are fine."

"I don't feel consoled," said Clovermead. "I hurt a lot."

"Let your middle rest today, as much as you can." Saraband knotted Clovermead's bandages, and Clovermead stuffed her shirttails back into her trousers. "You'll heal. I'm worried more about how to stay clear of the bear-priests." Saraband pointed to the lowering in the crest of the Reliquaries directly to the west. "Silverfalls is there. Should we risk going straight to it?"

"Why ask me? You're the one who's been here before."

"You're the fighter," said Saraband. "I'm not. There could be another hundred bear-priests out there waiting to catch us and I wouldn't know."

"I wish Sorrel were here," said Clovermead. "He'd know what to do."

"I do too," said Saraband. There was a thread of grief in her voice. "I liked him very much, Demoiselle."

Against her will Clovermead felt a burst of sympathy for Saraband. "He'll turn up. He's escaped from bear-priests before, and he can do it again." Clovermead didn't believe a word she said, and Saraband looked like she didn't either, but she nodded her head and pretended to be reassured. Clovermead looked at the oncoming storm-clouds. "We'll wait for the rain to arrive before we start walking toward Silverfalls," she decided.

"The bear-priests won't be able to see us in that downpour."

"That sounds remarkably cold and uncomfortable," said Saraband. She looked at her dirt-stained blouse and trousers, and sighed. "I wish the bear-priests had given me time to grab a change of clothing!"

Clovermead couldn't help but laugh. "I wish I could have grabbed some food and another sword! Clothing doesn't matter that much."

"I suppose so, farm-girl." Saraband shrugged. "But I cannot control my heart. It wants clean clothes more than food or weapons."

"I'm not a farm-girl," said Clovermead, annoyed. "We raised sheep up in Timothy Vale and I worked in Ladyrest Inn. We had a garden out back, but we weren't farmers."

"I don't care, farm-girl," said Saraband. "You've never acted like a Demoiselle, and I'm tired of calling you by the name. You're a farm-girl to me."

"I should just leave you for the bear-priests." Clovermead couldn't keep her dislike for Saraband out of her voice. "They deserve you."

"Do what you like." Saraband lay down on the Heath. "I presume the rain will wake me. If you're still here when I get up, I'll do my best to guide you to Silverfalls." She closed her eyes and fell asleep.

I ought *to leave you here,* thought Clovermead. *You wouldn't feel so high and mighty when you woke up!* Then she sighed. *I'm not that petty. Much though I'd like to be! Milady, why did you get it into your head to send Saraband along? My wounds aren't that bad, and there can't be a more annoying traveling companion in Chandlefort.*

Clovermead couldn't get back to sleep, so she took her sword out of her scabbard, wiped away the blood-stains on the dewy grass, then dried the metal with a clean corner of her shirt. She looked at the dull metal curiously and ran her fingers along the edge. It had cut through steel armor, but it was as sharp as ever. Clovermead eyed the sword with new respect. "You're quite something. Milady said you were an ordinary Yellowjacket's sword, but I don't think normal swords cut through steel like that." She looked at the plaques her father had carved, the boy freeing the bear and the man with his sword raised to the moon, and she remembered how light had reflected into the bear-priest's eyes. She raised the sword high. "Shine!" she said.

The sword stayed dark.

"I suppose it was just coincidence," said Clovermead. She put the sword back into her scabbard and patted the leather affectionately. "You're still a good, sharp sword, and I'm glad to have you." She settled herself into the earth, away from the wind, and waited for the rain to arrive.

When it finally came, Clovermead turned into a bear once more and Saraband got onto her back. Then Clovermead began to walk westward amid the spattering droplets. She trod cautiously over the hills: The mist had reduced their visibility to a few hundred feet, and the rain dug gullies in the earth. Clovermead tried to keep going in a straight line westward, but in the featureless, gray plain she quickly lost all sense of direction.

Soon the rain came down in determined, endless gray sheets. Sometimes it rained harder, sometimes softer, but it never stopped. Saraband shivered on her back. Clovermead felt wet enough, but she was sure Saraband felt worse. *Serves you right,* thought Clovermead vindictively. *Suffer! Sneeze!*

Despite the chilling rain and the constant ache from her wounds, Clovermead was enjoying herself. *I do like being a bear!* she thought. *It's like there's a pane of glass around me when I'm human, but when I turn into a bear, the glass is gone and it's just me in the world. Everything's so vivid and I can hear my heart pump my blood as loud as thunder. Oh, it's so wonderful to stretch my legs, to just run and be free!* She ignored her complaining ribs and bounded faster—until she slid down a muddy slope while Saraband yelped in sudden alarm. She kept her balance and trotted a little slower after that.

Once she saw a mounted figure in the grayness ahead. She stopped and crouched low while he rode by. She could hear Saraband moan her fear, softly and uncontrollably, until the figure disappeared into the distance.

Toward evening the rain finally tailed off, but clouds still swirled thickly over the Heath. Clovermead's stomach rumbled, and she stopped by a streambank. Saraband slid off her and huddled on a tuft of grass by the stream. She looked so bedraggled and miserable that Clovermead turned human just long enough to tell her, "I'll go get us some food." She shifted back into a bear and bounded upstream.

She could smell fish below her and fruit ahead of her. She pounced after minnows lurking in the stream, but they eluded her claws. Then she came to a length of wild strawberries growing by the stream. She turned human, pulled her shirt out of her trousers, and filled it high with strawberries, nibbling as she gathered. She saw a honeycomb high up in the branches of a nearby poplar tree, and all of a sudden her mouth watered. "A little honey wouldn't hurt," she said wistfully. Then she laughed. "Don't be silly, Clovermead. You know what happens when bears go after honeycombs. It all ends in tears and bee-stings." She finished filling up her stomach and her shirt with strawberries, then returned to Saraband. "Here, dancing girl," she said gruffly, and she dumped them into Saraband's lap.

"Thank you, farm-girl." Saraband began to pop strawberries into her mouth, at first with a semblance of delicacy, but then just wolfing them down. When she had gone through a respectable amount of them, she sighed happily. "That's much better. I'd almost be comfortable if we had a fire."

"I don't have any tinder with me, and I don't know how to rub damp sticks together to make a fire," said Clovermead. "Anyway, bear-priests might see the flames."

"I suppose that makes sense," said Saraband unhappily. She went back to gobbling strawberries. After a while she looked up at Clovermead. "Do you think the bear-priests knew we were coming?"

"A deliberate ambush?" Clovermead thought about it, then shook her head. "No. They'd have sent more bear-priests after us, to make sure they caught us all. I think that troop we saw ride past us must have caught our trail somewhere and taken the opportunity to attack us, whoever we were. It was just bad luck."

"Bad luck." Saraband stared despondently out at the darkness. "That seems an awfully bland way of putting it. I know I should not complain too much—after all, I am still alive—but right now I cannot help but wish that Milady had sent more Yellowjackets to escort us. Then we would not have been vulnerable to this sort of misfortune in the first place."

"Milady didn't have much choice," said Clovermead. "Chandlefort's awfully weak. She doesn't have many Yellowjackets to spare." She looked up at the dark sky. "Anyway, it should clear up tomorrow. And then—" She paused for dramatic effect.

"Then what?"

"Then we see the way clear to Silverfalls, or we see a whole lot of bear-priests, dancing girl," said Clovermead.

"Thank you so much for that cheerful thought," Saraband grumbled. She finished eating her strawberries while Clovermead turned into a bear and fell asleep.

In the middle of the night Clovermead woke with the smell of bears all around her in the Heath. There were dozens of them, pungent in the dampness, running westward toward the Reliquaries. Clovermead rumbled wistfully and wished she could join them—but Saraband had huddled up by her furry body again, clinging to her for warmth, and Clovermead couldn't move without disturbing her. *You really do have a positive knack for being annoying, dancing girl,* thought Clovermead. But she stayed still and let Saraband sleep on. After a while she fell asleep again too.

The next morning was overcast with gray clouds, but clear enough. Clovermead turned human and peered out over the Heath. She could see the Reliquaries closer than ever—but even nearer was a line of horsemen beading the plains. The nearest was only half a mile away. There was only one rider every mile or so, but that was enough to keep watch on that flat land. There was no way through to the Abbey.

"Lady's kirtle," Clovermead swore. "I didn't think there really would be bear-priests." She frowned as she looked at the expanse before them. "My best idea is to wait until nightfall and then try to slip between them."

"Will we be safe here during the day?" Saraband looked along the low streambed. "We won't be able to hide if a bear-priest comes for a drink."

"No." Clovermead laughed unsteadily. "Just pray to Our Lady that none of them gets thirsty."

"I will," said Saraband. She glanced at Clovermead. "Farm-girl, are you as scared as I am?"

"I've got gooseflesh from my forehead to my toes. Even when I'm a bear and I'm big and furry and strong, I just want to whine and run. I'd let my teeth chatter when I'm a bear, but my fangs would cut my lips."

Saraband smiled. "I'm glad to know I have company." Her hand pressed lightly on Clovermead's for a moment. "Thank you for protecting me, Cousin."

Clovermead felt suddenly ashamed, and her cheeks flared red. "I wouldn't really leave you to the bear-priests." Then she laughed abruptly. "I don't mind dance class *that* much!"

Saraband almost laughed too. "I'm glad you don't. I would hate to have my tombstone read, 'She corrected her students once too often.'"

"Just remember I got you strawberries the next time

I elbow my dance partner in the stomach. I want you to tell young Lord Whoever-It-Is that he needs to be a bit more agile when he dances with me, that's all."

"I will," said Saraband fervently. "You have my word on that."

Saraband took off Clovermead's bandages and cleaned her scabs with stream-water. She shook her head with amazement as she saw the new flesh knitting together. "I wish I knew how you did that," she said. "If I didn't know better, I'd say your wounds were two weeks old." Then she tied Clovermead's bandages back on, making sure they fit comfortably over her scabs.

They lay in the streambed all day and grew hungrier as they waited. Clovermead stayed small and human, for fear her bear-bulk would be too conspicuous. She tried to rest, but she couldn't fall asleep. She let her thoughts drift.

Hello, Clovermead heard someone say amiably in her mind. She could tell that he was a young bear not much older than she was. His name was Brookwade. She saw the way he looked in his own eyes—sleek and handsome, with long black fur and elegant fangs. He was entirely satisfied with himself.

With good reason, Brookwade thought comfortably. *There isn't a better-looking bear in all Linstock, if I say so myself. Who are you and how did you get into my mind?*

Clovermead, she thought. She sent images of herself as a human and as a bear.

The changeling? The one who turns furless?

That's me, said Clovermead. *I'll show you if I see you. Where are you, anyway?*

In the Heath. Brookwade sent Clovermead a confused image. There were mountains to the west, but his bear's vision was so dim that they were scarcely more than a blur of gray and green. He looked to be a few miles north of Clovermead and Saraband, but Clovermead couldn't tell for sure. *Have you been caught, too?*

Caught? What do you mean?

Caught, exchanged, given, said Brookwade. *Lord Ursus let us go, and for a moment we thought we were free. Then new coils came down upon us.* For an instant Clovermead could see Mallow Kite's white netting slither around Brookwade. It was slack now, but ready to command him whenever the dead man chose. *He summons us to meet him in the Reliquaries. Don't you feel his call?*

Clovermead tried hard to sense it, but she couldn't. *No,* she said. *I suppose I'm lucky.* She wrinkled her forehead. *He's in the mountains?*

In Kite Hall, said Brookwade. *By his grave. Lord Ursus gave Mallow only a little of his power when he raised him from the dead. Mallow can summon bears only when he is by his tombstone. He needs more bears for his second assault on Chandlefort, so he has returned to Kite Hall and calls us to join him.* Brookwade sighed. *It will be a wonderful thing to see so many other bears, but it will be sad and terrible to know we all are slaves to a dead man.*

I wish I could help you, said Clovermead. She remembered how she had crouched by the prison-carts in the Army of Low Branding and used Sorrel's blood to break the bonds Lord Ursus had clamped upon his bears. It had felt wonderful to drain Sorrel's blood, and she had almost killed him. She shuddered. *I won't use a bear-tooth again. I don't know anything else that can free you.* She frowned. *How does Mallow control you? It doesn't feel as if he uses blood.*

Mallow calls us with his misery, changeling, said Brookwade. *He calls us with the ache of his dead heart.* Clovermead gasped. She could see the white coils again, and now she could feel Mallow's jealousy and loneliness course through them. From the coils came a blurry image of her mother, the memory of blood dripped from his heart, and she felt a howl of pain and a punch of hatred—

Clovermead severed her connection to Brookwade. She was crouched with her knees to her chest and her hands to her ears. Her mouth had stretched wide in a silent scream. *I'm sorry, Brookwade,* she thought, tears leaking from her eyes. *I can't take any more of that. You poor thing, how can you stand to feel that all the time?*

And then she thought, *Poor Mallow. It must be worse for you.* She wanted to just hate him for deceiving her, for trying to kill her mother, but she couldn't. He hurt so much that she had to pity him.

The clouds swept away by nightfall and left the Heath sparkling clear. The stars shimmered above her in their thousands, and a shooting star arced over the southern sky. The waning moon was not much more than half-full: In a little more than a week it would be gone.

The medicines I gave you can't slow the poison much beyond the waning of the moon, Saraband had said.

Clovermead growled with helpless anger and tried to think about anything else. She could see the bear-priests' silhouettes on the horizon. "If we can see them, they might see us," she said to Saraband. "Maybe we should wait for the next rainfall."

"It doesn't rain often on the Heath in summer," said Saraband. Her stomach rumbled. "And I'm getting hungry. I'd rather make the effort while I've still got some strength left."

Clovermead's stomach growled too. "I guess I'm also hungry," said Clovermead. "I wish Father were here. He'd gather up half a dozen herbs, find a potato growing in a hillside, and make us a wonderful stew. Then he'd tell a story or sing a lullaby, until we'd fallen asleep without any worries at all."

"I'd like that," said Saraband wistfully. "I haven't had a lullaby sung to me in ages. My mother used to—" She stopped abruptly, then started again. "I haven't had a chance to talk with Lord Wickward. I've seen him around the Castle, though. He speaks to a scullery maid as politely as he speaks to Milady, and he wipes dust from the furniture when he thinks no one is looking. He's a curious man. I don't know him at all, but I think I might like him."

"Ask me extra politely and I'll introduce you when we get back to Chandlefort," said Clovermead. "If you're lucky, he might like you, too." Ahead of them a horse neighed, and Clovermead turned to peer into the darkness. "If we get back to Chandlefort. I think the bear-priests would see me if I went as a bear, so I'm going to keep my head down and crawl on the grass in human shape. How are you at slithering?"

"Ssimply sssplendid." Saraband smiled wanly at

Clovermead, then ruefully stroked her damp sleeves. "Oh, my poor blouse. I'll never get the grass stains out of it now."

"If we make it back to Chandlefort," said Clovermead, "I will wear nothing but green outfits. Green will become the Demoiselle's color and very fashionable, and then everyone will envy you your elegant grass stains. Does that reassure you, Cousin?"

"You're too kind." Saraband's eyes flicked over Clovermead. "You wouldn't look bad in a green dress," she said thoughtfully. "Not grass, but emerald, to show off your golden hair. Once the mud's been cleared out of it."

"Come with me to the seamstress when we're back home. You can tell her how to dress me up."

"Or I could just get a new blouse." Saraband shivered. "Shall we go? It's getting colder by the minute." Clovermead nodded agreement and they began to crawl.

The grass here was sometimes waist-high and sometimes nibbled down to the Heath. Where it was higher, they trotted forward on their hands and knees; where it was lower, they scuttled on their stomachs. Clovermead felt her scars stretch once or twice as she wriggled forward, but this time they didn't open. Then she led Saraband toward a gully that lay between the two nearest patrolling bear-priests, so steep that neither one brought his steed down into it, but only looked down into it from horseback. Clovermead could hear the rustling of small birds and field mice in the clear night air. She and Saraband moved ever more slowly and quietly as they came nearer the bear-priests.

They were only a hundred yards away from the bear-priests when Clovermead felt a sneeze coming on. It tickled at her nose, then loitered down into her throat. She felt herself convulse and she suppressed it with a desperate struggle. She moved forward another foot—and it was coming on again. Clovermead put her hand over her mouth. *Dear Lady, help me!* cried Clovermead in her mind, but this time she couldn't stop the sneezes entirely. Three muffled, snuffly *chuf-chuf-chufs* forced themselves through her clenched teeth into the Heath, and Saraband whimpered with fear.

For a moment there was silence. Then the *clip-clop* of the nearest bear-priest's horse started up again. He was coming closer.

Not again, thought Clovermead. *It was my fault Mallow struck down Milady, it's my fault again, and now Saraband will die because I couldn't control myself. I can't let this happen.* She put her hand on her sword, but she had a dreadful feeling in her stomach that it wouldn't do any good. More bear-priests would come the moment they heard the sound of battle. Maybe Clovermead could protect herself, but she didn't think she could protect Saraband as well. *If only she'd fight!* thought Clovermead with dread and anger. *Maybe we'd have a decent chance then. Why am I trying to keep someone alive who won't fight, and who'll take Sorrel away from me if he's still alive, and—*

She felt a twinge of jealousy and hatred in her heart. It was familiar. She had felt the same misery in the cords Mallow Kite used to bind Brookwade. *He calls us with the ache of his dead heart.*

Maybe I can do the same, Clovermead thought desperately. *A bear would be awfully useful right now.* She opened her mind and her heart. *Living heart, dead heart, what's the difference? Anyway, I don't have any better ideas.* She could feel jealousy and loneliness pulse in her, grief for her mother who was dying and grief for Sorrel who might be dead, and she flung her aching heart into the night. She felt a tug inside her, as if she had cast a line into a stream and caught a fish. The fish wriggled on the hook and she pulled back with all her heart.

What do you think you're trying to do? asked a voice like dried bones. Mallow spoke inside of her. Clovermead tried to break away from him, but white coils lashed out of the darkness and held her mind. She felt him rummage through her mind, like a bony hand turning the pages of a book. *Ah! Imitation is the sincerest form of flattery. But you are naïve, Demoiselle. My agony survived my death; do you think your little griefs are stronger than the grave? You cannot hope to wrest my bears from me.*

Let me go, said Clovermead. She struggled, but she could not move. She could hear the bear-priest coming closer still, *clip-clop. Let me fight before I die.*

Another minute, if you please, thought Mallow. He picked up strands of her memory—her anger and shame, her misery and uncertainty, her pity. *Pity? "Poor Mallow"? Why, Demoiselle, whatever gave you that curious notion?*

I don't want to think that way, said Clovermead unhappily. *You used my father's name to make me help you, and you tried to kill Mother, and I hate you! But you hurt so much that I can't help feeling sorry for you.*

I wish I hadn't needed to deceive you, sighed Mallow. *I must have my revenge against your mother, but I don't hate you, Demoiselle.*

Clovermead could hear the bear-priest's horse neigh. Terror had transfixed Saraband. *I don't care what you think about me,* moaned Clovermead. *The bear-priests will kill us in a minute if you don't let me go.* She tried to move her arms, but they were frozen stiff.

You should not die like this, said Mallow. Then he cried out with queer good humor, and longing, selfishness, and kindness mixed strangely in his laugh. *You will not die. I shall make you a bargain, little Demoiselle. Give me the heart's blood you would have thrown away on my bears, and I will send these bear-priests on their way.*

No! cried Clovermead. But now she could see the bear-priest. He was twenty yards away. His teeth gleamed in the darkness, and Saraband moaned with fear. *What do you want it for?*

A little bit to moisten my dry veins. The rest to cherish. Oh, Demoiselle, you do not know how sweet your pity is. Your mother never could feel pity for me. She destroyed me, and when I looked into her eyes, I knew she only felt a pale regret. He whispered wistfully, yearningly to Clovermead. *Let me take some of your pity to warm me. I am always so cold.*

How much? asked Clovermead. She could hear the bear-priest's breath. She saw his scimitar. *You can't have it all.*

Just a third, Demoiselle, said Mallow. He paused a moment. *And in return I will give you some of the dust that flows through my veins. Will you take my bargain?*

She thought of Waxmelt and Lady Cindertallow, and

her father and mother both seemed to be yelling at her not to do anything so foolish, but she didn't have time to think of another way to save Saraband. *It's not that I like her,* she told herself. *Most of the time she's the most aggravating person I ever met. But like it or not, I'm responsible for Saraband now. It doesn't matter what I think of her: I'd have nightmares for the rest of my life if I just let her die out here.* Clovermead didn't have a choice.

I will, said Clovermead frantically to Mallow. *Do it quickly. Hurry!*

Dust for blood and blood for dust, said Mallow. A hand of bone reached into Clovermead's heart, ice spread through her chest—and then the hand was gone. So was part of Clovermead. She felt light-headed, lighthearted, and something cold and dry ran in her veins.

I thank you for your gift, said Mallow. *Don't worry, Demoiselle. It will be safe with me.* He chuckled. *Now for my side of the bargain. I will play some music to call away Ursus' dogs. Farewell, Demoiselle.*

Clovermead heard a distant horn sound. It rang with the roar of bears, the clash of swords, and the clatter of marching skeletons. The bear-priest paused, only ten yards away. He lifted his head, then turned his horse around and galloped toward the distant hornsman. Elsewhere on the Heath, Clovermead saw more bear-priests abandon their patrol.

"Praise Our Lady," whispered Saraband. Feverishly she made the crescent sign over and over again. "Bless her and thank her. I was sure we were doomed."

"She had nothing to do with it," whispered Clovermead. She felt at her chest. It was still cool, and her heart beat strangely slow. "Let's go," she said more loudly to Saraband. "Don't waste the opportunity." *It was dearly bought,* she thought. She wanted to cry, but only a single tear came from her eyes. It was sticky with dust.

As the bear-priests galloped away, Clovermead and Saraband crawled forward through the Heath.

Chapter Nine

Among Bears

At dawn Clovermead and Saraband found themselves between two fallow fields. Behind them herds of cattle munched on the Heath. To the north little mountain streams ran into a broad, black lake, where boats creaked on the surface and fishermen cast their nets deep into its waters. The nearby foothills were dense with trees, but here on the plains there was only the odd shade tree over a farmhouse or a gnarled old oak overhanging a stream. Sturdy wooden frame farmhouses dotted the landscape.

"I don't care if we're safe yet or not," said Saraband. She collapsed onto the ground. "I want to sleep."

"I guess we can," said Clovermead. A cowherd lassoed a wandering calf and dragged him back to his mother. An otter stalked a fishing boat, hoping to seize a sturgeon from its timbers. A chaffinch cheeped from a nearby meadow. There were no bear-priests in sight, and the world was astonishingly, marvelously normal.

Her heart was still light. Her chest was still cool. She gulped for breath, but she wasn't short of air. Blood and dust mixed in her chest, and the joy she felt to see the

Heath clear of bear-priests was thin and desiccated. She looked numbly at the world.

I didn't let Saraband die, Clovermead told herself. *She'll be around to annoy me for a good long time. That's what matters.* She flung herself down by Saraband's side and fell asleep.

They woke toward noon with the sun beating down on them. "Now I am starving," said Saraband. She stood up and stretched her limbs, then sighed as she looked at her muddy, ragged clothes. "At least we can walk upright today."

"See, you should wear trousers all the time," said Clovermead. "They're comfortable. They're useful. They don't get in the way when you crawl through muck."

"Silly me, I didn't expect I would spend much of my life crawling." Saraband picked her trousers from her skin. "I'll grant you useful, but not comfortable. The mud's glued the cloth to my legs."

Clovermead pulled her own trousers from her legs and groaned. "You're right. I feel like I'm walking in bricks. Let's go—the sooner we get to Silverfalls, the sooner we can get new clothes to wear."

The blazing sun warmed most of the chill out of Clovermead's bones as they walked westward between the farms. Her wounds were nearly healed and only twinged occasionally. She began to feel cheerful as the fields grew thicker, the grassland of the Heath fell behind them, and the farmhouses clustered closer together. They found a country lane and started to walk along its packed hard earth. Saraband's clothes had become tattered, but her posture was elegant as she walked along the path, and she still looked beautiful beneath her grime.

"Tell me, Saraband," said Clovermead, mopping sweat from her forehead, "did you ever have a crooked tooth?"

"I beg your pardon?" Saraband felt at her mouth. "No, I don't believe I have. Why do you ask?"

"Just wondering," said Clovermead. Her own missing tooth ached in her. "Do you know that you still look just perfect? Your face is covered in mud, but you haven't gotten a scratch. I'm sweating so much that I'm breaking out in pimples, but you look like you've never gotten hot in your life. How do you do it?"

"Magic," said Saraband solemnly. "I sacrifice toads at midnight. It's excellent for the complexion." Clovermead gaped at her, and she laughed, high and silvery. "Don't believe everything you hear. What can I tell you, Clovermead? Our Lady gave me straight teeth, and she has preserved me from pimples so far. I suspect I spend more time in front of the mirror than you. Do you spend any at all?"

Clovermead looked at her scarred reflection in the mirror. She lashed out with enormous paws, and the mirror shattered.

"Not so much," said Clovermead. "But what's the point? I could spend all day and I'd still be a sight. You look all perfect in ten minutes."

"Thank you for the compliment," said Saraband drily. "I won't let it go to my head." She glanced at Clovermead. "I didn't think you cared about such things."

"I don't," said Clovermead. "Most of the time, anyway.

But—" She hesitated, trying to think how best to put it. "People look at you all the time, and they don't look at me at all. It must be nice to have people paying attention to you."

"By 'people' I take it you mean 'young men.' Lords and cadets and other easily impressionable sorts. Yes, it is nice. I try not to let their attentions turn my head, but I am flattered when they ask me to dance, or give me flowers, or, well, any of a thousand small courtesies. It's exciting and it makes my heart beat faster. I like it very much." Saraband smiled at Clovermead. "I like to flirt, too. It's fun to look coyly at a young lord or drop a handkerchief in front of him and see his knees go wobbly. I try not to be cruel or to lead anyone on, but I do enjoy making them admire me."

"And you enjoy making other girls jealous of you?" Clovermead couldn't keep all the bitterness out of her voice. Saraband's words churned icy dust in her heart and sent it racing through her blood.

Saraband raised an eyebrow. "Of course. Their jealousy compliments me as much as the young men's flattery. And it's not as if they object to the way I behave. They just wish they could allure as well themselves." She paused a moment. "I won't complain too much—I'm happier with straight teeth and a clear complexion. Still, I wish I knew which young men would be courteous to me if my teeth were crooked and my forehead full of pimples. It's difficult to tell which compliments I should take to heart."

"Don't you worry," said Clovermead. "They're all genuine."

"I wish they were," said Saraband. "Take your friend Sorrel, for example." Clovermead's heart stumbled. "I like his sense of humor. I like the way he dances. I like the way he compliments me—he's polite and teasing and, oh!, very flattering, all at once. There isn't a lord in Chandlefort with a prettier way about him. But how can I tell which compliments are for my face and which are for me?" She laughed lightly. "There's a certain hypocrisy in my worries. I scarcely know what Sorrel's like, and I wouldn't care for him nearly so much if he weren't so handsome himself. When I see him again—" A shadow crossed her face. "*If* I see him again, my heart will leap up to see his face, though he is still a stranger to me."

I could tell you about him, thought Clovermead, but somehow she couldn't say that out loud. She wasn't that generous. "I still wish I had your troubles."

"I said I didn't intend to complain overmuch." Saraband smiled wryly. "All in all, I am happy to have my problems. They are very ordinary, and I'm told most young ladies solve them in the fullness of time."

"I'm sure you will," whispered Clovermead. *You should hear the way Sorrel talks about you,* she thought. *The two of you make a proper pair of lovebirds. I can see the two of you are falling in love already.* The thought sent more dust raging through her veins, to her arms and legs, behind her temples—

"Silverfalls drops four hundred feet to a pool by the Abbey," said Clovermead, but she wasn't Clovermead, she was someone else. She rode alongside a young man with honey-blond hair and a wispy mustache among a troop of Yellowjackets in the fields

outside Chandlefort. The day was cold and the fields were brown. In the distance a few thickly clad farmers had begun to sow the spring corn. "It's three days' ride south of Kite Hall—two if you don't rest. It's magnificent."

"I hope I get the chance to visit it, Lord Kite," said the young man to Clovermead, and now Clovermead could feel stubble on her chin and powerful, rangy muscles in her arms and legs. She was Mallow Kite! The young man's eyes flashed. "There's so much of the world to see! I want to go to Queensmart and Snowchapel, to the Western Ocean and the Tansy Steppes. Can you speak to Milady about it? She sends messengers everywhere—surely I can be one of them?"

"I'll see what I can do, um, what's your name again, Trooper?"

"Ambrosius Beechsplitter, My Lord," said the young man.

"I know that name," said Mallow. He snapped his fingers. "Ah! I remember. Melisande mentioned you. Didn't you win the hurdles race last week?"

"I had that honor, My Lord," said Ambrosius. Then he smiled. "Does Milady really know my name?"

There was something in the way he said "Milady" and smiled that made Mallow's heart seethe. Impudent coxcomb, *he thought, but he tried to keep the frown off his face. "She does indeed, Trooper. Melisande always recognizes talent. So you want to be a messenger? I'll give you a good word." He kicked his horse and rode ahead, but his blood still boiled.* I'll have her send you to the Jaifal Archipelago, *he thought angrily.* How dare you smile that way at her? —

Clovermead was walking on the country lane as herself again. She had traveled a few-score yards, and Saraband was looking worriedly at Clovermead and talking to her, but Clovermead couldn't hear the words she said. Cold dust swirled behind her eyes, her heart was pounding, and her hand was on her sword hilt.

"Are you all right, Cousin?" asked Saraband. Now her words came through to Clovermead faintly, as if through cotton padding. "You look pale. Are your wounds worse?"

"I had a daydream," Clovermead began, but then she couldn't say another word. She looked at Saraband, and she was choking on bile. It flooded through her strong and pure, and flowed silkily smooth on a bed of dust. All the dislike she had ever felt for Saraband was back and more violent than ever. *How dare you smile at Sorrel that way?* Clovermead asked angrily. Her hand tightened on her hilt.

She jerked her fingers away and made them fall by her side. *That's not me,* she told herself. *That was how Mallow felt toward Ambrosius. That was just the dream.* She looked away from Saraband, so as to let the bile drain from her. "I had a nightmare," she said thickly to Saraband, and it was on the tip of her tongue to tell what she had seen.

How can she help you? Mallow whispered. *No sickness ails you, Demoiselle.*

What are you doing inside my head, Mallow? Clovermead asked in panic. *Why am I seeing your past? I didn't trade my heart for your eyes.*

My memories are graven in my heart, said Mallow. *My dust bears their imprint and sends them coursing through me. Now they flow through you, too. Love, and you rouse my memories of love. Hate, and you rouse my memories of hate.* He laughed bitterly. *Despair as you watch others fall in love, and you must see your parents through my eyes.*

Get out of my head! thought Clovermead angrily. *I didn't agree to this.*

Have pity on me, Demoiselle, said Mallow. *Take my memories from me a minute longer. It's been so long since I've been free of them.*

I don't care, said Clovermead. *Take them away.*

Our hearts beat as one, said Mallow. *I cannot. I will not.* Then he said softly, his voice fading into darkness, *What can your cousin say to comfort you? She doesn't know how you feel.*

Clovermead was alone in her mind again.

"Cousin?" asked Saraband anxiously. "Are you dreaming again?"

You don't care, thought Clovermead. The sun beat down. Clovermead was sweaty, but she was cold. She looked at Saraband's raven hair, and she saw a shadow of Ambrosius' honey-blond locks. *You like making other girls jealous, and Sorrel smiled when he said your name, and I'm on the outside, like Mallow. Just like him.*

"I'm awfully tired," said Clovermead. "Don't worry about me. I'll be fine."

"Are you sure?" asked Saraband. Clovermead nodded. Saraband looked at her intently another moment, then reluctantly turned away. They walked on in silence now. Every so often Saraband gave Clovermead another worried look.

Clovermead brought her hand up to her heart. It beat cold and slow. Her fingers grew chill, and she let them fall.

The sun rose high into the sky, then began to descend. They passed an orchard with ripe plums hanging over the path, and they plucked a handful apiece for lunch. In the sweltering afternoon, as they walked between two broad hayfields, Clovermead heard a long, low whistle from her right. At first she thought it was a bird, but then it repeated, longer and more urgently. Then she heard what sounded very much like "Clovermead! Saraband!" She turned to see who was calling them.

At first she thought it was a lumpy haystack. Then it was a lumpy haystack surrounded by fur carpets. Then one of the fur carpets yawned and Clovermead saw that the hayfield was full of bears. Fifty of them lay scattered through the field. At the top of the haystack, surrounded by sleepily curious bears, stood Sorrel and Brown Barley. Both of them looked as if they would very much like wings, so they could fly away without further fuss. Brown Barley didn't let his nerves get in the way of his nibbling hay.

Clovermead's heart leaped with joy to see Sorrel alive, the ice in her receded, and helplessly she started laughing. Saraband let loose a not very ladylike giggle. Sorrel turned red and glared at them indignantly. "It is not so funny when you wake up to find yourself made a prisoner by a whole flock of bears. Herd of bears. Gaggle of bears—whatever you call them!" The bear nearest him stretched his paw toward the haystack, and Sorrel and Brown Barley edged away from him. "Clovermead, would you please ask them to let me out of here?"

"Certainly, oh doughty warrior," said Clovermead. She left Saraband at the roadside and strode up to the bear nearest the haystack—and she recognized him! His lean, black face and sleek fur were just as he had pictured them the day before. He really was a remarkably handsome bear.

I told you so, said the bear, sleepily and comfortably.

Brookwade! exclaimed Clovermead. *What are you doing here?*

Resting. Brookwade yawned wide, and Brown Barley retreated another inch. *Mallow will call us again in the evening, but for now we are free of him.*

I'm glad to meet you in person, said Clovermead. She looked at all the bears and her heart leaped. *I've been wanting to spend time with bears for months now. Tell me—no, wait, would you first let my friend go?* She pointed at Sorrel. *You're giving him an awful scare.*

The nervous little snack? Brookwade yipped at Sorrel and chuffed with laughter as the Tansyard flinched. *It's been so much fun growling at him. Are you sure?*

Please, said Clovermead.

Brookwade got to his feet. He took a step away from the haystack—then stopped. He grinned at Clovermead. *Will you fight for him, changeling?* He stretched and his claws extended a good two inches from his body.

"You're in demand, Sorrel," said Clovermead. "Don't come down just yet." She shifted into bear shape and extended her own claws. *Certainly,* she said. *To the death,* she added defiantly.

Oh, he's not worth that, said Brookwade, laughing. *I just meant a friendly bout.* He roared to the surrounding bears, *Come and watch! The changeling's come among us, and she'll brawl for the two-legs on the haystack. Let's see how well she can fight!*

Hush up, youngling, said one old she-bear at the far end of the field. *I'm napping.* She flopped over onto her side and put a paw over her ears.

Nip his ears, changeling, said a small brown bear nearby, who blinked, sat up, and looked at the two of them expectantly. *Brookwade's mouthy, and he ate all the fresh plums on the ground of that orchard this morning. All he left us were the rotten ones.* He sounded very much the sniffy gourmet and startlingly like Waxmelt. For a moment Clovermead thought she was back home in Timothy Vale, listening to her father on market day as he complained about the second-rate garden greens the Valemen tried to fob off on him.

Give her a hiding, Brookwade, said another black bear, with white fur around her eyes that looked like spectacles. *I was dreaming that I was in the land of the Stingless Bees and gorging on honey when she woke me with her chatter. Whale her!* There were more encouragements to both of them from different bears, and in a minute some twenty bears had formed a circle around the two of them. Another score, mostly older bears, continued to nap and grumble at the far end of the hayfield.

I'm ready, said Clovermead. She stalked toward Brookwade and smiled as she walked among the other bears. She was alert, but somehow relaxed at the same time. It was nice to be just one bear among many. *I love their different scents,* she thought to herself. *I can tell every one of them apart! Why, I can even tell what makes my own scent Clovermead and not just bear-scent.*

Brookwade yawned again—and leaped! His claws were mostly drawn in, and he hammered Clovermead's back with paws to bruise and scratch her, but not really to hurt her. Clovermead smacked at him with her own paws and bit his ears just hard enough to make him yelp. Then they were batting, biting, and tumbling head over heels in the hay. Saraband gasped with fear by the roadside, Sorrel's hand was on his sword hilt, but Clovermead snorted with laughter as they whirled around and got wonderfully dizzy. Her ribs mewled at her a little bit, but they scarcely slowed her down at all. Her head was spinning, she was all in a muddle, and she didn't want to stop.

Then Brookwade pulled at her tail with his teeth, and Clovermead jumped straight in the air with shock and outrage. *That hurt!* she cried out, and she flailed at Brookwade as she fell back to earth. Her stinging tail gave her real fury, and she was battering at him, growling and smacking, until he fell to the ground laughing and whining.

Mercy, changeling! said Brookwade. He flailed his back legs in the air and put his forelegs over his eyes. *I'll never bite your tail again. You can have your snack and welcome to him!*

Stop calling him a snack! said Clovermead indignantly. *He's my friend!*

More of a light lunch, said an old he-bear with a torn ear and worn claws. *Brookwade's always so hungry! He'd eat a cow and call it an appetizer. You'll get fat and start to waddle, boy. Fruits, nuts, grass, and the occasional fish are the proper diet for a self-respecting bear. Humans give you indigestion. It's the clothes and the buttons.*

Do you really eat humans? Clovermead asked, horrified.

Brookwade struggled out from underneath her paw, righted himself, and licked his fur. *Not usually,* he said. *Sometimes we maul them a bit, sometimes we even kill them—but we don't eat them unless we're ravenous.* He paused a moment. *In our right minds. Ursus makes us do many things.* He shivered. *Never mind that,* he said briskly. *Time to let the snack go.* Brookwade growled out a command, and he and his companions moved away from the haystack.

Very cautiously Sorrel and Brown Barley descended from the haystack. Brown Barley took a last nibble of hay as they came to solid ground. "Thank you, Clovermead," said Sorrel. "I will be sure to return the favor if ever you are surrounded by a herd of hungry mustangs. Your friends won't leap at me if I head toward the road?" Clovermead shook her head. "Then I will be off!" He looked around at the bears dotting the field, gulped, and led Brown Barley as quickly as possible toward the edge of the field, where Saraband stood.

Saraband smiled like a sunrise to see Sorrel safe, and his eyes reflected her joy. Unregarded, Clovermead struggled to contain a choking spasm of dust.

She turned back to Brookwade. *Thank you,* said Clovermead. *I'm grateful.*

Brookwade shrugged. *It was nothing, Haybrawler.*

Clovermead! said Clovermead.

Haybrawler Clovermead, said Brookwade affably. He grinned at her. *It was a pleasant bout. We should do it again sometime.* He sauntered toward her and rubbed noses. Clovermead drew back a second, then rubbed noses back. It was wonderful to have bear-touch and bear-scent all around her. She felt warm through and through.

Can I talk with you a bit more? Clovermead asked wistfully. *You're the first bears I've had a chance to spend time with since I found out that I could change shape. I'd like to learn what it's like to be a proper bear. I can't do that by myself.*

Of course you can stay with us, said the small brown bear. *And, really, you should. You're dreadfully ignorant of etiquette. When you were fighting Brookwade just now, you leaped and snarled, when really you should have snarled and leaped. It's these small courtesies that distinguish a well-bred bear.* Now he sounded like Waxmelt had when he fussed around Ladyrest Inn, dusting furniture. *As for the way you groom your fur—*

Not now! said Brookwade. The small bear whined, dropped his eyes, and shuffled away from Clovermead. Brookwade looked toward the lowering sun, and there was sudden, awful sadness in his eyes. He turned back to Clovermead. *Not ever. We cannot teach you how to be a proper bear, for* we *are not proper bears any longer. The dead man has us in his power. This interlude is a dream of freedom, nothing more, and we will wake up soon enough. You do not want to be with us then.* Clovermead began to protest, and he growled in sudden anger and despair. *The day will be over soon. Go while we're still ourselves. I'd rather you remembered us as we are now.*

All right, said Clovermead. She rubbed his nose once more, with all the gentleness and affection and regret that she could give him. *I wish—*

What can't be helped must be endured, Brookwade said quickly. *Go.* He dropped to his side and yawned. *I'm glad you had the chance to find out just how remarkably handsome I really am.* He winked at Clovermead, then closed his eyes and began to snore. Around him the pack of bears were all yawning, settling into the hay, and dropping off to sleep.

I had a lot of fun, too, said Clovermead, and she turned human. "Blast Ursus!" she said to herself as she retraced her steps to the roadside where Sorrel and Saraband were waiting. "And blast Mallow Kite, too! How can he be so cruel?" Her heart had warmed as she fought with Brookwade, but now its heat began to fade. She was cold and sluggish, and she was starting to feel bruised exhaustion from her bout.

The three of them tiptoed several hundred yards farther down the country lane, out of sight of the bears, and then Clovermead flopped down under a pear tree by the side of the road. "Can we sit for a while?" she asked. "I've had a good hard fight just now and I'm tired."

"Hurt?" asked Saraband.

"Just winded," said Clovermead. She touched the scars over her wounds. The scabs were still whole, though now they did feel more tender. "Maybe a little strained." She also felt an ache in what had been her tail, but she didn't think she'd mention that while Sorrel was around.

"I feel a certain amount of strain myself," said Sorrel. He stayed on his feet and looked nervously back toward the hayfield. "Clovermead, what exactly did they intend? Sometimes I thought they were being playful. Other times—" He shivered. "It was very difficult to tell."

"Mostly playing, little snack," said Clovermead.

Sorrel turned red. "I am not a snack! And please don't start calling me one. It is undignified."

"One of the other bears called you a light lunch," said Clovermead, and Saraband snickered. "Never mind that. You're alive!" She wanted to seize him and hug him—but that might give Saraband an excuse to hug him too. Jealousy conquered joy and she kept herself still. "How did you get away from the bear-priests? Did anybody else survive?"

"I think I saw three Yellowjackets ride for Chandlefort," said Sorrel. "I could not look closely. First I fought one bear-priest, and then when I had thrown him off his horse, I had to flee two others. They chased me for miles before I could outrun them. The next morning there was so much rain that I could not find my way back to the shanty. Instead I rode toward Silverfalls Abbey, thinking to alert the Abbess and bring out her soldiers to find you, to liberate you, to avenge you at the worst. Yesterday I saw bear-priests on the Heath and I could not ride very far, for fear of alerting them to my presence. When I woke this morning, I found that this pack of bears had surrounded me in the night. I could not find a tree, so I went up the haystack with Brown Barley instead. Once I was up, the bears would not let me down. So I stayed there all day, until you came walking along. But how did you get free? Or rather, how did the Lady Saraband survive? I know Clovermead is irrepressible, indestructible, and dangerous to her foes—but, Lady, you are no fighter like Clovermead. I do not know how to express my joy that you are alive."

"I feared you were dead too, Cadet," said Saraband quietly. "I am very happy to see you well." She blushed a little, then hurried on. Clovermead felt a little colder and turned to stare at the grass. "The Demoiselle saved my life," Saraband continued. She recounted quickly what had happened that night and since then.

"And here you are!" said Sorrel. "Clovermead, you do not cease to amaze."

Clovermead shrugged uncomfortably. "It wasn't much." *Just a third of my heart,* she thought. Then she sat bolt upright. "If those Yellowjackets make it back to Chandlefort, Milady will think we're dead!"

"Yellowjackets are trained to say precisely what they saw and no more," said Sorrel. "They will say we were attacked, but they will not say they saw us die. Perhaps one even saw you escape." He sighed. "But, yes, she will fear the worst. We must hurry to bring you safe to Silverfalls, so a messenger may be sent to prevent such misconceptions from lingering. Are you ready to go, Clovermead? You do look pale."

Clovermead felt at her cool cheeks, then at the scab on her side. The ache there had dulled. "I'll be all right," she said as she got to her feet. Her heart beat lazily. "Let's go."

And she froze. A line of bears had come into view. They trampled through the fields by the roadside. There was the old she-bear, there the bear with spectacle-pattern fur. The sun was setting, and golden streaks lit every furred back. They padded forth regularly, all in the same rhythm. Their steadiness was terrifying.

Clovermead saw Brookwade in the middle of the line. He looked neither right nor left, and his tongue lolled out to pant every five seconds. Like clockwork.

What's wrong with you? Clovermead called out to him. *What's happened?*

Every single one of the bears paused for a moment. Their heads all turned to her in unison and they stared at her silently. *Mallow summons us,* she heard Brookwade say at last. *We must go.*

Clovermead blinked and she could see the white net in the air again. It was a lasso made of bones that hummed with Mallow's voice and played around every bear. *Disobey him,* Clovermead called out frantically. *Slip his knots!*

No, Demoiselle, they roared in chorus, but it was Mallow's dry whistle speaking through their throats. Then all fifty of the bears began to pad toward the Reliquaries. They left behind a hayfield pockmarked by the trampling impress of their enormous feet.

I enjoyed the bout, Haybrawler, Clovermead heard Brookwade say in her mind. Then there was only the rattling of bones.

"What was that, Demoiselle?" asked Saraband softly. "I've never seen bears act that way before."

"Mallow makes them march as his puppets," said Clovermead. She felt her heart would break.

"I find myself feeling pity for them," said Sorrel. He grimaced. "They terrify me, and I do not like being called a snack by such overgrown rodents, but they do not deserve this horrible fate."

"They were so happy and alive!" said Clovermead. "I could tell what each of them was like." She growled with indignation. "I wish I could—" But what could she do? *I enjoyed our fight too,* she called out to Brookwade. There was only the slightest growl in response beneath the clacking bones of Mallow's net.

Chapter Ten

SONG AT THE ABBEY

SORREL BROUGHT OUT SOME BISCUITS FROM Brown Barley's saddlebag and shared them with Clovermead and Saraband for a late lunch. Then Sorrel put Saraband onto Brown Barley and walked alongside Clovermead into Silverfalls Valley. The Reliquaries loomed over the Valley on three sides; it was planted solidly in vegetable gardens and fruit orchards beneath the forested slopes. From far away Clovermead could see a waterfall spill over a rocky scarp at the end of the Valley and down to a foaming pool. When she squinted, she could see beside the pool the stone walls of Silverfalls Abbey itself.

Sorrel frowned as he walked. "I have not said yet how sorry I am that I abandoned you," he said to Clovermead at last, in a low voice. "I said I would fight at your side against the dead man, but when the moment came to fight mere bear-priests, somehow I found a good reason to flee. I am ashamed."

"I don't expect you to kill a dozen bear-priests before breakfast. You behaved sensibly, and I'm not blaming you for anything. Besides, Saraband and I fled too."

"I am a Yellowjacket cadet, Clovermead. I think

Milady expected more swordplay from me when she gave me her livery." Sorrel paused a moment. "Did I ever tell you why I decided to stop being a messenger for Lady Cindertallow and instead to enlist as a cadet in her Yellowjackets?"

"I thought it was because you liked the uniform."

"That, too." Sorrel smiled a little, but then his smile faded. "You know that I killed a bear-priest during the battle outside Chandlefort last winter?"

"I was unconscious by then," said Clovermead. "You've never said much about what you did the rest of that day."

"He is the only person I have ever killed. I raised my sword against him, and all my sorrow for my dead family was in my blow. So too was my shame for my cowardice when I ran from the bear-priests' assault upon my Horde. When I killed him, I thought to myself, *I am a grown warrior at last. I am blooded and revenged.* Then I knelt in the snow and I began to cry. When dusk came, and Yellowjackets began to comb the ground to gather up the wounded and the dead, I asked myself, *Well, Sorrel, what will you do now?*

"I looked at the spires of Chandlefort and I thought, *I wish to have a home again, to have comrades who will search for me when I am wounded, and to live for something more than bloody memories.* I looked at the Yellowjackets weeping as they recognized their dead comrades, as Tansyards would, and I said to myself, *I want to be more than just a foreign messenger riding in Milady's service. I want to be a Chandleforter myself. Their lords are arrogant and cruel, and lords and servants alike can be callous and selfish in their worst moments, but Lady knows they are still as kindhearted a people as I have seen in my travels. I wish to be one of them and not only to serve them from convenience.*

"I felt my tattoos, and I remembered that there is not much trust for horse-thieving Tansyards among townsmen and farmers. First I thought, *I will scrape off my tattoos to prove my love of Chandlefort.* But then my love for my family and my Horde revolted in me, and I thought, *That will make me a traitor to the people who bore me. I will become a Chandleforter, but I will not give up being a Tansyard. I must earn their trust another way. I must do good service for them.* So I stood up and went to help the Yellowjackets bury their dead. The next day I enlisted in the cadets. I told myself as I put on my uniform that it was an oath in the eyes of Our Lady that I would not flee again when danger threatened." He picked disconsolately at his yellow sleeves. "But still I run. I left behind a friend, which is bad enough, but also I left behind Chandlefort's Demoiselle, which I think is dereliction of duty. I have not made a promising start of my new life."

"You should talk with Father. He was just terrified the servants wouldn't make good soldiers when we left Chandlefort, he was all gloomy and biting his nails, and the two of you would make good company for each other. You'd listen to each other, you'd say, 'It can't be as bad as all that,' and then you'd realize you were both right." Clovermead paused a moment. "I think I'd have run away from Chandlefort if you weren't here, Sorrel. I love Milady and Father, but I've needed a friend. You don't need to prove yourself to me or be a hero or anything. You were here when I was lonely, and that's more than enough."

"Thank you, Clovermead." Sorrel's voice was thick with emotion, and he took her hand and squeezed it tightly in his. "I have never had a kinder friend."

"Must you fight, Cadet?" asked Saraband. Startled, Sorrel and Clovermead turned to her. Sorrel abruptly let go of Clovermead's hand, and she could scarcely keep from crying out loud. "Forgive me," said Saraband, pinking slightly. "I couldn't help but overhear you. Cadet, there are more ways to serve Chandlefort than by fighting."

"What other skills do I have to offer, Lady?" asked Sorrel. He fell back by Saraband's side, forgot even to say good-bye to Clovermead, and all his warm, friendly words froze in her. Dust yawed through her blood. "I was raised to ride, to steal horses, and to fight. Riding makes me a messenger boy, but nothing more, and thievery is not esteemed by you Chandleforters. I cannot read and write like a clerk. I cannot farm, forge horseshoes, or do anything Chandlefort values except fight. Take that away, and I am useless."

"You dance well and you are courteous," said Saraband. "But I suppose those qualities are not usually accounted among the civic virtues, though I value them highly. Is it too late for you to learn another trade?" Her eyes dropped. "I could teach you something of medicine."

"That would be kind of you, Lady." Sorrel's eyes were suddenly alive with possibility. "That would be a quite respectable trade to take up in place of Yellowjacketing."

I don't have a choice, thought Clovermead. *I'm a*

Cindertallow, and I have to fight and rule. I thought you'd be fighting with me, Sorrel. She felt more alone than ever, and coldness crackled through her. *I still need you to be my friend. Why are you abandoning me?* But she knew why. *She bats her pretty eyes at you, and you forget me.* Her scar was a slash of hoarfrost on her arm; her missing tooth an icicle.

"I would be glad to see you turn doctor, Cadet," said Saraband. "I respect your current profession, but I confess I do not like it. I find killing distasteful."

For a moment Sorrel looked very tempted. Then, reluctantly, he shook his head. "I have trained since I was a boy in the Hordes to fight and to kill. When I do not run away, I flatter myself that I am a competent fighter. The warrior is the best part of me, and I should not offer Chandlefort anything less. A little bravery is all that is required to make me be of service." Sorrel looked anxiously at Saraband. "I trust your distaste for my occupation will not prove a fatal bar to our acquaintance?"

"You wore a soldier's coat the first time I spoke with you. I did not care for it, but it did not prove an insurmountable obstacle." She and Sorrel smiled at each other, and Clovermead was colder than ever.

They had come closer to the Abbey by now, and Clovermead could see a black ring around the Abbey and the pool. She squinted at it, but it stayed stubbornly out of focus. "What's that dark loop?" she asked Saraband.

"I don't know." Saraband frowned. "I don't remember anything like it."

Sorrel checked his sword. "Let us go carefully," he

said. He pulled a little ahead of Clovermead and Saraband.

Clovermead let her nose turn a little into a snout—then hastily turned it back to human. "Ugh! There's an awful smell. It's like bears and rotting meat."

"Is it Lord Ursus?" Saraband asked fearfully.

Reluctantly Clovermead sniffed again. "No, this is something different," she said with relief. Then she shuddered. "The wind's coming straight down the Valley. Whatever's rotting is by the Abbey." Saraband looked more unhappy than ever, and they went on in silence.

Earlier they had passed a number of farmers weeding their fields, but now the land was empty. The doors of the nearest farmhouses were all shut and barred. Farther away Clovermead could see groups of farmers filing stealthily past distant fields of corn, toward the foothills of the Reliquaries. Dozens of different groups went this way and that, but they all inched farther and farther from the Abbey.

"Those must be bear-priests around the Abbey," said Saraband. "When I was young, a band of Low Branding cavalry surprised the nuns' men who guarded the Abbey and burst in to ravage the Valley. I saw the farmers flee to the hills then, too. Demoiselle, should we turn aside?"

"You can, Cousin," said Clovermead. She struggled to keep an even temper as she spoke to Saraband. She wanted to snap at her. Any excuse would do. "I don't mean that to be nasty. It was Mother's idea that you come along, not mine. If you want to go to the hills with the farmers, I won't blame you. But it's my fault Mother got wounded, and I'm not going to give up just yet. I'll see if I can get through to the Abbey."

Saraband shook her head. "You are either brave or boneheaded."

"Both, I think," said Sorrel. He winked at Clovermead.

"I suppose I have to stay with you," said Saraband. "You'll get yourself wounded if you keep going, and I'll be needed to patch your wounds." She laughed tremulously. "Please be careful. Remember we're not all as brave as you, Cousin."

"Although we are as boneheaded," Sorrel added cheerfully. "Otherwise we would leave her to her own devices."

"Don't you worry. We'll be cautious as anything." Clovermead grimaced at Saraband. "You're on Brown Barley. Run if worse comes to worst."

"I am not a coward," said Saraband with dignity. Then she looked toward the Abbey and she shivered again.

They came to a last arbor of apple trees and peered across a lush meadow to Silverfalls Abbey. To one side of it were the waterfall and the pool, which lapped at its walls, flowed underneath the Abbey, and emerged from the other side as a stream that rushed down the Valley toward the Heath. The Abbey itself was a stout rectangle whose walls were gray granite slabs lashed together with strips of black iron, with arrow-slits carved into the walls every dozen feet. The buildings inside the walls were made of red bricks and sported gaily painted tile roofs.

The ring around the Abbey was not bear-priests but

a hundred black bears. They padded restlessly outside the Abbey walls and by the shore of the pool. One or two scratched idly at the Abbey gates; others wandered a little ways into the surrounding arbor. They passed each other silently.

They made no sound at all. They didn't growl and they didn't roar. Clovermead pricked up her ears, and she realized that they didn't even breathe. She looked more closely at their fur and she saw that it was roiling shadow. Sometimes it slid aside and she saw white bones underneath. The bears smelled of rotting flesh. Clovermead looked into their eyes and all she saw were empty eye sockets.

"They're dead," she said, horror-struck. She was in a cold sweat. *What have you done, Mallow?* she called out in her head.

The grave is no sanctuary, whispered Mallow. *My servants must come when I summon them, no matter how deeply they sleep.*

Poor bears, thought Clovermead. *Have you no decency at all, Mallow?*

Let them suffer as I suffer, said Mallow harshly. *I don't care.* Then he laughed mockingly. *You are to blame for their predicament, Demoiselle. You made your bargain, you let me into your mind, and I saw why you were heading to Silverfalls. Did you think I would let you cure Melisande? You had to be stopped. I need my living servants for Chandlefort, so I called up dead ones to stop you. Their agony is your fault.*

You raised them, not me, said Clovermead. *I'm not to blame for everything!* But there was only laughter in her mind, and then Mallow was gone.

"Can you persuade them to let us past?" asked Sorrel.

"I don't want them in my mind," Clovermead began, then stopped. *It's my fault again,* she thought drearily. *Every choice I make seems to end up with someone else suffering.* She shuddered. "I'll try." She sent out her mind to speak to them.

She felt cold like a knife and smelled rotting flesh all around her. There was pain, agonized and exhausted wakefulness, and a terrible hunger. She wanted to be warm, she wanted relief from the terrible dryness, she could not hear or feel or smell the world, only see it through shadows. A terrible compulsion rested on her, and she moved to Mallow's orders, moved to Ursus' roar—

Sorrel had seized hold of her, and she struggled in his grip. She was trying to walk out of the arbor to join the bears. "Don't go, Clovermead," said Sorrel. "Don't go. I'm sorry, please stay with us." She was flailing against him, but he held on to her with a grip of iron. "Are you there, Clovermead?"

Clovermead went limp. "I'm all right. I just—" The pain crowded in on her again, and she forced herself away from it. "There's just enough of them left inside their bones to know what's happened to them." She was crying.

Cautiously Sorrel let her go. "You will not go rushing to join them?"

"No," said Clovermead. She growled long and low. "I don't feel sorry for Mallow anymore. He doesn't deserve my pity. He knows what it's like to be up and walking with no blood in your veins, no heat to warm you—" She gulped as she felt her own heart pump lazily slow. "It's unforgivable."

"They've killed a nuns' man," said Saraband. She pointed to a body lying in the grass. The dead soldier wore a silver crescent on his uniform. Saraband's face was green. "I wonder if I knew him?" She looked around the meadow. "I think I see more. Not everyone got behind the walls in time." She looked up to the parapets. "So near! Isn't there any way we can get past these bears?"

"They are very thick around the door," said Sorrel grimly. "I would not risk it, Lady Saraband."

"I wish there were a way to let them know we're here," said Clovermead. "Maybe we could tell the Abbess to ride out of the walls so we could talk to her. But I don't know how we can keep the bears from noticing." Then she remembered how silent it had been inside the bears' minds, and she snapped her fingers. "They can't hear! We should stay out of sight, but maybe we can yell a message to the Abbey."

"I believe I could throw my voice to the walls fairly easily," said Sorrel. "Ventriloquism is an old Tansyard trick."

"Really?" asked Clovermead.

"No. I am very frightened of these dead bears, so I make bad jokes. Please forgive me." Sorrel stared dubiously at the meadow. "It is a long way and my voice is not so loud. I do not think they could hear me in the Abbey at this distance."

"I could roar," said Clovermead, "but they wouldn't

know what I meant. They'd just think I was another bear."

"I can sing," said Saraband.

"You can dance, too," said Clovermead. "You're quite entertaining."

Saraband grimaced. "Thank you, farm-girl. Nuns know how to sing very loudly and very clearly. They use the knowledge to praise Our Lady properly in their hymns, but they can also communicate with each other that way. I learned a fair bit of song-speech before I left the Abbey." She looked at the distance to the walls, and she turned to Sorrel. "I would have to go into the meadow to be heard properly. Cadet, can we both ride there on Brown Barley? If the bears decide to chase us, then you can have us gallop away before they catch up to us. Clovermead, can you keep an eye on us from the meadow's edge?"

Now the two of you get to ride together. Clovermead tried to banish that thought. "I'll come to the meadow with you," she said. "That way I can try to distract them if they come after you."

Sorrel and Saraband got onto Brown Barley, and Clovermead walked by their side. Cautiously they emerged from the arbor. The bears looked at them but did not move. They went ten yards, twenty yards, thirty yards, and then Saraband began to sing.

Her voice wasn't particularly loud, but it penetrated through the twilit air. The liquid syllables of the Moontongue rose and fell. Saraband sat erect, absolutely still but for the opening and closing of her mouth and the expansion and contraction of her diaphragm. Sound filled the meadow.

Hurts, Clovermead heard in her mind. *Pain.* A bear stood up and tried to howl. No sound came out. He snuffled in the air but smelled nothing.

"I think they know you're there," said Clovermead. "They can't hear you, but they can feel the music. It scrapes against them somehow, like hot needles. Try to hurry." Saraband nodded and sang a little louder.

People scurried on the walls of the Abbey. Clovermead saw nuns' men with pikes dash to the parapets, then nuns. A nun sang a snatch to Saraband, listened, then went running. "She's going to get the Abbess," said Saraband. She stopped singing, and the bears sat down again.

Help, Clovermead heard. *Please, Lady. Moving bones and no rest.* Tears trickled down Clovermead's cheeks.

A small figure came to the walls. She wore black robes from her neck to her feet, and an elfin head peeped above her jet-black dress. Even at this distance Clovermead could tell that she was a wisp of a woman. She sang and her voice filled the air. The leaves of the arbor behind them rustled. The sound of her voice was beautiful, but it throbbed with old pain. It roused the bears again, to howl silently. Now they looked around them with maddened, empty eyes, searching for the cause of their agony. Saraband sang to answer the distant Abbess, and the bears took a few steps toward the three of them.

Clovermead turned into a golden bear. She walked in front of Sorrel and Saraband and waited for the bears to come. Before her and behind her Saraband and the Abbess sang to each other, and Clovermead was surrounded by a sea of music. It was beautiful and it was torture to the dead bears. More and more of them wandered into the meadow, their jaws snapping and their throats rubbed raw by their noiseless wails. Clovermead stiffened herself against the pain and the stench, then let herself see through the eyes of the nearest bear. She saw a shadowy wasteland. The trees of the orchard were a distant blur, but she could almost see the three of them in the murk. Soon the bears would be able to make them out.

Lady, free us, the bears cried. *Let us rest. Please, Lady.*

Saraband sang a query, and the Abbess answered. Saraband sang another; the Abbess sang again. The bears howled in torment. Now they saw Clovermead and Brown Barley, Saraband and Sorrel, and they bounded toward them with a clatter of bones.

"Are you finished?" asked Sorrel. He had gathered Brown Barley's reins in his hand, prepared to ride in an instant.

"One minute more," said Saraband. She sang with redoubled strength.

Silence! howled the bears. *Beauty. Life. Song. Not ours. We hate.* They ground their teeth together. *Bite down. Kill. Join us in dust.*

Stop! cried Clovermead, and she sent her mind once more into their agony. *We don't want to hurt you. Just leave us alone.*

Bite down, the bears roared. *Kill. Hurt. Free us, Lady.*

They were very close—Clovermead could see their open jaws—and Saraband was still singing. *I will free you,* Clovermead called out in desperation. *I promise I will. I don't know how, but I'll do it. I won't let any of you stay subject to Mallow, or Ursus, or anybody. Dead or alive, I'll free you all.*

The bears stopped. The nearest was only ten yards away. He stared at her with empty eyes and scoured the grass with his claws. *Swear?*

I swear it in Our Lady's name, said Clovermead. *I don't know a better way to spend my life. I promise you.* As she spoke, she felt a blaze of joy that pierced through the chill thickening in her flesh. She clutched it to her. *I'm responsible for an awful lot that's gone wrong, Lady,* she prayed. *I know I haven't been worse than foolish, mostly, but let me be responsible for doing something right as well. I want to do something good in this world.*

Hurry, said the bear. *Hurt.* He turned around and roared at his fellows. The shadow fell from his jaws, there was only the pure white bone in the night, and Clovermead actually heard a thin calcified echo of a bear's roar. *Guard Abbey. Our orders. Nothing more.* He paused a moment, then rattled out another growl. *Leave singer alone.* The other bears stopped. They howled more pain that scraped in Clovermead's mind, then stepped away.

Saraband stopped singing. "Let's go," she said, and Sorrel began to ride and Clovermead began to run. The dead howled behind her, and Clovermead nestled her burden and her joy to her heart. *I don't know how I'll do it, but I said I'd free them and I will.* She fled from their pain, but she told herself, *It won't be forever. I swear it, Lady.*

Saraband whispered instructions to Sorrel and he turned toward a path that led away from the Heath and into the Reliquaries. They rode among deserted farms and into the foothills as the twilight deepened into night. Clovermead loped beside Brown Barley, and the three of them didn't stop until they had reached a meadow a league into the Reliquaries.

Sorrel helped Saraband off Brown Barley, and she slumped to the earth. Clovermead turned human. "What did she say?" she asked.

"She told me that the bears surrounded them early this morning," said Saraband. "She had no idea where they came from until I told her of Mallow Kite. Then I told her of Milady's illness. I couldn't be very detailed in song, but I believe she got the gist. She said she had no cure for Milady. Her knowledge is of medicine. She doesn't know the poisons of the dead."

"Then we've come all this way for nothing?" Clovermead felt despair sweep over her. "All those Yellowjackets died and she can't cure Milady?" *I bargained away one third of my heart and I haven't helped Milady at all?*

"No. But she told me how she can be cured." Clovermead felt a wave of relief flood through her. "The Abbess says there's a well in the back courtyard of Kite Hall, which Our Lady blessed when she walked through Linstock. It's supposed to lift enchantments, break curses, cure wounds caused by any sort of uncanny man or beast. She said we should get a cup of water from the well and bring it to Milady. She thought that might cure her, if anything on this earth can."

"'Thought'? 'Might'?" Clovermead shook her head. "Doesn't she know?"

"There's been no need for such water the last hundred

years and more. The Abbess cannot promise that the well retains its power."

"Milady didn't trust the Abbess," said Clovermead. "Are you sure she isn't sending us on a wild goose chase? The way Milady talked, I thought I'd have to apologize to the Abbess for an hour straight and wear out my knees before she'd agree to help."

"Milady is not always a good judge of character." Saraband shrugged her shoulders wearily. "If she isn't telling the truth, then Milady is doomed."

"Then I suppose we have to go traipsing into the mountains," said Clovermead. "I guess it's better to clutch at straws than have no hope at all."

"So much for my instructions!" said Sorrel. "'Bring the Demoiselle safe to Silverfalls Abbey,' they said, and I am sure they would have added, 'If you can't get her to Silverfalls, at least hog-tie her and keep her safe in some out-of-the-way barn.' But I have no rope with me." Sorrel sighed. "Somehow I always seem to have trouble obeying my orders where you are concerned. I suppose I will have to satisfy myself with trying to keep you safe as you bound into the Reliquaries. Lady Saraband, did the Abbess mention any dangers on the road to Kite Hall?"

Saraband shook her head. "Mallow's returning to Kite Hall," said Clovermead. "A bear told me so." Sorrel groaned. "I'm not happy about it either. I suppose he'll be just delighted to let us skip over to his well, draw up a bucket that will rattle and creak the entire way, and wish us a good journey back to Chandlefort when we're done. Where is Kite Hall, anyway?"

"A few days' ride from here," said Saraband, and

Clovermead almost screamed. She glanced helplessly at the waning moon. Her mother had so few days left. "I can lead you there," Saraband continued. "I was there once, when I was young, and the Abbess also gave me directions."

"Thank Our Lady for small favors. Did you sing all that time just to say that?"

"The Abbess and I had some words for each other as well," Saraband said quietly. "We haven't seen each other for seven years."

"Couldn't you wait for a better time? The bears—"

"Seven years!" Saraband's tears glistened in the moonlight. "Do you grudge me one minute to talk with my mother?"

Clovermead's mouth was agape and so was Sorrel's. "You're her *daughter*?"

Saraband laughed, tremulous and bitter. "You call me Cousin, but you don't know how we're related? My father was Athanor Sconce, only cousin of Milady. The Abbess is his widow, and I am her daughter."

My cousin Athanor came with me, Lady Cindertallow had said. *He loved the hunt as much as I did, though he had excused himself from hunting the winter before, in order to dote on his newborn babe with his wife, Meadowlark.*

Their newborn Saraband.

Meadowlark entered the Silverfalls Abbey soon after. She has never forgiven me for their deaths. Do you think she raised her dead brother from the grave?

"Your mother is Mallow's sister. You're his niece." Saraband nodded, and Sorrel whistled long and low. "Seven years. In Our Lady's name, what's kept you away from your mother for so long?" She tried to imagine what it would be like if Waxmelt had shut his mouth, shut the door of Ladyrest, and locked them both against Clovermead. Just thinking about the possibility made her want to scream in horror and loneliness.

"That is not your business," said Saraband. And she shut her mouth and said nothing more.

Chapter Eleven

EMBRACES IN THE RELIQUARIES

SARABAND CHECKED CLOVERMEAD'S WOUNDS when they woke up the next morning. "You can take off your bandages," she said. "You're well again. Your mother wouldn't have sent me along with you if she'd known how quickly you heal." She turned abruptly away from Clovermead. Clovermead stretched and didn't feel the slightest pain. She left the cloth strips on the crumpled grass where she had slept.

They went farther into the Reliquaries on a narrow stone road. Saraband was still exhausted from her singing the day before, so she rode on Brown Barley while Clovermead and Sorrel walked. The mountains north and south of them were high and jagged, and snowcapped at the peaks, but ahead of them the hills remained short and gentle.

"How far is it to the ocean?" asked Clovermead.

"Fifty miles," said Sorrel. "There is a hardscrabble fishing port called Stonehaven at the end of the road."

"What's the ocean like?" asked Saraband. "I've often wondered."

"It is an endless lake, filled with enormous Sorrel-eating fish," Sorrel said. Clovermead punched Sorrel lightly in the arm. "There is nothing but waves, rising and falling," Sorrel continued. "It smells of salt. I went out in a boat, I could feel the boat bobble on the water, and my stomach got queasy. I would not be a fisherman for any reason."

"For someone who travels a lot, you're a remarkable homebody," said Clovermead. "Sometimes I think you would be just as happy galloping round and round the walls of Chandlefort. Then you could get your fill of riding, but you wouldn't have to go anywhere."

"I like traveling very much," said Sorrel. "It is just that I am particular. So long as a place closely resembles the Tansy Steppes, I am happy to visit; otherwise, I would just as soon stay home. A small quibble, I assure you."

"He does speak the most remarkable nonsense," Clovermead said to Saraband. "Have you noticed?"

"I prefer to look at his eyes," said Saraband. "I trust they tell no charming stories but only the truth?"

"They charm by telling the truth, Lady," said Sorrel. He said something more to Saraband, but Clovermead started to walk faster and strode a little ahead. She didn't want to listen to them talking to each other.

They came at midmorning to a fork in the road and stopped to look at the two routes. The main road went left; a smaller road wound up and to the right, into the heart of the forest. Saraband pointed them onto the smaller road. Clovermead tried to peer through the thick greenery—and she heard a bear roar. Another did so soon after. She lifted up her nose and turned it into a bear's snout. Now she could smell bears walking all through the woods. They waited patiently to see if the humans would intrude.

"What is out there?" asked Sorrel. "Many slavering jaws, I expect."

"They smell of dust," said Clovermead. She frowned. "Mallow controls them all."

Another bear roared.

Their path curled higher as they ascended westward and northward into the Reliquaries. First they walked between aspens, birches, and cedars, but as they rose they entered a land of pine trees. The ground for twenty feet to either side of the road had been cleared a hundred years before, but it had grown up since then in bushes and saplings. A few branches reached out over the road, but most still had some feet to go before they would crowd travelers. In the breaks in the forest they could see the rock slopes of the Reliquaries, north and south, edging closer to them. Clovermead felt a twinge of homesickness: The land here was very like the forested slopes that rose above the green meadows of Timothy Vale.

In the evening Sorrel led them off the path and into a glade. It had been a long day and they were exhausted: The three of them tumbled to the ground, gobbled some biscuits and beef jerky from Brown Barley's saddlebag, and sprawled out on the grass. Sorrel fell asleep without any fuss at all. Light snores began to fill the air.

Saraband sat by Sorrel's side, looked down at his face, and laughed. "He's a queer mixture, isn't he? So polite, but he doesn't stand on ceremony." She trailed her fingers in the air by his cheek and smiled. "And so handsome, too."

"Be careful," hissed Clovermead. "Sometimes when he snores he's only pretending to be asleep. He could be wide awake." Saraband turned bright red. "You have to pinch him to be sure," Clovermead continued softly. Saraband reached out a hand—then lifted an eyebrow at Clovermead and withdrew her fingers. Clovermead grinned. "Almost worked. You dancing girls are gullible."

"So we are," said Saraband. She looked at Sorrel again, smiling once more. "What do you think, Demoiselle? He's your friend. Are his eyes to be believed?"

"Don't ask me," said Clovermead roughly. "I wouldn't know. You'll have to find out for yourself." She watched Saraband gaze at him tenderly, and Clovermead wanted to slash at her with her claws. *He doesn't care about girls with scars, you know,* she thought bitterly. *He'll ignore you. Then you'll know what that feels like.*

Clovermead scrambled away from the two of them to the other side of an old pine tree. She peered into the night and she saw the glowing eyes of bears creeping in the darkness among the distant trees. *Are you going to attack us?* Clovermead called out in her head. *Or are you just going to pad around out there and make us nervous?*

Pad, pad, said the nearest bear, and she chuckled. *You're safe for the night.*

Give me some warning if the dead man changes his mind, said Clovermead irritably. *Good night!*

Pleasant dreams, changeling, said the bear, and she chuffed with laughter.

Clovermead woke in the early morning with sunlight streaming onto her face. She stretched, looked around the trunk of the pine tree—and saw Sorrel and Saraband kissing at the other end of the glade. Clovermead turned away as if her eyes had been scalded, and she ducked back behind the pine tree, so all its thick wood stood between her and them. She couldn't look, but she felt a horrible curiosity. Her ears poked up, large and furry, and she couldn't help listening.

"Have I been too forward, Lady?" asked Sorrel. "I would not wish to ruin my reputation for tact and discretion." It was the same teasing voice he used toward Clovermead, but with a sort of affection in it he had never directed to her. Clovermead shivered with longing. She wished he had.

"Call me Saraband, Cadet," said Saraband. "Sorrel." She lingered over the name. "No, you haven't been too forward—but you haven't been too backward, either," she added hastily. "I admire you very much for your tact, Sorrel. It's rarer than I would wish among the lords of Chandlefort."

"Then I will be as tactful as ever, Saraband. Though I would give you a token of my affection every now and then." There was a sound that could be nothing but another kiss, and Clovermead's fist leaped to her mouth to stifle a scream. She could feel her claws digging into her palms. "I trust that is properly discreet?" he inquired after a moment, quite roguishly.

"Eminently," said Saraband, sounding rather dizzy. "I do appreciate your discretion," she said, and there was another kiss. Clovermead felt tears running down her cheeks, but she couldn't draw in her ears. She had to keep listening.

"I was not certain I would ever dare speak to you openly," Sorrel said after a while. "You are very noble and I am a commoner, a Tansyard, and I thought I must confine myself to discreet flirtations. But then the bear-priests ambushed us, I thought you were dead, and I told myself I was a fool to have kept quiet. I swore that if I saw you alive again, I would speak to you of the stirrings of my heart." Clovermead heard him laugh with delight. "I am so very glad I did."

"I'm also glad you spoke," said Saraband. "I grieved terribly when I thought you were dead. I was hard put not to weep in front of Clovermead. A lady of Chandlefort isn't supposed to speak first to a young gentleman, but I swore that I would if ever I saw you alive again. I care for you more than I care for decorum." Saraband spoke with such passion, and it was just like the way Queen Aurette spoke to Sir Tourmaline in *The Astrantiad,* but Clovermead had always imagined herself as the Queen, and here she was like the Reiver Prince, listening behind the door while the Queen and the knight told each other of their love—

A dozen lords and ladies were in an orchard picking apples. There were Yellowjackets standing guard all around them. Mallow stood on a short stool underneath a high branch and held a basket full of ripe, red fruit, just plucked from the stem. Lady Cindertallow stood at the next tree and jumped at a high round apple, perfectly formed and just out of reach. She laughed. "How provoking. Mallow, what will I do?"

"Give me a second and I'll get it for you," said Mallow. He started to get down from the stool.

"No, no, don't move. Your job's to get all the apples on that branch. Beechsplitter!" Lady Cindertallow called out, and the honey-blond Yellowjacket stepped forward from where he stood guard. "Fetch me that apple," she said to him.

"Certainly, Milady," said Ambrosius. His sword flashed out of his scabbard, the white birchwood medallions flashed in Mallow's eyes, and then the apple had fallen into Ambrosius' hand, the stem sliced cleanly off. "May I serve you in anything else?" He held out the apple, and if only Mallow had had his sword with him, he could have killed Ambrosius. The look on Ambrosius' face—and on Melisande's—

Saraband giggled, and Clovermead was back in the forest again. With one hand she had drawn her sword half out of its scabbard. She fumbled at the hilt, but her fingers were cold and clumsy. Her other hand had turned into a paw, and her claws scratched against the tree-trunk's bark. She had opened four wounds in the wood, and they were bleeding sap.

"I want you to look at me that way," she whispered to herself, admitted it to herself at last. "Oh, Sorrel, I want you to kiss me, not her." She laughed at herself, angry and forlorn. "Stupid little girl! Why would he? Saraband's all grown up and she's not scarred, and it turns out he likes girls who are demure and mannerly. I'm not and I won't change. It's just a stupid crush. You're so nice, Sorrel, and Saraband was right, you are awfully handsome. I don't want to be just your friend. I want you to dance with me and flirt with me and, and, I don't even know! But you won't wait until I'm old enough. You've found someone already." She scratched deep into the tree again. "I want—I want—" She was all bile and dust inside, aching in her heart and cold in her flesh, and even if Waxmelt or Lady Cindertallow had been there, she couldn't have gone to either of them for comfort. This wasn't something she could talk about with her parents. She called out with her mind, *Mallow! Where are you, Mallow?*

His cool voice was in her head, bitter and mocking and tender all at once. *Waiting for you in Kite Hall, Demoiselle. Why do you call on me?*

I feel so miserable, thought Clovermead. She sent him a jumble of pictures in her mind, of Saraband and Sorrel together and dancing and kissing. *I hate you, but you're right, you're the only one who knows how I feel. Talk with me. Tell me how I can stop feeling so stupid and angry and jealous.*

I'm not the best person to come to for sensible advice, Demoiselle. I watched Melisande and Ambrosius fall in love with each other, and I could not bear to live. Death came as a relief.

I know what you mean, thought Clovermead in utter misery. *Mallow, I hurt so much.*

You'd hurt more if I didn't have a part of your heart in safekeeping, Demoiselle, said Mallow softly. *Let the dust flow in you. It doesn't hurt.*

No, said Clovermead, but then she could hear Saraband and Sorrel laughing in the distance. Their laughter stabbed at her, but it was true, the dust in her veins didn't feel. It was cold and dead, and it was a relief. *Yes,* she said. She filled her heart with dust, let it flow in and out of her until the pain in her dulled. *I do feel better.* A dusty tear congealed on her cheek. *I'm glad you have part of my heart.*

Your heart comforts me as well, said Mallow. *It's so bright and cheerful! Even your sadness is innocent and sweet. I've felt less alone the last few days. I'm glad to have your companionship in a cold world.*

Thank you, said Clovermead, and then she felt confused and angry. *You shouldn't speak that way to me! You're a killer and you're cruel and you're, you're—*

Heartless, said Mallow, and he laughed. Then he said wistfully, *I was until we made our bargain. I am no longer.* He paused a moment. *I begin to feel some remorse for my actions.*

Then stop! Say you will. Mallow was silent, and Clovermead's sympathy for him drained suddenly away. *It doesn't matter what you say. You're so sympathetic, you understand me so well, but you won't change what you do. Monster! Get out of my head.* Clovermead slammed her sword back into her scabbard.

As you wish, said Mallow, and then he was gone.

Sorrel and Saraband were still laughing in the distance.

I don't care, Clovermead told herself. *My dust will keep me numb.* She soothed her aching heart in cool sand.

Clovermead banged loudly on the tree-trunk and walked around the tree, scuffing leaves noisily as she went. She looked ever so casually toward Sorrel and Saraband, and now they were a very decorous distance apart. "There you are!" she said as cheerfully as she could. "I was sniffing for bears. There aren't any around right now." Which was true enough; they had disappeared during the night. "What should we do for breakfast? Shall I catch some fish?"

"If you can," said Sorrel. "I will see if I can trap anything in the woods. Lady Saraband—" He looked at her puzzledly. "Can you light a fire?"

"Do I look as if I can?" asked Saraband. She showed him her delicate, soft hands.

Sorrel rolled his eyes. "What can you do for breakfast, Lady?"

Saraband shrugged. "I can gather sticks. One of you two can light them."

"That will do," said Sorrel. He cast a worried eye at Clovermead, as if afraid she would make some sarcastic comment. Clovermead blinked her eyes at him innocently—*Who, me?*—and headed toward the nearest stream.

She returned with two trout and Sorrel with an unfortunate rabbit; then they made the fire and roasted their catch. Clovermead tore at her fish with relish, while Saraband picked at hers fastidiously. Clovermead packed their leftovers in Sorrel's saddlebag, then washed her hands thoroughly to get the grease and scales off of them.

They climbed through ever-thicker forest. The road went up and down over the ridges of the Reliquaries. As they rose, Sorrel fell back and spoke softly with Saraband. After a while Saraband began to giggle softly. Clovermead wasn't even trying to eavesdrop when she heard Sorrel say, "*He imali ta sekawa*—you resemble a white dove."

They finished off their fish and rabbit for lunch, then continued walking in the afternoon. Sorrel strolled for a while with Clovermead while Saraband rode slowly after them. He smiled at nothing in particular and started to whistle an entirely too jaunty tune.

"*He imali ta* ninny," said Clovermead crossly. "*He imali ta* rooster, his crest all puffed up as he stalks around the coop and thinks about hens. What do you call a rooster in Tansyard, anyway."

"Cucuru," said Sorrel. "I do not look like a *cucuru* at all."

"You do now," said Clovermead, chortling. "Your face is as red as one, anyway." Sorrel turned even redder. *"He imali ta cucu*rooster like anything."

"Have you been listening to my private conversations, Clovermead?" asked Sorrel as sternly as he could, but his face was still extraordinarily scarlet.

"As little as I can," Clovermead lied. "Anyway, I couldn't miss the *He imali* line you were feeding her. So you think she looks like a pigeon?"

"A white dove," said Sorrel, with what tatters of dignity he could assemble. "They are quite different birds."

"Pshaw," said Clovermead. "A dove is a pigeon that fell into a bucket of white paint. Everyone knows that." Sorrel glowered at her, and there was a spark of real anger in him, so Clovermead added hastily, "I'm not saying anything against her. I'm just giving you guff."

"Be gentle, Clovermead," said Sorrel. "I am tender on the subject."

"Don't you worry," said Clovermead. "I wouldn't do anything to hurt you." She turned away from him suddenly as her face flushed red.

Sorrel didn't notice. His expression had grown thoughtful. "I wonder if I was too hasty," he said ruminatively. "There is much to be said for the art of curing men."

Clovermead could not speak.

"Saraband—*Lady* Saraband says it does not take so long to learn the rudiments of healing," Sorrel continued.

"I could be of use to Chandlefort as a nurse even before I completed my studies in medicine."

"She'll be awfully busy," said Clovermead. "Between teaching dance to me and medicine to you, she won't have any spare time at all."

"That is a good point," said Sorrel, quite seriously. He frowned. "I suppose I would have to study with the nuns of the city hospice, too. It would be unfair to demand too much time of her to act as my tutor."

"You'd stop being a Yellowjacket? Who'll be my sparring partner when you're gone?" Clovermead tried hard not to whine.

"Someone else," said Sorrel. He smiled at Clovermead. "You would become a better fighter than me in months, little hellion! Does not the thought delight you?"

"No," said Clovermead miserably. "I want to beat you fair and square."

"And I still want to spend many years whacking you on the ribs, Clovermead," said Sorrel with a smile. "But there are other things I want as well."

"And *she* doesn't want you to be a Yellowjacket," said Clovermead, with an angry jerk of her thumb back at Saraband.

"Soldiering does distress her deeply."

Then you'd better follow her apron strings, thought Clovermead, and she clamped shut her mouth. She didn't think Sorrel would forgive her if she said that out loud.

She couldn't think of anything else polite to say, and they hiked forward in silence for the rest of the afternoon.

Toward evening Saraband peered ahead and said, "We've come close. We can't be more than an hour from Kite Hall."

They heard a roar behind them. Clovermead whirled, and she saw a bear laze across the road.

Sorrel had seen it too. "What does that mean, Clovermead?" he asked nervously. "Are we told that trespassers will be nibbled?"

"It's just roaring," said Clovermead. "It doesn't always mean something." She cast her mind out into the night. *Mallow?* she asked.

Join me in Kite Hall, said Mallow. *I have sent these bears to escort you.*

Bears? asked Clovermead, and then she could smell them and hear them everywhere around them, bounding closer, growling and roaring. They came out of the woods by the dozens—brown bears and black bears, white bears and russet bears, circling them all around. Sorrel drew his sword and Clovermead drew hers, too. They stepped to either side of Saraband and Brown Barley.

"Mallow's sent them to take us to Kite Hall," said Clovermead. She looked at all the bears around her, saw the white tendrils digging into their heads, and she swallowed hard. "I don't think they mean to hurt us."

You are invited, whispered a great brown bear. *The others are not.*

Lord Kite has left them to us, said a leering black bear who was missing two fangs.

You can't have them! said Clovermead indignantly, but now it was just Sorrel she cared about. Dust swirled in her and brought her the pleasing vision of Saraband torn apart, limb from limb. *I'm still responsible for her,* Clovermead told herself, told the tempting dust. *It doesn't matter if she's kissing Sorrel now. That doesn't change anything.* But the words scrambled for purchase in her emptiness. The black bear laughed at her contemptuously and stepped forward into the path.

Saraband brought Brown Barley back a step. "If they don't mean to hurt us, Clovermead, what are they doing?" she asked. Sorrel moved between her and the bear.

"I got the message a little wrong, dancer." Clovermead raised her sword up high. "Mallow wants me in Kite Hall, but not the two of you. We have to fight them off."

Her sword flared in the moonlight, and the bears stopped where they were. The plaques gleamed and the metal of the sword shone like molten silver. Clovermead waggled her sword at the bears, and they stumbled away from its light.

Sorrel kept his sword at the ready, but he took a quick glance at Clovermead and smiled unsteadily. "Now you are a firefly! You show no end of talents. How does your sword come to glow?"

"I don't know," said Clovermead. "It shone once before. It just happens." She took a step forward, and the sword's light moved with her. The bears ahead of her fell back while the bears behind her came forward, crowding at the edges of the sphere of swordlight. "They don't seem to like the light. The two of you had better stay close to me." She took another step forward,

Saraband and Sorrel hurried after her, and now she saw the path divide again. "Which way to Kite Hall?" she asked Saraband.

Saraband pointed to a path ahead and to the left. "That way." Clovermead nodded, and started up the narrow road.

Twilight ended, night fell, and the stars appeared. Sorrel walked just ahead of her and Saraband rode right behind on Brown Barley. They went ever deeper into a grove of giant oaks, the thinnest tree four feet across and the thickest seven. The ground was still covered with brown oak leaves from the last fall. Owls hooted from the branches above and sometimes dove after small, squeaking animals dashing among the leaves. Clovermead saw a raccoon trot confidently through the night. The silent sphere of bears followed them steadily, like great moths hovering around a lantern.

At last they emerged into a hollow where a round pool stood. Forests rose around the three nearest sides of the pool, but a greensward lay on its far side. Beyond the pool the land fell away. Leagues away and far below, Clovermead saw the lights of Silverfalls Abbey pierce the endless darkness of the Reliquaries. The pond spilled over a stone lip to form a small waterfall that spattered down rocks with a constant roar. Two narrow white stones lay by the water's edge.

The travelers came closer to the grass, Clovermead's sword still held high, and now Clovermead saw that the stones were gravestones. They were marble and they glowed in the swordlight. The words MALLOW KITE were graven on one and ATHANOR SCONCE on the other.

Mallow Kite straightened up. He had been lounging against his tombstone. He was no longer a voice in Clovermead's head, but solid and visible; no longer wore a bear-priest's furs, but the golden raiment of a lord of Chandlefort.

"Welcome to Kite Hall," he said.

Chapter Twelve

Kite Hall

Mallow glanced at Saraband and Sorrel with mild surprise, then at the glowing sword and the circle of bears. "I didn't invite your friends, Demoiselle. They aren't welcome here."

"Uncle," whispered Saraband. "It really is you. How can you be here?"

"I don't quite know how it happened, Niece," said Mallow thoughtfully. "The sword of a soldier of Low Branding came toward me, there was pain and darkness—and then I heard a piper play. Her instrument was very cold and very far away. Her tune grew louder, and then it melted into the roar of a bear that tore me from my sleep.

"*Wake,* he said. *I have need of you.* 'Let me sleep,' I said. 'I had enough of doing and loving before; no more of that.' *But I can offer you something very sweet,* he said. *Wake and you can take revenge against Lady Cindertallow.* That caught my attention somehow, even in my sleep. I had forgotten a great deal under the earth, but I remembered how Melisande had let me come to love her and then spurned me for the craftsman's son. That still gnawed at my heart. 'Wake me, My Lord,' I said.

"I stood on the ground once more, by this gravestone.

'How much time has passed?' I asked him. *Eleven years,* he said. 'So long asleep?' I cried. 'I must be very active for the next eleven to make up for lost time. How may I serve you, My Lord?' *I have an army that needs a commander,* he said. *Will you lead them?* 'Gladly,' said I. And here I am." He bowed low to Saraband.

Saraband shuddered and made the sign of the crescent.

Mallow lifted up a bear-tooth that hung on a leather cord around his neck. "I am immune to such conjurations, Niece." He rubbed his hands briskly and turned back to Clovermead. "Put away your sword and come with me."

"I'm not an idiot," said Clovermead. She kept her sword up. "I'm not going to leave my friends to die."

Mallow tried to enter the sphere of light. He winced in sudden pain and drew back into the darkness. "It appears that we're at an impasse." He smiled. "I surrender, Demoiselle. Put down your sword. I won't harm the Tansyard or my niece."

Clovermead laughed harshly. "You think I'll believe anything you say?"

Mallow hissed impatiently, then raised his right hand and said out loud, "I swear by my fear of Lord Ursus' vengeance that I will not harm your friends while they remain on the grounds of Kite Hall." He made a gesture and the bears fell away from the light. Slowly, growling softly, they melted back into the woods. Very hesitantly Clovermead lowered her sword. Its light went out as she sheathed it. She looked warily at Mallow.

"I am no oath-breaker," said Mallow. He strode from his grave and beckoned them to follow. "Come with me to Kite Hall. Quickly, now! Your friends have delayed our business here long enough."

A stone path led from the greensward through more woods. Great roots stretched under the path and tore its stones apart. In a few hundred yards they came to a great lawn of grass thick with sprouting saplings. Ahead a long timber house stood half-collapsed. The tiles had fallen from its roof, and its shattered windows were dark. Sorrel helped Saraband dismount from Brown Barley and tied the horse to a sapling on the front lawn.

Mallow strode through the sagging front door and into the dining room of Kite Hall. He led them past a table long enough to hold thirty guests, covered with leaves that had blown in through the broken windows, then back through cold, dark rooms to a kitchen thick with ancient dust and grease. A partridge that had made a nest in an abandoned pot fled out the broken back door as they came in. Through the door Clovermead saw a very ordinary stone well in the middle of a rectangle of grass.

"You want to cure Melisande with a cup of water from my well? There it is." Mallow pointed to a row of dusty metal flasks on a shelf. "Take one," he said. "Keep it away from me. Only living flesh should touch the flask until the water is poured in."

Clovermead reached out her hand toward the flask, then looked at Mallow suspiciously. "You'll just let us take the water and go?"

"Of course not." Mallow stared at Clovermead with glittering eyes. "You and I will make a bargain for this favor."

"That does not sound like a good idea, Clovermead," said Sorrel hastily. "Please do not decide too quickly to accept his offer."

"Wise words," said Mallow. "Prudent words. Be judicious while Melisande dies." His laughter was colder and more joyful than ever.

"Be merciful, Uncle," said Saraband. "Let Milady live without conditions. Haven't you had your fill of revenge yet?"

"No!" blazed Mallow. Red spots rose on his bloodless cheeks. "She tore out my heart. She showed me no mercy and I will show none to her."

"She has been kind to me, Uncle," said Saraband. "She has—"

"I don't care how she's cosseted you, Niece." His raging eyes whipped across Saraband's face, and she whimpered and fell back toward Sorrel. He opened his arm to embrace her and she huddled by his chest. Prudent Sorrel, cautious Sorrel, frightened Sorrel unhesitatingly stepped between Saraband and the dead man's rage.

They're good for each other, thought Clovermead. *She needs someone to be brave for her, and he needs someone to make him brave.* She sighed, cold and empty. *Sorrel doesn't need me.*

I have been very lonely, Demoiselle, said Mallow silently. She could feel his solitude etched in every grain of dust that flowed through her veins. *I would be glad to have a companion.* He looked at her wistfully. *Give me more of your heart, and I will give you water enough from my well to cure your mother.*

Anyone would do for you, said Clovermead. *You don't need me either.*

I know what your heart is like. I've felt it beat in me these last few days, and I like it very much. I would not make this offer to my niece or the Tansyard. Only to you.

I wish Sorrel had said that to me, thought Clovermead, but at least someone had. He was a dead man eaten up with hatred and revenge, but he wanted her. Clovermead felt blood rush through her, she was all fire and ice, and the words darted out of her mouth: "I accept your bargain, Lord Kite." Saraband and Sorrel gasped, but Clovermead didn't regret what she'd said. She walked briskly over to the shelf, picked up a flask, and brushed the grime off it. "What do we do now?"

"Draw up the water," said Mallow. He led them through the broken back door into the grassy courtyard, then stood aside as they approached the well. A sturdy bucket attached by a rope to a winch sat on the well. "I trust you know how?"

"We had a well at Ladyrest," said Clovermead. "Drawing up the water was one of my chores, but I was always forgetting, and Father had to remind me just about every day of my life." She gave the flask to Saraband and began to lower the bucket down the well shaft. When the bucket hit water, far down, she turned the winch to bring it back up.

The bucket was extraordinarily heavy. "This isn't water," said Clovermead. "You've put lead weights into the well. I know it." Her arms ached as she turned the winch, and she found herself panting. *I want to turn into a bear,* she thought.

"Don't, Demoiselle," said Mallow. He leaned comfortably against a windowsill outlined in climbing ivy. "You must stay human while you bring the water up." Clovermead obeyed and kept on turning the winch.

Her entire upper body was in agony by the time the bucket was halfway up. "I can't go on," she gasped. "Please, Sorrel, take the winch."

"Lady, give me strength," Sorrel murmured. He took the winch from Clovermead's hands and wheeled it around while Clovermead massaged her aching arms and the chafed skin of her hands. It was no easier for him than it had been for Clovermead. The bucket came nearer and nearer to the surface, and sweat glistened on Sorrel's forehead. He twisted it once more—and his fingers came loose! Sorrel cried out in despair as the winch began to slip backward, and Clovermead grabbed the handle. The bucket had fallen only a few feet. Some water must have spilled out, but the bucket was as heavy as ever. Clovermead and Sorrel held the handle together and kept the bucket from falling, but neither of them had the strength to lift it the rest of the way.

"Let me do the rest," said Saraband.

"You?" asked Clovermead. "You're not strong enough."

"It only needs to come a few more feet," said Saraband. "I can do that much." She put the flask down on the grass and set her hands next to Clovermead's on the handle. "I owe your mother for her kindness to me," she said quietly. "Let me pull."

"I don't need your help," said Clovermead, but she

felt her arms buckling. Unwillingly she stepped aside and let Saraband take her place. "Don't let the bucket drop," she growled. "I can't pull it up a second time."

"I won't fail Milady," said Saraband. Then she began to pull. Sorrel tried to help her, but he, too, was limp with weariness, and Saraband's slender arms had to bear the weight of the bucket. She began to tremble at once, and Clovermead could tell that her cousin didn't have half Clovermead's strength. Weak as she was, she didn't falter, didn't cry out, didn't say a word of complaint. Inch by inch she raised the bucket until it was even with the top of the well, then held the winch steady while Clovermead and Sorrel grabbed the full bucket and set it gently on the grass by the well. When Saraband let go of the handle at last, Clovermead saw she had rubbed half the skin off her palms. Without fuss she bled in the darkness.

Clovermead dipped the flask into the bucket. When it was full, she drew the cap tight. The flask was still as heavy as lead, as heavy as gold.

Mallow gazed at the flask. "I drew another bucket a fortnight ago," he said. "I spilled the water through my fingers upon my sword. With the touch of my flesh it became the water of death, and I opened Melisande's veins with it. The water you have drawn up will counteract that other flask, heal any wound I have caused. If you reach her." He smiled at Clovermead. "That is not so certain."

"Ah," said Clovermead. "I hear the catch coming on."

Mallow turned to Saraband and Sorrel. "Niece, Tansyard, it is time for you to go. Take the flask and leave my home. You will not be attacked by bear or bear-priest until you come in sight of the fields of Chandlefort. If you dare that, I will not be held accountable for what happens to you. Chandlefort is under siege, and Melisande is answerable to my vengeance. My armies will fight against you if you attempt to bring that flask to her." He turned to Clovermead with glittering eyes. "You and I have made a bargain. You will stay to fulfill your part of it."

Clovermead nodded, eager and fearful at once. Then she picked up the flask and thrust it into Sorrel's hands. "Go," she whispered.

"Clovermead," Sorrel began, and there was fear and tenderness and affection in his face.

"I know what I'm doing. Hurry to Milady!"

"We will ride like the wind, Clovermead," said Sorrel reluctantly. "I promise you, you will not have bargained in vain." Then he and Saraband turned and ran from the courtyard back through abandoned Kite Hall and toward the front lawn where Brown Barley stood waiting. In a minute Clovermead heard Brown Barley neigh, and then she heard hoofbeats sound, dwindle, and disappear.

Clovermead and Mallow stood alone in the cold courtyard, and Clovermead shivered. "You're only offering my mother a chance of survival. That means you'll only get a part of me. Is that understood?"

"That seems fair," said Mallow. He smiled. "What do you offer?"

"Will you take another third of my heart, Mallow?" Clovermead was trembling worse than ever, with cold, with fear, with anticipation.

"Yes," said Mallow. "And I will give you more of my dust." He reached out his hand, and a pulse of red light leaped from her chest into his waiting fingers. Clovermead gasped as ice thickened in her. She was very far from the world now. Mallow closed his pale fist and her light disappeared into him.

"I don't mind, you know," said Clovermead as her teeth chattered. "I want Milady to live, and I don't want to hurt, and this way I get both." She made herself think of Sorrel and Saraband embracing, but it didn't hurt at all now. The dust was thick and soothing; the ache in her blood very thin. She tried to make herself smile. "It won't be so bad if I bargain the rest of my heart away? If we become companions forever?"

"Once I was reputed to be a witty man. I dance well. I was pleasant to look upon, before I grew so pale and cold." Mallow bowed and kissed Clovermead's hand with his lips that were not cold to her any longer. "And you will be an agreeable companion to me. You are brave, kind, and pleasant to look upon."

Clovermead colored, and anger and embarrassment stirred in her chilled heart. She drew away from him. "Don't lie. I know I'm not pretty."

"Then you are a fool," said Mallow roughly. He seized her hand in his and he held up her scar. The mishealed flesh tingled hot in his grip. "This is nothing. You will be a beautiful woman." There was a sad look in his eyes. "As beautiful as Melisande."

Clovermead jerked her arm away from Mallow, though she wasn't entirely sure she wanted to. She liked the way his palm had warmed her scar. "I want *Sorrel* to like me. Maybe he does, some ways, but he likes Saraband better. I don't care what anyone else thinks. You didn't—why should I?"

Mallow smiled crookedly. "I cannot argue with that," he said. "Ah, Demoiselle, we will provide good solace for each other when I have had my revenge."

Anger flared in Clovermead, and it melted some of the ice in her. "I want to like you, but then you talk about revenge and I know you're as hateful as ever. I won't stop fighting to save Milady."

"You can't resist me." Mallow grinned at her and his flesh was shadowy on him. The skull beneath the skin stared through at her. "All you'll do is hurt yourself if you try." He looked at Clovermead, and now there was only compassion on the dead man's face. He extended his hand toward Clovermead. "Don't struggle. Let me end your pain."

Clovermead felt her heart beat slower as ice spread through her chest. For a moment it was welcome. *I do hurt so much,* she thought wearily. *Besides, how can I save Milady in time? The moon's less than half-full, and she doesn't even have a week left. Maybe it would be easier to let this happen.*

Death, she thought as Mallow's pale fingers approached. *This is death.* And suddenly it didn't matter how much she hurt. *I'd rather hurt than be dead,* she told herself in fear and anger. *Anything's better than that!* Her mind was slow and frozen, but she blurted out, "No! I don't want to die."

"You don't know your own mind," said Mallow. She could feel the cold of the grave as his fingertips came close.

"You can't harm me," said Clovermead. "You swore you wouldn't."

"I swore not to harm your friends. I said nothing about you. Don't be afraid, Clovermead. I'm doing you a kindness."

"So am I," said Clovermead, and she drew her father's sword from its scabbard. The birchwood medallions shone in the moonlight, and Clovermead swung in a blaze of heat. Her sword glowed in the night as she sliced through Mallow's fingertips.

Mallow screamed and stumbled back from Clovermead. "My hand!" he moaned, and the top halves of his left pinky and ring finger were gone. A dribble of blood came from the severed flesh.

"Leave me alone," said Clovermead. She stepped away from him.

She heard a rasp of metal as Mallow drew his sword. Dusty tears ran down his cheeks, he howled again, and his sword smashed at Clovermead. She jumped back, then tried to parry his next blow, but it struck so hard against her father's sword that she went tumbling on her back. Mallow raised his sword to finish her off—and Clovermead shot up a great paw to catch his hand and keep his blade suspended in midair.

I need to fight berserker, thought Clovermead. She had kept herself human when she fought with Sorrel on the Training Ground, but she didn't need to bother with that now. She growled and rose to her feet, and now she was as tall as Mallow and far thicker. She held her father's sword with claws that could barely grip the handle, and she shoved Mallow away from her. He flew from her like a rag doll, and Clovermead threw herself at him with a howl.

She was far clumsier this time than she had been when she fought Sorrel. All her training was as a girl, and her bear body was the wrong size, the wrong shape. She could barely keep from completing the transformation and just attacking him with her claws and jaws. Instead she used her father's sword like a battering ram. They fought shambling from the courtyard into the kitchen, then through the house and out to the lawn beyond. Clovermead roared with rage as great as Mallow's, and the dead man and the bear had scarcely a human thought between them.

Clovermead smashed her sword at Mallow and it went six inches into the earth. She howled as Mallow danced away from her. His rage had subsided at last, and now he grimaced at her with a ghastly light in his eyes. "Do you want to play at being a bear?" he gasped. "Lord Ursus has given me power over them." Clovermead felt something slithering in her mind, a hand out of the grave began to pull at her like a puppet, and against her will she felt her paw loosen on her sword hilt. She screamed in horror and turned herself back to human—but as she turned she lashed out one last time with her sword. She crunched through Mallow's palm and half his wounded hand fell to the ground. Three fingers of his severed hand still scrabbled at the air, and his severed stump dripped thin blood. Mallow screamed louder than before, and the coils that had settled around Clovermead's mind jerked away.

"Not again, Ursus," he cried out wildly. He backed

away from Clovermead and raised his sword to defend himself. "Don't let another Beechsplitter defeat me."

Have faith in me, Mallow, she heard Ursus roar in the distance. The words were a hot and foul wind from the south. *Use my strength wisely.* His growl made the trees shake.

"You've already failed," said Clovermead, in taunting triumph. "Sorrel and Saraband have the flask, and Sorrel's the fastest rider I've ever seen, and they'll cure Milady. You won't get your revenge."

"You're right, Demoiselle," Mallow said wonderingly. "Your friends will rob me of my vengeance. I should concentrate on that. What do a few fingers matter?" He whistled shrilly and Clovermead heard neighing. Mallow's dark horse galloped up to him, and Clovermead saw that he was like the dead bears, made only of shadows and bones. Where the flesh should have been was churning darkness that moved over his pale and glowing skeleton. His harness glowed silver in the moonlight, his eyes were dark hollows, and his tail was switching blackness. He neighed like clacking tombstones.

Mallow jumped lightly onto his steed's back and he was confident once more. "I must return to Chandlefort quickly, and I must keep you and that sword away from me." Clovermead saw white coils flash through the night, and she heard Mallow's bony rasp loud in her mind. *Kill the changeling!* he cried out. *Chase her, bite her, crush her, eat her, tear her limb from limb. I command you, in Lord Ursus' name!* Lord Ursus roared with glee, and a hundred bears roared with him as they started padding toward her.

"Run for your life, Demoiselle," said Mallow. "You will find me in Chandlefort with your mother, if you survive. And perhaps then I will have the last bit of your heart from you, and we will spend many pleasant hours in the grave together." He wheeled his horse and galloped down the valley after Saraband and Sorrel.

The bears roared again and Clovermead turned pale. *Time to get out of here,* she thought, and she turned into a golden bear and started to run. She could see the first bears come into sight at the other end of the lawn, and she fled for dear life.

Chapter Thirteen

HIDE AND SEEK

CLOVERMEAD CHARGED INTO THE FOREST, ANGLING away from the road back to Silverfalls. *Sorrel and Saraband will be riding that way,* she thought. *They don't need a lot of bears chasing them.* Branches clung to her and slowed her down as she ran through pathless hills pursued by a straggling arc of bears. She heard steady roaring from one or another of the bears following her. Sometimes they lagged behind, sometimes they gained on her, but they never fell out of hearing.

Clovermead struggled through streams and over rock faces, between thickets and trailing vines, and after a while she came to a dirt trail that was scarcely a path at all, but marked with blazes on trees every now and then. Clovermead could smell human scents on it—*A smuggler's trail, I suppose,* she thought. *This'll be easier.* She accelerated, and finally the bears fell out of earshot. She felt her fear ease a little.

She knew she must be colder than ever, but she couldn't feel the chill anymore. She knew that her paws struck the ground and that her whole upper body was still sore from pulling up the bucket of water, but she felt no aches. Her tongue lolled out and she wanted to drink, but she felt no thirst, either. Her heart was slow, her blood was dust, and inch by inch her body was growing numb.

Toward dawn Clovermead couldn't keep her eyes open. *I have to sleep,* she told herself as she lay down underneath an overhanging boulder. *I haven't heard any roaring for hours, so I think I'll be safe. It's sleep now or collapse later.* The moon had set long since, and even the stars were dim. She shut her eyes—

Mallow charged toward the heart of the Army of Low Branding. No! *he heard Athanor cry behind him, but he didn't care anymore.* Better to die this way, *he told himself.* Better this than a lifetime watching them. *He lowered his spear—*

"No!" cried Clovermead, and she woke gasping. "Lady, I don't want to dream of Mallow. Let me sleep in peace." She wiped dusty tears from her cheeks. "I beg you, Lady, with all my heart." She fell back against the twigs and closed her eyes. She felt real sleep descend on her, sweet and refreshing, and she smiled with exhausted gratitude. "Thank you, Lady," she said, and she slipped into unconsciousness—

She dreamed that she and Waxmelt stood on the walls of Chandlefort and watched a regiment of servants in armor fight a horde of bears. "They don't have the hang of it yet," said Waxmelt, rather woebegone. "Look, they're supposed to put up their shields to defend themselves, but they keep using them as trays. See? They've loaded them up with small sandwiches and—Dear Lady, they're feeding them to the bears! I told them this morning, 'Fight *the bears, don't* feed *the bears,' but they don't listen to me. Oh, dear, they've used the salmon sandwiches. Those were meant to be saved for the next ball."*

"It seems to be working," said Clovermead. "The bears have stopped attacking and, goodness gracious, Father, they've started dancing! They're not orthodox tactics, and I don't suppose Sir Tourmaline would approve, but it does seem to work. You should be proud of them."

"I commend you, Lord Wickward," said Lady Cindertallow, who had just come down from the clouds, mounted on an enormous buzzing bee. "You will be rewarded. I dub thee Prince of Pastries; your escutcheon will be a cream-puff rampant. Clovermead, don't forget that we're supposed to go hunting spotted orchids after lunch. You have to watch out for orchids, they'll rip your heart out if you're not careful." She waved farewell to Clovermead with her bleeding hand and flew, bee-back, off to her tower.

Clovermead shivered suddenly. The bears were dancing to the sound of a distant piper, whose music was beautiful and cold. "Spotted orchids?" she asked Waxmelt. "What are those?"

"In Timothy Vale we call them dead men's fingers," said her father sadly. "Clo, I wish you wouldn't go hunting. If I've told Milady once, I've told her a thousand times, you're too young yet to be murdered. Stay home with me in Ladyrest where it's safe."

"I wish I could, Father," said Clovermead. She seized him in her arms and hugged him, but he wore cold armor that kept her away. The bears roared to the piper's tune, the cold pipe-music blew a hail of dust at her, Ursus laughed—

And Clovermead woke to the sound of distant roars. The bears were catching up to her again. She started to her feet; the sun was barely above the horizon. *I liked the sleep, Lady,* she thought, *but the dream at the end wasn't so nice.* Her stomach rumbled, but she didn't feel much hunger. She started running again.

The trees thinned after a while, but the ground grew more precipitous. Clovermead stopped at a rushing stream for a drink of water, then ran faster over the rocky slopes. Here the soil was chalky, and dry gulches alternated with pure white cliffs that heaved out of the earth. When Clovermead went into a gulch, the earth seemed quiet; when she rose to the top of a ridge, she could hear bears roaring behind her.

At noon she came to the top of a granite scarp and saw the Salt Heath just beyond a last few miles of broken ground. She could see herds of cattle and horses wandering the grassy outskirts of the Heath, and beyond them the bare rock and sand of the Heath's heart. She could run flat out once she reached the Heath—*but so can they,* she thought. She bounded down the slope a little faster and wondered how far Sorrel and Saraband had gotten by now. *Next time,* she told herself, *I will arrange matters so Saraband flees through the forest and I get to ride on Brown Barley with my arms around Sorrel. Share and share alike is fair: She's had the fun parts of adventuring long enough, and now it's my turn.*

All through the long afternoon Clovermead made her way down the slope of the hills toward the Heath. Here the trees gave way entirely, on a slope so steep and rocky that not even grass could grow on it. She skidded down among boulders and thanked Our Lady for her thick fur, which protected her skin from abrasions. It would have been safer to turn human and use her fingers to clamber down, but that would have slowed her down too much. The roaring grew ever closer.

At dusk she came to the bottom of the hills at last,

and the plain stretched out before her. She ran as quickly as she could across it, and for the first time all day the roaring dwindled. After a few hours it struck Clovermead that she had heard nothing for a while. *Maybe they're asleep at last,* she thought hopefully. She was terribly tired. She came to a stream, turned, and splashed upstream for a few hundred yards before turning into a muddy bank obscured by reeds. *Even if they do come after me, that should obscure my scent long enough for me to get away.* Then she prayed again: *Give me better dreams tonight, Lady*. She fell asleep—

Mallow watched as Ambrosius carved figures into a birchwood plaque. They had just fought together in the Training Grounds for a solid hour, and Ambrosius had beaten Mallow six touches to four. It had been a good bout, and Mallow didn't much mind that he had been beaten by a commoner. Now they sat together on a bench at the edge of the sands while figures emerged at the touch of Ambrosius' knife. "What is that, Master Beechsplitter?" Mallow asked.

"A reminder to myself," said Ambrosius. He dug his knife deeper into the wood and etched out the features of a captured bear. "I once freed a bear's leg from a trap when I was a boy. I don't precisely know why—she was a monstrous creature, and I should have been terrified. But somehow I wasn't. All I saw was that she was hurt, and I had to help her. I felt happier going home that day than I ever had in my life." He shook his head and laughed. "My father whipped me for ten solid minutes when I told him what had happened, and he told me never to do anything so foolish again."

Mallow laughed. "Sage advice. Did you follow it?"

"Until the day I insisted on becoming a Yellowjacket."

"That's an understandable folly," said Mallow, and for a moment the two of them looked at each other almost as friends. Then Mallow remembered how Melisande had looked at Ambrosius, and he dropped his eyes. "So this plaque is vanity? You have a swelled head, Lakelander."

"Undoubtedly, My Lord," said Ambrosius merrily. "I try to put cold cloths on my forehead, but it will bubble up with pride." Mallow had to laugh, and Ambrosius laughed with him. Ambrosius put the first plaque onto the bench and pulled a second one from his pocket. He showed it to Mallow: It was a rough carving of a young man who offered up his sword to Our Lady. "Seriously, My Lord? I joined the Yellowjackets because I loved the idea of fighting, and I have enjoyed myself splendidly as a cadet and trooper these last few years. But we have not fought in any actual battles yet. I used to think I would welcome a real fight, but now—" He shook his head. "I see Milady and the Mayor drift closer to war, and I find my joy diminishes as the prospect of battle comes closer. I find myself thinking back to how happy I was when I freed that bear. I felt like I was doing something in Our Lady's service. I like to think that when I do fight, it'll be in her service too. I'm carving these medallions to remind myself to consecrate my sword to Our Lady."

"You wear Melisande's livery, not Our Lady's," said Mallow. "You must fight when she orders you, whether or not the cause is good. If you cannot do that, perhaps you should take off your yellow coat and become a nuns' man."

"Perhaps I should, My Lord, but somehow I don't wish to leave Milady's service." Ambrosius smiled, Mallow scowled, and Ambrosius flaked away another piece of birchwood. "Call these medallions a prayer in wood. I carve them and pray that Milady will never ask me to draw my sword in a cause which is not Our Lady's—"

Bears roared, terribly loud. Clovermead started awake with the moon high above her, and twitched her ears. The bears were no more than a mile away and coming closer terribly fast. She was still muzzy-brained, and she stumbled in loose soil before she hit her stride. *Time to run again,* she thought as she dashed out onto the plain, but she wasn't quite sure who she was as she ran. She seemed to be riding on a horse of bones somewhere else on the plain, and she felt her blood course through Mallow's veins. It took her a minute to be sure she was Clovermead and not Mallow.

Now she could see the bears behind her. Fifty of them had spread out upon the plain. She couldn't run any faster, and the bears were gaining on her. *A little help wouldn't hurt, Lady,* thought Clovermead. The bears roared, and each growl was a message that she had no hope of escape.

Finally Clovermead could run no farther. She stopped upon the plain, heaving with exhaustion, and turned to face her pursuers. They bounded toward her, howling, and she could see Mallow's white coils bright against the darkness. They were a cage of bones in the sky.

I'd rather die as a human, thought Clovermead. She changed shape and drew her sword from her belt. She could kill at least one bear before she died. The moonlight struck against the birchwood plaque of the boy freeing the bear.

"Shine, sword," said Clovermead. "Keep the bears away from me." The sword remained obstinately dark. "Isn't there anything you can do, Lady?" asked Clovermead despairingly.

It was a white cage in the sky.

"Lady's kirtle," whispered Clovermead. "I'm not the one who has to get free. They are." She lifted her father's sword to the moonlight and she cried, "Free them, Lady. Not me, but them. In your service, Lady."

The moon was brighter than Clovermead had ever seen it, and the worn birchwood glowed like silver fire. The bears were very near to her, but they had stopped, blinking in the glare of the light. Clovermead could no longer look at what she held in her hand. The light pressed against her eyes, into her mind, and rooted through every corner of her. *How shall I free them?* it seemed to ask. *What shall I do?*

Clovermead lifted up her sword and pointed it at the white coils. "Shatter those chains, Lady," she cried. "Free these bears from Mallow Kite. Let them go!"

I'll need your help, the light asked. *Will you give it to me?*

"So long as I have something to give, Lady," said Clovermead. Then she gave her heart up to the light, without bargaining and without dismay, and she swung her sword wildly at the white cage of bones in the night sky.

What was left of her heart pushed out of her, and the sword flared white. Lightning blazed out along the arc in which her sword swung and pierced the white net, shattered it, and swept beyond the horizon. Clovermead heard a distant howl of rage, and the bears around her roared in sudden delight. Light came to rest on each of the bears nearby, glowed in their fur for a moment, then settled in them. For a moment Clovermead felt all their hearts beat in hers, and her chest wasn't empty at all, but fuller than it ever had been. Then the bears' hearts were only memories in her chest, but her own heart came back to her, as thin and dusty as before, but no weaker.

I'm free, she heard a bear roar. *So am I,* shouted another, and then a joyful roar rang from one to another all across the Heath as the bears abandoned their pursuit of Clovermead and turned to run, to leap, to do whatever they felt like.

Clovermead slumped onto the Heath with her sword by her side. The light faded slowly from it. She had exhausted herself. *It would have been easier if I'd had all my heart to give,* she thought—but there was no point worrying about might-have-beens. She sat and watched the bears enjoy their freedom, and a little joy warmed her cold weariness.

After a few minutes the bears stopped playing. One by one they came forward to sit around her. *Thank you, changeling,* they said, one after another. *Thank you. Thank you. Thank you.*

Brookwade stepped out in front of the others and shuffled toward her. *How did you free us?* he asked in wonder. *I thought there was no way to break our chains.*

There's something special about this sword, said Clovermead. She touched the hilt of her father's sword and tried to make lightning blaze again, but the metal stayed dull. *I don't know how it broke Mallow's bonds.*

Will Lord Ursus come after us again? asked another bear. *Will the dead man?*

I don't know that either, said Clovermead.

You look so tired, said Brookwade. *You should rest.*

I will, a little, said Clovermead. *But I can't for long. I have to try to save my mother. My friends have a cure to heal her, but there's an army between them and Milady. I have to find my friends and figure out how to get them past the bear-priests and into Chandlefort.* She laughed despairingly. *There's no hope, but I have to try.*

Bear-priests? asked Brookwade. He growled angrily. *I would be glad to take a bite out of some of Ursus' jackals.* He grumbled thoughtfully for a moment. *Do you think this sword of yours has freed our minds forever? Or just for a while?*

I wish I knew, said Clovermead. *If Ursus or Mallow try to enslave you, I'll ask the sword to free you again. I don't know if it will, but I'll try my hardest. I give you my word for that, Brookwade, in Our Lady's name.*

That's good enough for me, Haybrawler, said Brookwade with a grin. He turned to the other bears. *Let us fight him,* he roared. *We owe the changeling for her service to us. Besides, I want Lord Ursus to know just how much I dislike being enslaved. I want his servants to feel it as my jaws bite down on them.* He growled low and terrible.

This moonlight can't stand up to him, said a stout bear. *We can't resist him. Leave us alone, Brookwade. At least we can enjoy ourselves until he comes for us again.*

We can defeat him if we fight together, said Brookwade.

The stout bear laughed with scorn. *No one can resist Lord Ursus.*

We can try, said Clovermead. She clutched at her father's sword, and she felt hopeful again. *Anyway, what have you got to lose?*

My life, said the stout bear. *My freedom. We'll only attract Lord Ursus' notice if we fight him, and then his net will come down on us again. He may overlook us if we hide. No. Now that I have my freedom, I won't throw it away. I won't be a fool.* She turned from Clovermead and Brookwade and trotted toward the Reliquaries.

I will, said Brookwade. He roared with glee. *I'm tired of running away, and he'll come for us all in the end. I'd rather die fighting than be a slave again. I'll take the risk.* He took a step forward. *And I do want to bite a bear-priest,* he said hopefully, hungrily. A rumble of laughter spread among the bears.

Some bears drifted toward Clovermead and Brookwade, others toward the distant mountains. They were slow to decide. At last, twenty bears sat in front of Clovermead.

Clovermead looked at the remnant around her and sighed. *There aren't nearly enough of you to do much damage to the bear-priests. Maybe you should go off to the Reliquaries with the others.*

Brookwade rumbled consideringly. *There are other bears who have hidden far from sight and stayed free of Ursus and Mallow. I might be able to persuade them to come to Chandlefort.*

Clovermead looked up at the waning moon. Lady Cindertallow's life was waning with it. *My friends and I need to be in Chandlefort as soon as possible. We only have a few days.*

That isn't much time to search out my friends, said Brookwade. Then he looked at the other bears around him and he grinned. *But then, it won't be just me looking for them.* He turned to the bears and roared loudly. *Do you know where the free bears of Linstock hunt?*

In the snow-bound heights of the Reliquaries, growled a cinnamon bear.

In the muddy pools of the Harrow Moors, said a black bear with one ear.

In the wastes of the Salt Heath, sighed a grandame the color of ashes. *In the hungry corners of the land, where Ursus does not think a bear can live and does not look for us. I should have joined them when I had the chance.*

Go search for them, said Brookwade. *Tell them a few of us are going to rise up against Ursus and bite a few of his bear-priests. We may be slaves to him the next day, but we'll have let him know the edge of our teeth first. Ask them to join us in the fun.*

Where? asked the cinnamon bear. *When?*

Clovermead looked up at the narrow moon again and calculated what was the most time she could spare. Her mother would be dead in days. *Can you meet me four days from now at the teardrop pillars west of Chandlefort?*

We'll do what we can, changeling, said the grandame. She went over to Clovermead, rubbed her nose in a friendly manner, and growled at her comfortingly. Then she went bounding away onto the plain. The cinnamon bear left a few seconds later, then the one-eared black bear. Soon all the bears were padding off in different directions.

I'll see if I can find my sister, said Brookwade. *Two years ago she was hiding among the salt pans in the South Heath.* He smiled at Clovermead. *There are more of us than you might think.* Then he, too, slipped away.

Clovermead let go her sword and it fell to the grass. "You're just full of surprises," she said to it. "I should give you a name. All great warriors have swords with names." She smiled as she remembered what Sorrel had said when he saw the sword light up. "I think I'll call you Firefly. You aren't a talking sword, are you? I think I'd find that unnerving. I can handle bears chatting, but cutlery should stay silent."

Firefly lay quietly on the grass, much as swords do.

"That's a relief," said Clovermead. She yawned. "I've never been so tired in all my life! I'm sure somebody else will be chasing me tomorrow, so I'm going to get a proper night's rest while I have the chance."

She sprawled onto the grass, closed her eyes, and fell asleep.

Chapter Fourteen

Battle in the Heath

Clovermead woke the next morning terribly cold. Sweat glistened on her forehead, but she felt no heat at all. The sun shone pale and the colors of the plains had faded to dull sepia. When she turned into bear form, the scents and sounds of the Heath were also distant. There was a shroud between her and the world.

Dead to the world, she thought, and she laughed hollowly. There was ice all through her, but it was hard to care. *I have to get to the pillars,* she told herself, and she lumbered into motion. Her self was distant from her flesh, and the way she moved her body was like pulling the strings of a marionette.

Clovermead ran southward, searching for the road from Silverfalls to Chandlefort. She passed alarmed farmers and cowherds, and sometimes arrows whipped overhead as she raced past herds of cattle. She stopped to gulp down some grasses at noon, and she gobbled them all the way down to the roots. They were rough on her stomach, but at least they filled it up. Clovermead smelled fish in the streams of the Heath as she forded them, but she was no longer captivated by their smell. *Just so I have food in my belly,* she thought, *I don't care what it is.*

Toward afternoon she reached the Chandlefort road. She sniffed at the flagstones, and she could smell Sorrel and Saraband. Their scent was two days old. She sniffed again, and she could smell Mallow's faint, stomach-turning scent. He had ridden through a little while after Sorrel and Saraband. Their scents intertwined with each other, and Clovermead followed them eastward along the road.

She spent the night by a stagnant stream where poplars grew over tall reeds. The air was muggy and mosquitoes rose in the darkness to nip at her. She scarcely felt their bites. She dreamed—

An arrow pierced Ambrosius' side, and the force knocked him from his horse. His chest ached and he saw an arrow sticking out of it. It ran through him. "I've been killed," *he said in amazement. Blood trickled from his mouth and he felt the world going gray.* "Tell Melisande I love her," *he said, and he clutched at his sword.* "Oh, Lady, I've never paid you for your gifts. Lady, I hurt." *And then grayness swallowed him up—*

Clovermead woke in the middle of the night shivering and weeping. She had turned human, and Firefly shone at her waist. She took it out and touched the birchwood plaques, and she could feel warmth in them through the coldness settling in on her. "Help me," she whispered, and she clutched the medallions to her cheek. She closed her eyes—but now she could not sleep. She tossed and turned in the darkness all night, helplessly wakeful, and at dawn she rose with a groan. *I'm going to be exhausted,* she thought, but then she realized that while she wasn't well rested, she wasn't sleepy, either. Dreamless, sleepless, she turned into a bear and ran eastward into the Heath.

At first the day was miserably steamy; then a storm boiled out of the Reliquaries, drenched her for five minutes, and blew quickly to the east. The sun came out and joined forces with a brisk wind to dry her off. The grass of the Heath grew thinner as the day wore on, and the soil thickened into a swirl of black and gray clays scattered over yellow sandstone. Clovermead gulped down a lunch of grass from the last patch before the Heath turned into bare and baking dirt. By dusk she had been running through flat clay for hours with only the odd clump of weeds to break the monotony. To the north more thin grasslands were barely visible, while broken hills covered the terrain to the south. Her paws pounded on the road's hard stones, and small puffs of dust rose around her.

She huddled by the plaques that night and closed her eyes, but still she could not sleep. When her eyes were closed, she rode through the night on a horse of bones, and the wind whistled through her empty rib cage. The world was dry, the world was frozen, but she was not dreaming. When she opened her eyes, she felt Mallow looking through them. *We'll be together soon,* he whispered. *Just a little longer, Clovermead.* She looked up at the horn moon, eaten away by night and time, and Mallow smiled. *Three days left? Four days? Then Melisande dies.*

"Let me sleep once more, Lady," Clovermead begged. "I don't care what I dream—just so I sleep. Please." She closed her eyes and she did dream—

She was a golden cub walking with a huge white bear through a mountain forest. It was late afternoon on an autumn day, red and yellow leaves fell from the trees with every gust of wind, and the pale moon shone in the clear blue sky. The white bear cried as she walked, and with every step a tear struck the ground. For a moment her tears turned the leaves they touched to rubies and yellow diamonds that glinted in the sunlight. Then the jewels turned back into fading, tearstained leaves.

Why do you care about them? *asked Clovermead, cold and discontented. She kicked at a leaf with a numb paw and tore it with her claws.* Dead is dead.

It's my nature to cry when they fall, *said the white bear.* I wouldn't have it any other way.

They're only leaves, *said Clovermead.* They don't deserve your tears.

They have them anyway, *said the white bear, and she roared with sorrow. Her roar was a great wind that shuddered through the forest and howled along the leaf-strewn floor. The leaves rose in the gale and swept around Clovermead's head. They glinted in the sunlight, jewels once more, then blew out of sight.*

The forest had been swept clean of leaves, save for one tree that stood right in front of them. It was spindly, bent, and cankered. Some shriveled, worm-eaten leaves clung to the branches with fierce determination; others had stuck to the soil beneath the tree and bent away from the white bear's breath. The tree's bark was rotting.

I've never seen anything so ugly, *Clovermead marveled. She felt a wave of revulsion sweep over her.* I've never seen anything so hateful.

Nor I, *said the white bear. She walked forward to the cankered tree, and her tears were a flowing stream. They washed toward the fallen leaves, but the leaves dug into the earth to avoid them. She brushed her head against the branches, but the branches shivered away from her fur. The white bear turned to*

Clovermead. I hurt so, Clovermead, *she said. Her tears soaked the earth, but the tree was dry still.* Help me.

I will be revenged, *the tree said in Mallow's voice. Its sap oozed with venom.*

No, *said Clovermead. She turned away from the tree.* Let it suffer for what it's done. It can't be forgiven. *But she could not walk. She was rooted to the ground, her arms had turned to branches, and venom ran through her rotting wood.* I'm trapped! *she cried in panic.* Help me! *But the white bear had disappeared, and there was only Clovermead and Mallow in the rotting tree, alone in the leafless woods.*

We are trapped together, *said Mallow.* Let us make the best of matters. Shall we dance? *Far away the piper began to play. The dead limbs of the tree writhed to her icy tune.*

Dead is dead, *sighed Clovermead, and she joined Mallow in the dance—*

Clovermead woke and her muscles had stopped hurting. She was not thirsty and she was not hungry. The world was shadows upon shadows, and the sun shone gray. "Dead is dead," said Clovermead out loud, and she turned into a bear. The world was just as dark and she began to run on nerveless legs. She snuffled for Sorrel and Saraband's scent. It was faint, but she could tell she was catching up to them.

At midday she came to a valley filled with red sand, rolling hills, spires, and in the far distance a smudge of pale green where the fields of Chandlefort began. The valley was a mile long, with broken hills rising to either side, and she could see Sorrel and Saraband riding ahead of her at last.

And then she saw them stop, turn around, and begin

to flee toward her, pursued by three distant dots. *It must be bear-priests chasing them,* thought Clovermead. *Mallow said they wouldn't be safe once they got within sight of the fields of Chandlefort. I need to run faster. Saraband's no good at fighting, Sorrel can't hold off three of them, and I need to help him.*

But then she thought, with ice in her heart, *Go slowly, Clovermead. You can take the flask from their dead bodies and then you can save Mother anyway. If I can't have Sorrel, let them die.* Her pace slackened, and the bear-priests came closer to the fleeing pair. *Dead is dead. Mallow is waiting for me.* In her mind's eye she could see the bear-priests strike them down, and she didn't have to feel a thing as dust blanketed her heart. It was the dust's fault she wasn't running, not hers. She let the kindly dust fill her. It was so sweet to have an excuse to do nothing.

You almost got Milady killed and you almost got Saraband killed, a part of her that was still alive whispered through the muffling dust. *You're not in your right mind, and you'll get Sorrel killed. Don't let that happen.* She thought of Sorrel who laughed with her and teased her, who had risked his life for her, whom she liked so much that his absence was an agony, and cold tears trickled onto her fur. *I don't care about Saraband, and I'll be miserable seeing you with her, but I can't let you die, Sorrel. I can't.* She shook the cloud of dust from her thoughts. Still weeping, still miserable, she sped up again, so Sorrel could live happily ever after with Saraband.

Sorrel's face lit up with desperate relief as he saw Clovermead approach, and he kicked Brown Barley to go a little faster. Brown Barley grew large, the bear-priests were only a hundred feet behind him, and then

Clovermead had reached her friends. Sorrel wheeled to face the bear-priests while Saraband clung to his waist and held the flask tight in her hands. Sorrel drew his sword, and then the three bear-priests were upon them, scimitars slashing.

Clovermead's opponent was a giant almost seven feet tall, with a scimitar nearly his height. He grinned at Clovermead with sharpened teeth, he swung his blade, and Clovermead crouched under its sweep and slashed the back of his hand with her claws. He cursed as they slewed around to fight again, and he lashed out and creased Clovermead's fur from her shoulder to her tail. The bear-priest growled his pleasure at Clovermead's yelp of pain, and hewed at her neck. Clovermead ducked underneath his blade, she was all cold dust and there was no mercy in her heart, and she slashed at the bear-priest's guts as hard as she could. She crunched through his chain-mail shirt and into his flesh, and her claws ripped open his stomach. The bear-priest looked at Clovermead in shock. The bloodlust slipped from his face, he was suddenly scared, and then he was dead and falling forward onto his horse's neck. In death he seemed to embrace his steed tenderly. She looked up with a snarl to fight the next bear-priest, but Sorrel had slain both the others. They lay on the ground, his sword was red to the hilt, and blood had spattered him from forehead to waist.

Saraband looked at him with horror. She had ridden behind Sorrel the entire time. There were drops of blood on her sleeves too, her arms still held him around the waist, and there was no affection in her embrace now.

"You killed them," she said dumbly. "You slaughtered them." Her teeth chattered in horror.

Sorrel, full of his victory and his back to Saraband, was oblivious. "I am not always a coward, Clovermead," he said exultantly. Now Clovermead could see that his cheek had been cut. "I do not always run away, and you see that I am indeed a skillful warrior." He looked down at his bloodied yellow coat and he grinned. "I have saved your life, Saraband! On the Steppes this victory would be worthy of at least a small song. I have not disgraced my uniform after all."

"I am grateful to you," Saraband whispered. She looked at the dead bear-priests, and she made the crescent sign with trembling hands. "Poor creatures," she said. "Lady have mercy on their souls."

Now Sorrel looked back at Saraband and a flicker of perplexity and anger crossed his face. "They do not deserve your good wishes," he said. He wiped his sword on his bloodstained clothes, sheathed it, then looked worriedly toward Chandlefort. "We must leave before more bear-priests see us," said Sorrel. He rode forward to grab the reins of the two dead bear-priests' Phoenixians, then cantered back with the horses stumbling after him. "Follow me, Clovermead. I know a place in the hills where we can hide."

Clovermead nodded her furry head yes—and then her stomach rebelled. She turned to one side and vomited up grass from yesterday morning. What little blood was left to her raced feverishly, she could not get the bear-priest's face out of her mind, and she was weeping. But there wasn't time to think about what she had done.

She ran after Sorrel and Saraband, and in a minute she left the man she had killed far behind them.

As the sun set, they cantered into a labyrinth of rocks in the middle of the hills. There Sorrel led them onto a path that was invisible from the Heath and led between huge boulders up to the top of a sandstone crag. When they came at last to the summit, Sorrel looked down to the Heath and smiled with relief. "No one is following us."

Clovermead changed back into human form. "I'm glad," she said. "Excuse me, Sorrel. I need to be alone for a little bit." Then she almost ran to the other side of the rocky hill. She found a flat shelf of rock, sat down, and stared out at the plain. She could not stop thinking about the bear-priest she had killed, could not stop seeing his face. She tried to spit out the sour contents of her mouth. Her back stung where the bear-priest's sword had sliced the skin. She was no longer cold, she couldn't stop feeling, and she wished she could be cold again. "I'm a Cindertallow now," she whispered, rocking back and forth. "I can kill, Milady will be happy, and I wish I were back in Timothy Vale with Father when I didn't really know what killing meant. Poor Father, he has to be a soldier and kill people too, and he'll turn bloody and hard like me. Oh, Lady, I don't want my blood anymore. Just dust." She heard a scrabbling noise behind her, and she was glad Sorrel had ignored what she'd said and come after her.

But it was Saraband who came scrambling over the rocks to join her. "I thought you might want company, Cousin," she said. She looked at Clovermead's back, satisfied herself that the cut was minor, then settled herself by Clovermead's side. "How are you doing?"

"Why didn't Sorrel come?" asked Clovermead. "I don't want you. I want him."

"The brave Yellowjacket is full of his victories," said Saraband. "He scarcely notices how I shrink from his bloodstained clothes, and he didn't see that you were upset." She grimaced. "I don't think he'd make good company for you now anyway. He's too cheerful."

"Why don't you stay with him, then? Go away."

"Don't tempt me, Cousin," said Saraband stiffly. "I don't like your rudeness, and I won't stay for it." Clovermead wanted to yell an insult to her face, but she bit her tongue. She wanted the comfort of Saraband's company more. "Sorrel's not good company for me while he's drenched in blood," Saraband continued. "If I stayed with him, he would realize how much I dislike his killing. He would not understand my revulsion, he would get angry with me, and we would quarrel. So I think I should stay away from him for a while." Her face twisted in repugnance and continuing horror. "I knew Yellowjackets killed, but I never imagined it would be as awful as that."

"What are you complaining about?" asked Clovermead bitterly. "You wouldn't even fight to save your own life. You made us fight for you. I had to kill for you." She said the word *kill,* her heart wept, and then Clovermead's tears were brimming over. She beat her fists against Saraband, but Saraband took Clovermead in her arms and held her and wouldn't let her go. Clovermead could not stop weeping, Saraband was weeping with her, and Clovermead let herself go limp. She huddled against Saraband's warmth.

"I felt him die," Clovermead sobbed. "My paw went into him and I *felt* it. I killed him." She took a shuddering breath. "Me, Clovermead. Not the Demoiselle and not Lord Ursus and not anybody else. Dear Lady, he was so frightened when he died." Her throat was thick, and she tried to clear it with a cough, but she hiccuped instead. The hiccups continued, and Clovermead laughed through her tears. She tried to wipe her nose, but her hands were bloody. "Saraband, what have I done?"

"You saved my life," said Saraband. She pressed her wet cheeks against Clovermead's yellow hair. "I'll always be grateful to you."

"We disgust you." More tears spilled out of Clovermead. "Sorrel and I are just alike. Killers. He told me how he cried the first time he killed a man, and now look at him! I'll be as jolly as him the next time I chop someone down. Oh, Lady, we deserve to disgust you."

"I think I could rather like you, Clovermead. When you forget you don't like me because I'm a prissy dancing girl, you can be rather nice, in a bumptious, farm-girlish sort of way." Clovermead couldn't help but giggle in her tears, and Saraband laughed with her. "See? We can laugh together."

"But I'm still a killer," said Clovermead. "Even when we're laughing, you'll always look at me and know that."

"I'll also know you hate bloodshed almost as much as I do," said Saraband. "That matters most." She paused a moment. "I wish Sorrel minded killing as much as you do."

"Tell him how you feel. Tell him to give up fighting. I'm sure he'll oblige you." Clovermead felt ice stab in her, and she shrugged out of Saraband's embrace. Saraband let her go, but she kept Clovermead's hand in hers. Clovermead clenched her fingers tight around Saraband's. She didn't want to let her go entirely.

"I don't know that he would," said Saraband bleakly. "When we were in the mountains, I thought he might. Now that I see how much Sorrel enjoys fighting, I'm afraid to ask again. I think he'd say no."

I wish I could believe that, thought Clovermead. *Sorrel would run to the ends of the earth for you—any fool can see that. Ask him anything and he'll say yes.* But she couldn't help but hope that Saraband was right about the Tansyard.

"He likes you more than he likes battles," she said out loud. Then she shook her head in perplexity. "Saraband, I can understand not wanting to be a soldier, but it seems awfully strange to me that you'd rather die than defend yourself. Why do you hate fighting so much?"

Saraband was silent for a long moment. "It's a matter of loyalty to my mother," she said at last. "I cannot fight and be true to her." She looked levelly at Clovermead. "I won't go against her wishes again."

"What did you do the first time?"

Saraband smiled bitterly. "Mother didn't want me to accept Milady's request that I become the Demoiselle Cindertallow."

"The Demoiselle? *I'm* the Demoiselle!" Clovermead stared at her cousin incredulously. "What are you talking about?"

"We're cousins, Clovermead. Who do you think became the Demoiselle when you were thought dead? Surely you knew." Dumbfounded, Clovermead shook her head. "Hasn't anyone mentioned this to you?"

"Milady didn't have an heir when I came to Chandlefort," said Clovermead.

"I was no longer Demoiselle by then."

"I'm very confused," said Clovermead. "How did you come to be Demoiselle and how did you stop being Demoiselle?"

"Your mother was responsible for both events," said Saraband. "It was like this."

Chapter Fifteen

SARABAND'S STORY

AFTER MY FATHER DIED, MY MOTHER AND I LEFT Sconce Keep and went to Silverfalls Abbey. Mother had wanted to be a nun before she met father; now she returned to Silverfalls and made her vows at last. Usually no nun was allowed to bring a child with her, but the old Abbess made an exception for me. I grew up in the company of nuns—I had fewer friends than most children, but the nuns delighted to have a girl around, and they spoiled me more than most too.

Mother was my friend as much as anyone. She taught me my letters, and we learned our prayers together. We also learned medicine from the Abbess: Mother had a fierce desire to be a healer, after father and uncle died in battle, and she had considerable talent as well. I think I was a fast learner too, for a child, but I never learned as much as Mother. She read books of medicine late into the night; I concentrated on nursing and what could be taught by example. I was happy enough that way.

And I learned to dance from Mother. She loved the music, she loved the motion, especially those nights when her sorrows lay upon her more heavily than usual. She would call in a nun who played the fiddle, and we would dance together. The frown would fade from Mother's face as she lost herself in the music. Sometimes she would even laugh.

Lady Cindertallow came to Silverfalls when I was nine. There was no warning: I had been sewing an altar cloth with my mother, and she suddenly dropped her needle. I turned and saw a lady with golden hair. I knew who she was: Mother had described her well enough over the years as she cursed her. Besides, I knew that no one else was allowed to wear a brooch with a burning bee. My mother set aside the cloth and stood still and pale, just looking at Lady Cindertallow. I curtsied, very awkwardly. I thought she might gobble me up or set me on fire just by looking at me.

"Hello, Meadowlark," said Lady Cindertallow. Her voice was astonishingly human. It was not gentle, but it was not the thunder I had expected. There was self-confidence, command, and pride in her face, but no deliberate cruelty. I did not understand why my mother feared her so.

"Lady Cindertallow." My mother tried to curtsy but could not manage it.

"Melisande," said Lady Cindertallow. "I have always wanted to be Melisande to you, Meadowlark." There was sadness and pity in her voice.

"That is impossible, Lady Cindertallow," my mother whispered.

Lady Cindertallow looked angry for a second. Her lips thinned, her eyes blazed, and now I understood my mother's fear. My mother would be helpless should Lady Cindertallow lose her temper.

"As you wish," said Lady Cindertallow at last. She turned from my mother and examined me. "Lady Saraband, I believe? I would recognize you anywhere. You have your father's strength and your mother's beauty. A better combination than the reverse, eh, Meadowlark?" She laughed, but my mother would not smile, just moved closer to me and put her arms around my shoulders. I let myself fall into her protective embrace. Lady Cindertallow scrutinized me again, and I felt like she was weighing my soul teaspoon by teaspoon. I wanted to run. At last she nodded. "You look fit enough," she said. My mother stiffened.

"Fit for what?" I asked. Everyone was silent. "Fit for what," I repeated.

"Some years ago I lost my husband and my daughter," said Lady Cindertallow at last. "My Council recommended that I remarry so that I might bear another heir. I asked them to give me a while to mourn. Now the time I asked them for is up, and I find that I have not ceased to mourn. I will not remarry. Still, I must provide an heir for Chandlefort. I have no brothers or sisters. Your father was my only first cousin, Lady Saraband, and you are my closest female relative." My mouth fell open with shock. She was going to make me the Demoiselle Cindertallow.

"You can't have her," said my mother. It was a whisper, a shriek, a saw slicing upward from her throat. "You can't take her from me too."

"Lady's diadem, what do you think I want of her, Meadowlark?" asked Lady Cindertallow. "I mean to have her trained as my successor, but I won't steal her from you. She'll live with you, dine with you, and sleep with you. I'm not inhuman."

"I don't want her to become a Cindertallow," my mother said, with a brittle determination that did not at all mask her fear. "I don't want her to justify her whims as the good of Chandlefort. I don't want her to learn how to break people without remorse. I want my Saraband to stay soft and gentle. I don't want her to become like you." She was trembling with fear, but still she spoke.

"Hold your tongue," said Lady Cindertallow sharply. "I've done you no harm."

"You killed Mallow," said Mother. "You led him to love you, then you cast him aside in an instant and his heart died. He threw his husk away in battle, but you killed him. Athanor died trying to save poor Mallow and you killed him, too. I'll never forgive you for their murders. And now you want to take my daughter from me. Don't think I'm giving her to you."

"I also grieved when Mallow died, Meadowlark," said Lady Cindertallow. "I did not love him, but he was dear to me. I loved Athanor as a brother, and I grieved yet more for him. I wish you had let me attend their funerals." She was clearly angry, but she made herself speak gently. "If I was thoughtless in my treatment of your brother, if I bear any responsibility for their deaths, I think that Our Lady has punished me well for my sin. I have lost my Ambrosius and my Cerelune, and I ache for them as much as you do for Athanor and Mallow. Meadowlark, let this hatred come to an end."

"No," said my mother. She was ablaze with anger and sorrow. "I'll never forgive you. I'm glad your husband died and I'm glad your daughter died. You deserve those sorrows and a thousand more. You may not have my daughter. I defy you."

Then I saw the fury truly gathering on Lady Cindertallow's face. There is a mosaic in the Abbey chapel of *The Wrath of Our Lady,* when she saw the mistress making her servant work during temple services, and all the light in Our Lady's face turned to terrible anger. Lady Cindertallow looked like that—majesty, power, light, and rage. I knew she would order my mother killed if she spoke. I knew I had to turn aside her wrath.

"It's not my mother's choice whether I stay or go," I said, and somehow my words managed to stay Lady Cindertallow's anger. "It's mine, Milady. Isn't it?"

She could not speak, from grief and rage. All she could do was nod her head.

"Then I choose to go," I said. I turned to where my mother stood frozen in despair. "Don't you understand?" I whispered to her. "She'll kill you otherwise."

"I'd rather die," my mother whispered, and some part of her was broken. Thanks to me. She took her arms from around me, backed away, and averted her eyes. "If you go, Saraband, I won't see you again. I'll have no truck with Cindertallows."

I hugged my mother and I kissed her terribly hard on the cheek. She shivered in my arms, small and delicate and wounded. Then I let her go. "Good-bye, Mother," I said.

My mother nodded and drew herself up to her full height. "Take the Demoiselle with you," she said to Lady Cindertallow. Then she left the room.

I came to Chandlefort, and I began to train to be the next Lady Cindertallow. I rode, I practiced fighting and ceremonial, I studied history and statecraft, I watched Lady Cindertallow in her various offices. She was civil to me but never warm: I was an unwelcome necessity. Whenever I told her I had to go, she never urged me to stay.

My mother was right: It was a terrible thing to be a Cindertallow. In ceremony they taught me never to make a mistake; in fighting they taught me how to kill; in statecraft they taught me to be ruthless. I cannot fault the schoolmasters who decided on this mode of education: For making a Lady Cindertallow competent to lead Chandlefort, it was excellent. But it also made a Lady Cindertallow terrible in her heart—a Lady Cindertallow who would destroy men in a second if she thought it suited the interests of Chandlefort. And when I saw those whom it was necessary to destroy, I saw my mother's face. I hated what I was being taught.

I far preferred to dance. I danced with children, at the balls with the lords and ladies, and for long hours by myself in my room. It wasn't only the urge to follow my mother in some part of my life that made me love dancing so. It was somehow the opposite of everything I had to learn during the day. It was beauty unalloyed with terror, prudence, or any of the hard virtues of the Cindertallows. Dancing, I could be soft. So it became my passion, and I spent many hours repeating dance steps, until they were ingrained in my body far deeper than any swordplay or matter of state.

I spent three years as Lady Cindertallow's Heir

Apparent. My last day in that exalted position came some four years ago when I saw a dozen prisoners from Low Branding in the great courtyard of Chandlefort playing the fiddle and dancing. They were patricians who had been captured in a skirmish and allowed on parole within the city walls while they waited for their ransoms to arrive. They had borrowed clothes from lords within the Castle, had their wounds bandaged, and now one of them had borrowed a fiddle and was playing a Low Branding tune while his companions danced with one another. The beardless youths took the women's parts.

I was due at Lady Cindertallow's study to review a particularly dull piece of ceremonial involved in receiving emissaries from the Empress of Queensmart. There was very little chance the Empress would ever send an emissary to Chandlefort again, but in case she did, I had to know the proper protocol. I was in no great mood for my studies, and the dance music tempted me as I walked. I was no truant, I told myself, but my feet turned toward the music, and then I was gawping at the dancers.

The music was fascinatingly different from that of Chandlefort—sometimes lazily slow, sometimes brisk, and sometimes rollicking and rolling, but never as stately as our Chandlefort court dances. The young patricians were no experts, but they clearly enjoyed themselves, and they had attracted an admiring audience. I stared at their whirling feet and clapping hands and listened to the fiddle play. My own feet started tapping to the tune, then imitating the patricians' movements.

One of the patricians looked up, saw me, and laughed. "Look at that girl dance! Come and join us—I want a real lass for my partner, not one of this lot."

"I wouldn't, little lady," said one of the beardless youths, grinning. "He begged me to dance, and now he throws me over in a second! That one's a rake."

"I promise I won't dance with anyone else all afternoon," the first patrician said to me, with his hand on his heart and a wink in his eye. "Come along, come along now." He stamped his feet, clapped his hands, and beckoned to me.

I knew my duties and I turned to go—but I could not. A surge of nausea almost overwhelmed me, and I felt that my heart would die if I went away. Instead I turned back to the patrician and stepped forward. I smiled, and my feet started to leap to the fiddle's tune. There was a murmur in the crowd, for they knew who I was, but no one spoke. The patricians did not notice, merely welcomed me with happy grins. And then we were dancing.

The rhythm was infectious, the pounding of feet as marvelous as the saw of the fiddle. The patricians gave me some words of instruction, but I scarcely needed them. It had been enough to watch them, and now I could melt into the dance. I kicked my legs, let the patricians whirl me in their arms, and I laughed more deeply than I had since I'd come to Chandlefort. I was careless, heedless, irresponsible, and I loved it. I surrendered to the dance, let all steel and power melt from me, and I was happy.

How long I danced I don't know, but there came a moment when the fiddle fell silent and the patricians shuffled to a halt. I looked up, and there was Lady Cindertallow. The crowd of Chandleforters gaped at us, expecting some great drama. She stood and looked at me—vexed, puzzled, and oddly smiling. I had expected terrible anger, not this curious expression. She did not often bestow smiles on me, and never any so warm.

"You are late for your lessons, Lady Saraband," she said out loud, and there was so much amusement in her voice that the crowd rustled with relieved laughter. Even the patricians grinned. "I didn't know you were so fond of dance."

"I apologize, Milady," I said, my eyes to the ground. I shuffled away from the patricians—rather, I meant to shuffle, but I half-skipped to her, still dancing, and the patricians behind me chuckled again. "I have no excuses," I said, my cheeks flaming.

"You certainly don't," Lady Cindertallow said loudly, but her eyes were gentle on me. "I must chastise you, Lady Saraband," she said for the crowd; "Come with me," she said more softly. We walked down the cobbles of the courtyard as the crowd scattered out of our way.

"Let me see," said Lady Cindertallow, once we had some privacy. "You were late for a lesson with your sovereign mistress, you were fraternizing with Low Branding prisoners, and you had a very abandoned look on your face that wasn't at all befitting for a future Lady Cindertallow. You've not shown yourself at your best today."

"No, Milady," I said. My heart fluttered within me, but I made my voice calm.

"Indeed," said Lady Cindertallow, "you shock me. I've never known you to act like this before. You've been a model of dutiful obedience."

"You're kind, Milady," I said, but already my heart was retreating from me. The music faded from my mind, and my feet forgot the dance they had so recently enjoyed.

"You reminded me of Meadowlark," said Lady Cindertallow. "She danced so, before you were born."

I could not help crying. Her words stabbed my heart. I would not acknowledge the tears by wiping them away, but let them float down my cheeks. "She taught me when I was younger," I said, and I spoke with calm steel. As a Cindertallow.

"It comes to me that I don't know you at all," said Lady Cindertallow thoughtfully. "I've never seen you . . . I was going to say so happy, but I don't know that I've ever seen you happy at all. You're capable of happiness—I saw that clearly today—but training to be my heir gives you no joy."

"How can it, Milady?" I asked. I had never thought I would speak so freely, but it was a strange day. "Yesterday I studied how to pronounce a sentence of death upon murderers. Last week I learned when it is expedient to burn peasants' crops during a war, and when it is not. Tomorrow I'll find out yet one more way to gut a man. I know this is all necessary, I know that my subjects will need me to do these things, but it's inhuman. How could I possibly take joy in these things?"

"I do," said Lady Cindertallow. She looked at me quizzically. "It's strange to hear you talk so. I don't like killing, Lady knows, but—yes, when I sentence a murderer to death, I feel satisfaction. I've dealt justice for his victim, and I've prevented him from ever harming another soul. When I fight in battle, I know I'm fighting so my subjects will be able to live in peace later. Yes, I feel delight when I fight for Our Lady, for Chandlefort, and for my people. I do take pleasure in my power as Lady Cindertallow. I try to use it justly, to use my power to do good, but I do feel joy. I thought everyone would feel the same. Don't you?"

"Not at all, Milady," I said. "I don't care for power. Milady, my mother was right. You wouldn't have cast my uncle aside so easily if you weren't so accustomed to power. I know. I'm learning how to cast people aside. After a while it becomes very easy."

"That it does," said Lady Cindertallow quietly. Then she suddenly smiled. "Well, Lady Saraband. You make me wonder if I was correct to appoint you my heir. Do you think I should revoke the appointment?" I could barely understand the words, but it was as if a stone had been taken off my heart, and I smiled all at once, all over my face. I felt light and giddy, and Lady Cindertallow laughed. "I've never seen a yes so clearly indicated."

I made my smile go away. "It would not be wise to relieve me of this duty, Milady," I said. "Chandlefort still needs an heir. My wishes don't affect the matter."

"I think they do," said Lady Cindertallow. "I don't doubt you would be quite competent as Lady Cindertallow, but more than competence is needed. Your heart must be engaged too. It's not fair to

Chandlefort to have a halfhearted Lady." She pondered matters for a second, then spoke again. "If you're convinced that your heart will never enjoy the duties of a Lady Cindertallow, I will disinherit you."

"Who will be your heir, then?"

A shadow came over Lady Cindertallow's face. "No one. I'll pray to Our Lady for another solution to Chandlefort's difficulties."

"I'll pray to Our Lady too," I said. Then I spoke to Lady Cindertallow with all the firmness I could muster. "I'm not fit to be Lady Cindertallow, Milady, and I never will be. Release me for the good of Chandlefort."

"For your own good," said Lady Cindertallow. "Chandlefort can shift for itself this once." Then she laughed with sudden jubilation. It struck me that if she had never seen me happy, neither had I ever seen such joy in her. I laughed with her, and we filled the courtyard with our merriment. Everyone heard us—the prisoners, the Chandleforters who had been watching the dance, lords and ladies in the balconies. We embraced, I cried amid my happiness, and so did she. I came to love her in that moment. She was a fearsome ogre still, she could not be Lady Cindertallow and not be one, but she had balanced her realm against my happiness and given my heart the greater weight. For that she has my love and loyalty forever.

"Listen!" cried Lady Cindertallow, and she took my hand in hers. "I disinherit Lady Saraband Sconce! She is not my heir and never will be. She is a dancer and nothing more. Let all know!" She squeezed my hand so tight it hurt, I squeezed her hand back, and all my mind was laughter and joy. Then we went around Chandlefort, and Lady Cindertallow repeated her words until she was hoarse.

I sent a letter with the news to Silverfalls. My mother had become the Abbess in the time I was gone, and I asked her if I could return to the Abbey. Her response came within the week: *I'm glad you're no longer Demoiselle, Saraband. Nevertheless, I will not change my mind. I will not see you again. Do not come back to Silverfalls. But tell Milady that I am grateful for what she has done.*

I told Lady Cindertallow, and then I burned the note. And since then I have not picked up a sword or opened a law book or done anything in the way of power. Nor will I act the Cindertallow again: I am my mother's daughter. We may never speak again, but I will not go against her wishes. I will remain true to her for the rest of my life.

"I'm sorry," said Clovermead quietly.

Saraband shrugged. "The past is past." She yawned and looked up at the star-filled sky. "I didn't think I'd talk such a long time! Are you all right, Cousin?"

"I'm fine," said Clovermead. She squeezed Saraband's hand a moment. "Thank you for coming to comfort me."

"Anytime, Cousin." Saraband ran a finger along Clovermead's cheeks, but the tears had long since dried. She yawned again. "Time for me to sleep. It's been a long day." She lay down on the rocks, still holding Clovermead's hand in hers. She smiled at Clovermead, and then she fell asleep.

Sleepless, Clovermead sat up through the night. But

when she looked down at her sleeping cousin, her beautiful cousin whom Sorrel preferred to her, dust swirled in her. *I should be grateful to you, I should like you, but I'm full of dust, and I don't have to care tuppence what happens to you. It's not as if I have a heart left. Dead is dead.*

She let go of Saraband's hand.

Chapter Sixteen

THE GATES CRACK

"SHALL WE TRY TO GET TO CHANDLEFORT AGAIN, Clovermead?" Sorrel asked the next morning. "We did not have much luck with our first attempt, and there are a great many more bear-priests around Chandlefort. Even with you by our side I am not sure we can make it through to the town."

"Don't worry about that," said Clovermead. "I think we'll have help." Quickly she told them how the bears had agreed to meet her at the teardrop pillars. "Can we make it there before dusk?"

Sorrel glanced to the west. "I think we will make good time. There should not be any rain today."

Clovermead looked up too. The world was black and white and gray. She turned to stare straight at the morning sun, looking for a hint of color, and she did not have to flinch. It was no brighter than a candle flame.

Saraband and Clovermead got onto the two captured Phoenixians, Sorrel rode Brown Barley, and they cantered down from the rocky hills onto the dry plain of the Salt Heath. This time they rode cautiously and watched for bear-priests riding from the distant line of Chandlefort's green fields. They stayed away from the road itself, took shelter behind low hills when they could, and dashed across stretches of open ground when they had to. Far ahead Clovermead could smell the moisture and life of Chandlefort, but it was well hidden in the dead husk of the Heath.

It's like me, thought Clovermead. *Dead on the outside but alive on the inside. But there isn't much left to either of us. Give it a little more time and we'll both be dead through and through.* She pinched her arm. She saw her abused flesh darken, but she could not feel it.

When the sun was near the western horizon, they came to the teardrop pillars. Clovermead looked around her, and everywhere she saw bears dotting the ground—bears padding, bears growling their thirst, bears napping, bears swinging their heads as they smelled the three riders approach. There were bear cubs and ancient bears, bears with the fierce glow of exile in their eyes, bears who blinked in the light, bears haunted and terrified. She tried to count them, but there were too many. Hundreds waited for them by the pillars.

"I don't think we'll have any trouble getting past the bear-priests," said Clovermead. A flicker of joy pierced her numbness and she smiled. *I'm so glad you've come,* she called out to the bears. The bears roared back complaisant acknowledgment.

I told you we'd be here, said Brookwade cheerfully as he ambled up from the pack toward them. He sniffed at Sorrel and chuffed laughter. *You brought your snack with you, changeling!*

Sorrel shied away from him. "Is that the bear who held me captive in the hayfield?" Clovermead nodded and Sorrel grimaced. "I know the look on his face. Tell him not to think of me as edible. It is not a polite attitude toward a comrade who will fight in battle by his side."

Clovermead giggled. *His name is Sorrel. Do try to call him that—he's sensitive.* Brookwade shrugged and Clovermead looked around at the bears. *Are they all here to fight?*

All, said Brookwade. He sat back on his haunches and rumbled uncertainly. *Now that we're here, what do you suggest that we do next?*

I'm not quite sure, said Clovermead. *I should have some sort of clever and complicated plan, but I'm no general.*

Just as well, said Brookwade. *I don't think we'd remember anything very complicated. Really, all we want to know is where to run and who to bite and when to start biting. There will be biting, won't there? I've wanted to chomp on a bear-priest for such a long time.*

You won't be disappointed, said Clovermead. She looked at the sky. The sun had nearly set. She calculated the remaining distance to Chandlefort, then smiled. *Start running toward Chandlefort now. It'll be dark by the time we get to the fields, and then we can surprise the bear-priests. Just bite down on any of them you find.*

I think I'll like this battle, said Brookwade. He roared to the rest of the bears. *Time to fight! We go to Chandlefort for our revenge. Quietly, now—give the bear-priests no warning. Only let them know we're there when our jaws are on their throats.*

At last, said another bear, and he sprang to his feet. He roared with anticipation, and the roar passed from bear to bear. It was soft but chilling in its settled anger, and Clovermead was very glad the bears weren't mad at her. The roar died out, the pack stood up, and they began to pad eastward toward Chandlefort.

Clovermead explained to Sorrel and Saraband what she and Brookwade had decided. "They won't hurt us." *Not unless Mallow seizes control of them again,* she thought to herself. She looked at the bears all around her, and her heart suddenly thumped with fear. "Don't dress as a bear-priest and you should be all right."

"I will try to remember that," said Sorrel. He gulped and shuddered. "I will never get used to these bears. They are so *big*! It is very unnerving."

Clovermead rolled her eyes. "Let's get after them, little snack," she said.

They raced toward Chandlefort among a sea of bears. The bears' powerful muscles ground away the miles, and their flesh and fur rose and fell like waves driven by a gale. Brown and black, golden and russet, even pure white here and there, two hundred bears pounded along the Heath. They kept eerily silent, and a storm of dust billowed high from the hammering of their feet.

They entered the fields, and Clovermead was shocked at how much had changed in the short time she had been away from Chandlefort. Most of the crops were still growing, but half the farms they passed were burned down. Olive trees had been necklaced by knives, and above the broken bark the trees were already starting to die. Cows and horses had been slaughtered and their corpses left to rot in the barns. Some fleet-footed goats peeked at them from behind distant trees.

The bears fanned out onto the smaller paths through the fields. In the deepening gloom Clovermead rapidly lost sight of them. Soon she began to hear growls and the clash of swords, screams and the sudden sound of retreating hoofbeats as the bears drove their erstwhile tormentors before them. Now Clovermead, Sorrel, and Saraband rode alone, and they came swiftly to the open land between the fields and the walls of Chandlefort. Clovermead reined in her horse at the edge of the fields. Ahead of her four hundred bear-priests had retreated into a tight circle in front of the gates of Chandlefort.

At the forefront of the mass of bear-priests Mallow Kite rode on his horse made of shadows and bones. Behind him were the dead bears Clovermead had last seen at Silverfalls. They mutely growled their terrible hunger, silently howled at the living world that mocked them with its vibrancy. They stood among the bear-priests, and even the bear-priests showed some unease at their new companions. The bears who had been pursuing the bear-priests came to a halt. They moaned in fear as they looked at the dead bears in front of them.

"I think they're too many for us, Cousin," said Saraband faintly. "What do we do now?"

Clovermead looked up at the moon. Only the narrowest crescent was left. "Milady doesn't have any time to spare," said Clovermead. She drew her father's sword and crouched forward on her horse, ready to gallop. "It doesn't matter how many there are. We have to try to fight through them."

"Wait," said Sorrel. "Perhaps I can distract them instead. I think I have told you that any Tansyard can ride faster than the wind? Well, I can ride faster than death itself."

"No!" said Saraband. She clutched at him. "Are you mad?"

Sorrel scratched his head, thought for a moment, then winked at Saraband. "I think I am not. Whenever I am with Clovermead, I get into scrapes where it makes sense for me to do mad things, that is all. And I am in service to Lady Cindertallow—there was nothing in my oath to her about an exception for dead bears, much though I wish there had been. I think I must go."

"I could use someone to help me nurse the wounded when the battle is over," said Saraband. Her eyes were hollow as she looked at Sorrel. "Stay with me, Sorrel. Let someone else fight."

For a moment Sorrel looked enormously tempted. He looked at the dead bears, and Clovermead saw how afraid he was. He looked at Saraband, and Clovermead saw how much he liked her, how little he wanted to hurt her. He looked at Clovermead—and Clovermead blushed and ducked her head when she saw the deep affection in his eyes. It was stronger than his fear of the bears, stronger even than his desire to please Saraband.

"I cannot play that role, Saraband," Sorrel said quietly. "I am sorry." Then he was galloping straight toward the dead bears, hunching under a shower of arrows sent by the bear-priests and riding from right to left twenty feet in front of the bears, whistling to them as he went. He circled around the dead bears, circled around all the bear-priests and Mallow, and the bears followed eagerly after him like dogs after a haunch of meat. Sorrel circled in front of the dead bears once more, the nearest bear snapped at his heels, and he fled around the castle with a stream of dead bears behind him. Jaws, bones, and shadows followed him, waiting for Brown Barley to stumble.

"How can he risk himself so?" asked Saraband. Her eyes were fixed with horror on his fleeing figure. "I couldn't bear to see him go," she whispered. "I'd never sleep at night while he was away."

Now that their dead brothers were gone, the living bears leaped forward again with howls of delight. The bear-priests readied their scimitars and stood on their horses, waiting for them to come. Clovermead glanced at the walls of Chandlefort—*Where are the Yellowjackets?* Last winter they had come charging from the town gates to rout Ursus' bear-priests just when they were most needed. *We could use the help,* she thought. *Now's the time to come out.*

The gates stayed shut. There were terribly few Yellowjackets on the walls. Against the distant torchlight she saw the faces of servants in ragged armor, plugging the gaps between each yellow coat. They were brave enough to hold the walls, but they would not be coming forth this time. That was too much to ask of them.

"Do you still have Milady's flask?" asked Clovermead. Saraband nodded. "I'll try to distract Mallow. Wait until the way is clear and then ride like blazes for the gates. You don't have to fight," she added hastily. "Just ride." Saraband hesitated and Clovermead almost yelled at her. "There isn't anybody else."

"Then ride I will," said Saraband resignedly. "I won't fail Milady."

"Thank you, Cousin." said Clovermead. She turned

away from Saraband, drew her sword, and rode toward the dead man.

Mallow sent his dark steed in a gallop toward her and raised his pale sword up high. They were hurtling toward each other, and Clovermead tried to keep straight the lessons she had learned at fight practice. *Be steady,* she thought. *Aim for his head, his throat, his chest.* She felt a terrified laugh struggling to escape from her. *Slice at his other hand. You can't kill him, but you can keep him from killing you.*

Their swords met with a shriek of metal. The force was so great that, numb as she was, Clovermead screamed with pain as her muscles wrenched. Her horse had galloped past Mallow, and Clovermead brought him up short. She gaped at her sword. It had been sheared off halfway, and the new tip was jagged splinters. She looked up at Mallow. His blade was unharmed. He laughed, almost gently. He raised his sword to salute a gallant opponent, then lowered it toward Clovermead again and charged.

Clovermead looked behind him—and saw Saraband riding on her Phoenixian! She had left the safety of the woods behind and was galloping for the gates between Mallow and the bear-priests. She was only halfway there. "Not yet," Clovermead whispered. "It isn't safe yet. You fool, you'll kill yourself! Dear Lady, don't let Mallow see her!"

Clovermead drew up her broken blade and charged toward the dead man once more. *Sir Auroche never had his blade break in the middle of a battle,* she thought crossly. *Why do these things happen to me? I don't want Mallow to see Saraband, but I don't want him to skewer me while I'm distracting him! How do I get out of the way of his sword? Wait, I remember a trick of Sorrel's.* Clovermead let her sword drop, slipped to the side of the horse so its torso was between her and Mallow's deadly blade, and hung desperately to the reins—but she couldn't hold on. Her fingers came loose and she fell to the ground, but it was just as well, for Mallow's blade had caught the Phoenixian in the head and he was already dead. His legs went forward another ten feet, then caught, and he fell to the ground. Behind him, Clovermead rolled on the earth.

Mallow brought up his horse. "Well done, Demoiselle," he said. "But not good enough." He grinned, raised his sword—then, as Clovermead smiled with triumph, he looked over his shoulder to where the gates of Chandlefort had opened and Saraband rode through.

"You're too late," said Clovermead. The gates began to close. "I don't care what you do to me. Saraband has the flask and Milady is safe."

"No," said Mallow. His voice throbbed with emotion. "Niece, traitress, how can you? I won't be denied my revenge. You'll die for this." He turned from Clovermead and galloped toward the gates.

"It's no good, Mallow," said Clovermead. She brought herself aching to her feet. "Mother will live." The gates clanged shut.

"You shall not keep me away!" cried Mallow. He had come to the gates. They stood massive and iron before him. "I have come back from death. I have vowed myself to Lord Ursus. No lump of metal will keep me from my vengeance." He lifted his sword and it shone with a bitter fury, brighter than the moon and the stars. The bear-tooth at his neck gleamed in its awful light. Clovermead felt his misery, his cankered love, and his despairing rage surging through his heart. Lord Ursus drank in Mallow's anguish and gave it back to his servant, transformed into destroying power. He had never hurt so much and he had never had such strength. Mallow brought his sword down on the gates of Chandlefort.

"No," Clovermead gasped. Mallow's sword sliced a vertical gash in the gates from eight feet high down to the ground. As she watched, the sound of creaking metal filled the fields, and the gash spread to the top of the gates, fifty feet above the ground. Mallow brought his arm back for another blow, and Clovermead shifted to bear form. She began to run—her front paws ached and she could not go at top speed, but at least it was faster than a human could go. Mallow struck the gates from left to right.

The gates screamed. The metal hinges tore off from the struts that attached them to the stone walls. Cracks spread along the frontispiece of metal. The metal shivered, wailed, and fell. The crash of metal chunks striking pavement rang in Clovermead's ears, and there was a gaping rent fifty feet wide in Chandlefort's walls. Inside, Clovermead saw servants and Yellowjackets in the entrance square fall back from Mallow. Saraband, at the far end of the square, turned and galloped toward the Castle.

"Nothing on earth can stop me," said Mallow. He kicked his dark horse in the flanks and rode through the crumbled gates of Chandlefort.

Clovermead chased after Mallow. Bears and bear-priests were fighting nearby and somewhere a trail of dead bears was chasing Sorrel, but she had no time to think of that. She bounded over the metal wreckage and into the square, where the servants gaped at her and a Yellowjacket drew his sword against her.

"Don't hurt my daughter!" said Waxmelt, and he slapped down the Yellowjacket's arm. He stumbled toward Clovermead. He was still dressed in his ill-fitting helmet and chain mail. "That is you, Clo, isn't it?"

Clovermead shifted quickly back to human form. "I can't stay," she panted. "I have to stop Mallow."

"Clo, he broke the gates," Waxmelt began, then checked himself when he saw Clovermead's weary determination. "Lady fight with you." There was a howling behind Clovermead, Waxmelt looked through the gates, and his face dropped in horror. "Oh, no."

Clovermead looked back. The bear-priests had turned from their fight with the bears and were charging horseback toward the crumpled gates.

"Can you handle them, Father?" asked Clovermead.

"We'll see, won't we?" asked Waxmelt. He turned to the servants around him. "Time for us to show these Yellowjackets how we defend our town," he cried out. "And it will be our town when this night's work is finished. There won't be any more talk about how we have to defer to the lords and ladies because they fight for us. We'll have done the fighting for ourselves." The servants cheered and rushed forward. They showed very little military discipline or skill, but they were there. They made a ragged line among the fallen chunks of the gates. Clovermead couldn't think of words to say. She hugged Waxmelt, kissed him on the cheek, then let him go. She was bounding off in an instant, a bear again, pursuing Mallow into the town.

She raced up the curving main street toward the Castle. The street was empty: If anyone had been on it before, they had fled at the approach of Mallow Kite. Clovermead tried to go faster, but she could not. *I need to practice these marathons,* thought Clovermead, breathing hard. *I'll catch up with him before he catches Saraband. I will. I will.* But she was terribly afraid she would not.

She burst into the chapel square—and there she saw both Saraband and Mallow. Saraband was only halfway across the square, passing in front of the steps that led up to the chapel, and Mallow was close behind her and gaining. Saraband looked behind her with a face full of terror, and she swerved up the chapel steps. The crescent moon high over Chandlefort lit up the high dome of Our Lady's chapel. The chapel's marble steps shone lightly pink in the moonlight, as if a stain of heart's blood suffused them. Saraband reached the top of the steps and half-fell from her saddle. She fell against the chapel doors, stumbled inside, and slammed them behind her.

Both Mallow and Clovermead veered to follow her. Mallow galloped up the steps and only stopped for a second as his dark horse reared up and smashed open the doors with its hooves. Mallow rode into the chapel, and Clovermead was still at the bottom of the chapel steps. She bounded up them, but she couldn't help feeling despair. *He's right,* she thought. *Nothing on earth can stop him.*

Clovermead leaped past the broken doors into the chapel. Inside, moonlight poured in through a great glass roundel. Near the door stood rows of pews where worshipers could listen to sermons and pray. Farther from the door a wooden pulpit carved to resemble a crescent moon rose ten feet from the ground. Tile mosaics of Our Lady's travels through the Thirty Towns decorated the rose granite walls. In the back half of the chapel a large open space of flagstones surrounded a shallow pool whose water came piped in from the well in the square. Pewter cups lined the edge of the pool; any Chandleforter could use them to take water from the pool and drink. The water of the pool glimmered in the moonlight.

Saraband stood before the pool. She glanced behind her, but there was no back way out of the chapel. She composed herself and stood with dignity. Mallow sat on his horse in front of her. He reached down with his free arm, tore the flask from Saraband, and crumpled the metal in his hand. He hurled the flask to the floor, then caught Saraband by the neck. "Traitress," he spat. He lifted her up in the air and held her dangling a foot in the air, his half hand around her neck. Saraband looked him levelly in the face, without fear. He smiled and twisted, and Clovermead heard a horrible crack. Saraband crumpled, and Mallow cast her to the floor.

Clovermead's heart leaped with delight. *Sorrel's mine*

now, she thought. Then she was horror-struck at what she had thought. She tried to forget she had ever thought it, but Mallow knew. She could see it in his mocking, compassionate eyes.

"Take her death as my gift," said Mallow. "She'll never trouble you again."

Murderer! roared Clovermead. Mallow was the murderer, not her, she would make it be Mallow, and she leaped at him with tears in her eyes.

Mallow slapped Clovermead with the flat of his blade and sent her crashing into a pew. "A murderer at your service, Demoiselle," he said. "I gave a friendly hand to a friend in need. Deny it, Demoiselle. Dear Clovermead, you wanted her dead." He waited for Clovermead to protest, but she could not speak. "How well I know your heart," he said. Then he laughed, spurred his dark horse, and galloped out of the chapel.

"It's not true," said Clovermead, shifting to human. She stumbled to the girl sprawled on the floor, and she felt Saraband's wrist. There was a faint pulse, Saraband's chest rose and fell a very, very little, and her neck was at the wrong angle. "I swear it isn't—" The piercing light of the crescent moon, nearly extinguished, fell on Clovermead through the roundel, and it dug at her through the layers of dead flesh around her heart. She turned away from the moonlight, but it was inside her now, setting what little blood still ran in her to boil with anguish and guilt, clawing at the bits of her that could still feel pain, and she could not lie.

"I did want you dead, Saraband," said Clovermead.

"Oh, Lady, I still do. You've been kind to me, a good companion and brave to the death, you love your mother more than she deserves, you're even funny, and I still hate you so much. Sorrel's fallen in love with you, and I'd rather you were dead and he were miserable than to see the two of you happy together. I want you dead and I want him to dance with me and look at me the way he dances with you and looks at you. Lady help me, I was happy when Mallow broke your neck. There's hardly anything left in me to care or love, but what there was, was happy. Mallow was right. He did what I wanted him to do. He acted as my friend."

A little blood trickled from Saraband's mouth.

"I'm sorry," said Clovermead, and now she was weeping. "I hate you and I love Sorrel, and I *am* like Mallow, all eaten up with jealousy, but I don't want to be. I want to love without hurting other people. I don't want you dead anymore, Saraband. Mother and I, we've chewed up your life between us, but we're not supposed to do that, are we? We're supposed to protect our subjects and keep them alive. Oh, Lady, it's too late now, but I wish I could keep you alive. You gave up everything for Mother, and I can't stop hating you with part of my heart, but I know it's wrong of me. You ought to live, you ought to be happy. Even if it's with Sorrel. Lady, isn't there anything I can do?"

The moonlight glittered on the crumpled flask that had fallen by Saraband's side, and Clovermead saw that it wasn't completely destroyed. *The water you have drawn up will counteract that other flask, heal any wound I have caused,* Mallow had said. Clovermead grabbed at it and sloshed it gently. A little water still lay in the bottom. There was only enough for one drink.

Sorrel doesn't need to know, thought Clovermead. The thought was a whisper of dust and hatred that struck at her from her freezing heart. *Do nothing and let her die. He'll never know you could have saved her.*

"But you'll know, Lady," Clovermead whispered. She fought back against the dust that rose high in her, which tried to choke all warmth from her. "I couldn't ever look you in the face again."

It won't be your fault, said the dust, roared Lord Ursus. Clovermead recognized his voice. It was familiar. Once he had come to her through her loneliness and desolation; now he came to her through her jealousy and desire. She could never rid herself of him entirely, no matter how hard she tried. *It will be mine. So little of your heart is left to strengthen you against my influence. How can you be expected to resist me?*

"Like this," said Clovermead. She lifted Saraband's head and brought the flask to her lips.

Milady needs the water, Lord Ursus urged her. *Saraband wanted her to live. How can you make her sacrifice be for nothing? Milady's need is greater than hers.*

Clovermead laughed bitterly. "Milady's need is always greater. My need will be greater too when I'm Lady Cindertallow. Maybe that's the way Cerelune Cindertallow should think, but I'm not her and I never will be. I'm Clovermead Wickward, Saraband is my friend, and I won't let her die. Not even if Sorrel spends the rest of his life with her. Oh, Mother, I'm so sorry." Her dry tears flooded down her face, and what was left of her heart was howling. "I don't know if I could even get this to you, and Saraband's dying now." Before she could change her mind, she poured the remaining water of the flask down Saraband's throat.

The pool was a sheen of silver, the flask was so bright that Clovermead couldn't look at it, and then the whole chapel flared with blinding light. Lord Ursus roared his disappointment. For a moment Clovermead heard joyful singing pounding in her ears, and then both light and music faded. There was color on Saraband's face again and she breathed more strongly. Her neck was in the right position again. She smiled in dim moonlight and slept normally and healthily.

"Thank you, Lady," said Clovermead exhaustedly. She put the empty flask down on the chapel floor, and she wished she could put herself down next to it. She was empty too. The light was dim, she could barely feel the last trickles of sluggish warmth inside her, and she wished they were extinguished once and for all. She looked again at Saraband, and cold resignation filled her. "There's no hope," she whispered. "She'll have Sorrel, and Mother will die. There's nothing left to live for."

She took Saraband's hand in hers a moment to make sure she was all right. She could feel how Saraband's blood jumped in her veins, hot and vibrant and exuberantly alive. Clovermead let Saraband's hand drop to the floor, squeezed it in farewell, then let it go. She turned into a bear and lumbered to her feet. *I'll get my revenge on you, Mallow,* she growled. She could feel hatred for him, even in her coldness. It was the only thing she could feel now, and she clutched it close to her. *There's no life in*

Mother and there's no life in me, but you won't have a chance to enjoy that. I'll tear you apart. I'll send you screaming back to the grave. She started to run down the aisle. She growled again, with merciless anticipation. *Mother and I will be revenged on you.*

In the waning moonlight she dashed from the chapel.

Chapter Seventeen

THE DARK WORLD

CLOVERMEAD COULD NOT SEE THE STARS, AND THE windows of the houses were flickering panels of gray in the darkness as Clovermead ran through the streets of Chandlefort toward the Castle. No one tried to stop her: A few soldiers lay dead, struck down by Mallow, and the rest had fled. The doors to the Castle hung loose on their hinges. Mallow's steed stood in the courtyard, and Clovermead rushed past him into the Throne Room. There she saw Mallow Kite as he loped toward the far door and the corridors that led up to Lady Cindertallow's apartments. Clovermead roared and leaped at him.

Mallow whirled, and his sword skated along Clovermead's side, shaving the fur from her and rasping the skin. Clovermead didn't feel any pain. She bit at Mallow's sword-arm, but he shook loose from her teeth and threw her with terrifying strength to the floor. Clovermead sat stunned for a second, then leaped at him again. He ducked to one side and boxed her ears with the hilt of his sword. As she fell, Clovermead bashed his legs and sent him rolling along the floor. Tirelessly he bounded to his feet, his sword once more at the ready. Clovermead howled and leaped at him again.

They fought among ever-thickening shadows. Clovermead had trouble telling Mallow's sword from a bone, and she could no longer make out the features of his face. He was a shadow, he was a skeleton, and the glow of his bones hardly lightened the murk around them. Out of the corner of her eye Clovermead could see her own bones beneath her paws. Her fur and flesh were turning into shadows too, but she hardly cared anymore. She only fought, heedless of the flesh wounds Mallow scored on her. He had wounded her a dozen times, as she had wounded him, but neither of them screamed, neither of them bled. They fought with the grim determination of the dead.

A high, thin pipe sounded in the darkness. It sang of crumbling bones and sepulchers, of gnawing worms and of terrible cold. Then the piping shifted and a growl mixed in with it. In that growl, chains creaked in a city of stone. Then, louder and louder, came the sound of crying prisoners and throbbing drums. Clouds rumbled; lightning crackled. The pipe played sharpened blades, the whimper of fear, the slaver of anticipation. Clovermead felt what little heat was left in her drain away.

What is that? she roared in fear, in repulsion, with strange longing.

"The music that woke me from my sleep," said Mallow. "A hundred slaves died to bring me from the grave. That is the sound of their death. That is the sound of Garum." He stumbled back from Clovermead and kept his sword up in a wary defensive posture. "So many died for my revenge. Should their deaths be in vain?"

I don't care about them, Clovermead growled. Her head swam and the darkness swirled about her. She tried to keep her eyes focused on Mallow and his sword. All she could see was a man-shaped blur of bones. *Mallow, what's happening to me?* she asked in fear.

"Why ask me?" she heard Mallow say. "Am I your friend to tell you so?"

No, said Clovermead. *Yes. Please, Mallow.*

"You're dying," said Mallow softly. "How can one third of your heart provide for all your body? It's failing, and you will die."

I didn't give you all my heart, said Clovermead. *I'm still alive. You're lying!*

"You will die one way or the other," said Mallow sadly. "You can only choose the manner. Will you die alone or will you come with me? I would rather you came with me, Clovermead," he added wistfully. "I thought the only thing I wanted was to revenge myself against your mother, but now I find that I have come to desire your companionship as well. We could be such friends. We can dance in the halls of the dead together for eternity. I would like your company very much."

I want to live, said Clovermead, but the words barely made it through her lips. *Save me, Lady,* she whispered, and she looked up desperately around her at the Throne Room's walls as the light dimmed, where the last driblets of moonlight shone on gorgeous frescoes painted a hundred years before to illustrate the Cindertallows' rule over Chandlefort. On the north wall a Lady Cindertallow and her Yellowjackets struck down bandits who had just killed a farmer and looted his hut. On the east wall the peasant's wife and children stood in a courtroom and begged the same Lady Cindertallow for justice. On the south wall the Lady Cindertallow listened to two of her advisers, one a stern judge who pointed to the words written in a code of law, and the other a nun of Lady Moon who begged for mercy. On the west wall the Lady Cindertallow sent a sneering bandit to the gallows and a repentant bandit in chains to work with other prisoners building a road. In every picture, moonlight shone down on the Lady Cindertallow to hallow her and ennoble her. Her features reflected the goodness of the moonlight.

"She cannot hear you," said Mallow. "She could not hear me, either. For such as us, there is no salvation." He paused a moment. "Why do you care so much about dying? What are you losing? Life is heartache. Our friends abandon us and our lovers spurn us. Life is beasts tormenting one another. We are happier in the grave."

It isn't so, said Clovermead. *You're lying*. But she could barely mouth the words. Cold and despair battered her, Sorrel and Saraband were smiling at each other down all the future's long years, and there was so little light left.

Mallow sheathed his sword. Slowly he walked toward Clovermead. "You see with eyes blinded by the light. Let me show you the world through my eyes, and you will not love it any longer." He held out his sliced half hand to Clovermead.

Clovermead drew back from him, but ice ground through her, the darkness was thicker than ever, and she was terribly afraid. She turned back to human. She was very small in the darkness, and the only light she saw was Mallow's bony hand. Shadowy flesh thickened on his face and she saw a kindly smile. His hand stretched out, open and welcoming, and she could not withstand the chill in solitude any longer. She reached out to grip his hand in hers.

The piper blew shriller than ever and Ursus' growl filled the world. There was a whistle of knives in the air, the crunch of metal into flesh, and the wail of dying men. Then there was an eerie howl amidst silence and a carnival cry of desire fulfilled, and a black veil covered the world. It extinguished the candle-flame and left the wax to melt from an unseen cause. The world was a subtle mixture of different hues of gray, one hue bleeding into the next, darker and darker, until the edges of objects blurred into black flame. The world was on fire, and the fire gave no light. The table, the chairs, the candle changed size and shape, and in seconds Clovermead had begun to forget their true appearance. No matter how they changed, they were hideously out of proportion.

Clovermead looked up at the frescoes, and she gasped in horror. On the north wall the Lady Cindertallow and her Yellowjackets, brutal thugs on horseback, struck down a peasant and looted his hut. On the east wall Yellowjackets dragged the peasant's wife and children into a courtroom while the Lady Cindertallow avariciously eyed the family's little purse of gold. On the south wall the Lady Cindertallow complacently looked on as a judge rewrote the words written in a code of law and a nun pointed to an empty sky while she slyly purloined the last coins from the wife's purse. On the west wall the Lady Cindertallow sent the wife to the gallows and her children in chains to work with other prisoners to build the foundations of the Castle of Chandlefort. In every picture gray flames haloed the Lady Cindertallow with an unhallowed, terrible light.

"You see?" Mallow laughed in disappointment and despair. "There's nothing to love in her when you see her aright. She deserves nothing but hatred."

"It's not so," said Clovermead desperately. "It's not how she looks in the light."

"Light deceives you," said Mallow. "It offers false hopes. Only the dead see the world truly, in darkness." The room swayed toward Clovermead, its myriad inconstant grays clear in her sight, and she could not answer the dead man. "Come with me," said Mallow. His hand tightened on hers. "See the world of the living as it truly is. Disillusion yourself. You will see how preferable are the halls of the dead." He pulled her to the door and the corridors leading toward Lady Cindertallow's rooms. Somewhere the cold pipe played on and on.

They walked on through a ghastly parody of the Castle. All was ill-fashioned, all was befouled, all was grayness besieged by darkness and flame. Gray corridors churned before Clovermead like quicksand; repulsive always, but in all else mutable. The sturdy walls looked as if they had been thrown together by ancient savages and left for centuries to rot. The finely crafted tables seemed besmeared with filth. After a while Clovermead noticed that the tables and chairs still left shadows, but no torch or candle cast them. Every shadow fell away from Clovermead herself and shifted direction as she walked. The gray light came from no outside source, but from herself. This world of shapeless, shifting shadows was all that she could see by her own light.

"How can you look at this?" asked Clovermead in a whisper. "How can you bear it? I'd shut my eyes."

"The halls of the dead await me," said Mallow. "They were built in darkness, and they look no different in darkness or in light. I can endure this vileness for a while."

"What do they look like?" asked Clovermead. She looked around her in horror. "Are they better than this?"

"They have walls plain as a pine coffin," said Mallow. "There are no windows and no furniture, nor trinkets made by men. There are no mirrors to see ourselves. The piper plays for us through eternity. That is all."

"Will we forget how our hearts ached?" asked Clovermead.

"Not if we go there alone," said Mallow. "We must go together to console each other." His hand clutched tighter to Clovermead's. "I would like to forget with you."

And I with you, Clovermead almost said, but then they had come to Lady Cindertallow's apartments, and Clovermead suddenly balked. "I don't want to see her like this," she whispered. "Let go of me."

"Ah, no, Clovermead," said Mallow. His hatred blazed in him once more. "You will see your mother with my eyes, and you will know why I have wanted my revenge. You will understand why she deserves death." Now Clovermead struggled to escape his grip, but Mallow's hand was a vise on hers. Her hand turned into a paw, she flailed against him, but she could not escape.

Mallow laughed at her futile efforts, then raised his boot and kicked at her mother's door. Once, twice, thrice, he kicked, and the door splintered into a thousand shards. Dragging Clovermead behind him, Mallow marched into Lady Cindertallow's apartments.

Lady Cindertallow turned from the window as the door came crashing down, and Clovermead wept as she saw her mother. Her mother was skeletally thin, with yellow skin and bulging eyes. She leaned upon a cane almost as thick as her poisoned arm. Her bandaged arm still bled, and her hair had dried to the color of straw. But the changes in her mother were not as terrible as what was familiar. Her face was lined with the long use of power, with selfishness and cruelty. Her hand was a talon clutched tight ahold of whatever she desired. She was a portrait of will and rule, of fear and brutality. The dark world had not changed her so very much. Clovermead had seen much the same in her by ordinary light.

"No!" cried Clovermead, and she tore herself loose from Mallow. Now his hand was slack on hers and he willingly let her go. The pipe abruptly fell quiet, and the portrait of tyranny that her mother had become flickered away. All that was left was a dying woman—proud, too much like the nightmare Mallow saw, but better in the light. Clovermead ran to her side and embraced her, though she could scarcely feel her. She clung to her for warmth as the ice closed in on her heart.

"You're alive, Clovermead," said Lady Cindertallow as she clutched her daughter tight to her. "I was so afraid the bear-priests had killed you on the Heath. Praise Our Lady, you're alive."

"Not for long, Melisande," said Mallow. His half hand extended toward Clovermead. "Join me," he said. "Now you know what your mother is like. Now you know what the world is like. My halls are a better place." He paused a moment. "Step outside into the corridor," he said gently. "You don't need to look. I'll join you when I'm done with my revenge. We'll go and we'll never look back."

"I'm so afraid, Mother," said Clovermead. Lady Cindertallow's arms were folded around her, but she couldn't feel them. Clovermead's teeth were chattering, but she couldn't hear them. She looked up and all she saw with her failing eyes was the gray outline of her mother's head. "I'm sorry. I tried so hard to save you, but it didn't work."

Lady Cindertallow felt her daughter's cheeks and exclaimed in terror. "How did you get so cold?"

"I had to save Saraband from the bear-priest, and I gave Mallow one third of my heart. I had to get the flask of water to cure you, and I had to give him another third. But then he would have killed Saraband, I had to give her the flask of water, and I'm dying anyway." Clovermead tried to laugh, but her throat rattled. "Forgive me, Mother. I wanted the water for you, but I couldn't let her die."

"I forgive you," Lady Cindertallow whispered. She squeezed Clovermead even tighter in her arms, and Clovermead's heart felt warmer for a moment.

"Let her go, Melisande," said Mallow. "She'll have company if she comes with me. Otherwise she'll die alone." Lady Cindertallow moaned and Mallow laughed.

"Don't worry, Melisande. You'll die before she does. You shan't see her dead." His hand was still extended. "Come away with me, Clovermead."

Clovermead whimpered. There was so very little of her left, and she was terribly frightened of dying alone. Darkness and cold surrounded her, and Mallow's hand was friendly. She knew that. She ached and she wanted an end to her suffering.

Her mother's arms were hot and tight around her. Her heart could not freeze while Lady Cindertallow embraced her. The dust could not dry up her blood entirely. Her skin prickled where her mother's flesh encircled hers.

She looked up and she could see light again. It wasn't the moon—she couldn't see that far. It was moonlight reflected off her mother's face—and not just moonlight. In the last flare of light she saw love, she saw old happiness, and somewhere she saw a glimmer of Ambrosius as he looked with blazing love at Melisande. The old fires still glowed in her mother, they magnified the distant moonlight, and lit by the embers of love she still was beautiful. Clovermead drank in the sight of her mother, clung to her heat and to the distant moon in her, and the ice receded. She wasn't afraid anymore. She wasn't alone.

"Keep on holding me, Mother," she said. "Don't you let go of me, and I won't stop fighting." She laughed, a painful wheeze through her frozen ribs. "Fighting's what I'm good at, you know. I wish I were soft and gentle like Saraband, but I'm not. I just fight. I'll fight for you. Don't let go."

"I won't," said Lady Cindertallow. She clung ever tighter to her daughter as Clovermead turned back into a bear. Clovermead fell to the ground and her mother clung to her neck, light as a thistledown. Clovermead faced Mallow with her mother on her back. Her bear's vision was worse than her human vision, and she could not see him at all in the darkness. She called on the berserker in her, she called on the bear, she called on the Cindertallow. She called on all the fury she had in her, all the unreasoning will to live and never stop fighting, and refused to let her legs buckle. It was a greater struggle than her bout with Sorrel, than her battle with any bear-priest, than her duels with Mallow. Death called on her to surrender, lulled at her sweetly with her pipe, but she would not give in.

I won't stop fighting, said Clovermead. *I won't leave my mother. I've seen the light in her and it's true. You go with your piper into the darkness. I won't go with you.*

Are you sure?

I'm sure.

As you wish, Clovermead, said Mallow. Clovermead heard his sword unsheath in the darkness. He walked slowly into sight. For a moment the shadow had whipped away from him and he was a skeleton with a sword. Then his flesh came back to him. Clovermead summoned up the strength to fight him again, but it was gone. All she could do was stand up. She waited for Mallow with her mother on her back.

She saw a red heart glowing in him.

Lady Cindertallow looked at the dead man with resentment and anger—but then her rage was overwhelmed by wonder as Mallow came close. "You are so young! You have sidestepped old age, Mallow."

Mallow looked at her with hungry eyes, still full of despairing love. "And you"—he looked at the crow's-feet radiating from her eyes, the ravaging lines of illness in her face, her strawlike hair—"you are still lovely. Ah, Melisande, you are the most beautiful woman I ever knew." He stood only an arm's length away, he reached out his hand over Clovermead's head, and his fingers brushed through Lady Cindertallow's hair. "How could you set me aside? I loved you so. I still love you so."

"I loved Ambrosius," said Lady Cindertallow. "I love him still." She was majestic in her courage. "You had no right to demand that I put my love aside." The remorseless words flew like daggers into Mallow, into Clovermead, the heart in Mallow flared in agony, and Clovermead nearly screamed with pain.

It was Clovermead's heart. She could feel it beating in Mallow, beating in her, felt her heart throb in two separate places, and she was looking out of Mallow's eyes as well as her own. She was a dead man who held a sword in bony fingers, and she was a bear who stood trembling on weary legs beneath her mother. She felt Mallow's hate and loneliness and pain surge through her, so strongly that she could barely keep from slipping away into the final darkness to escape it. She swayed and nearly fell.

Mallow trembled too. He lifted his sword toward Lady Cindertallow's neck. Clovermead tried to rear up, to bat his sword away, but her strength was gone. She fell onto her knees, and her mother slipped from her back. Now she stood by Clovermead with her arms still around her daughter's neck as Mallow's sword touched her jugular. She stood erect, proud and unwavering. Her hands were tight in Clovermead's golden fur. Her mother had suffered so much already, and Clovermead knew that she would plant herself in her endurance of her own suffering, stand like iron, and never bend herself to Mallow's pain.

The white bear turned to Clovermead. I hurt so, Clovermead, *Our Lady roared. Her tears soaked the earth, but the tree was dry still.* Help me.

I'm no better than he is, thought Clovermead. *I've been as stubborn and hateful as he is, and I could have let Saraband die if Our Lady hadn't been gracious enough to let me see the light in time. She didn't reject me, and I shouldn't reject Mallow. He deserves better from me.*

She roared with all her strength, *the white bear roared with sorrow, and a great wind shuddered through the forest and howled along the leaf-strewn floor.* Clovermead put all that was left of her heart into her howl. She howled pity for Mallow, she howled sorrow. She could not rid herself of hate and resentment, could not make herself as gentle as she wanted to be, but she imitated the white bear's roar as best she could and echoed it with everything she had in her. She tried to sound like Saraband and Sorrel, too. *They're gentler than I am,* she thought. *They're better at loving.* She howled Waxmelt's anxious care for all the servants of Chandlefort, roared Mallow's friendship for Ambrosius turned to ashes, growled widowed Meadowlark who had immured herself in unforgiving hatred and savaged her own daughter's soul. Above all, she roared all she knew of Mallow's agony to her mother and Mallow both. She gave her voice to the white bear. It was the only weapon she had left to use in her service.

When she was done, Mallow's sword had clattered to the floor and Lady Cindertallow's tears flowed down her cheeks.

"I'm sorry, Mallow," said Lady Cindertallow. "Oh, Lady, I'm sorry. I never told you that, did I? I never have apologized for anything I did to you. How could I have been so thoughtless? I shouldn't have led you on when I didn't love you. I shouldn't have cast you aside so brutally. Lady knows I never meant to hurt you so, but I did. It was cruel of me and I am so very sorry."

Mallow could not speak. He only howled. He put his hands over his face—then lifted up his head in anguish. "I cannot cry. I have no tears."

Lady Cindertallow let go of Clovermead and walked to Mallow. She kneeled by him and took her tears, and her wet hands rubbed them on Mallow's face. "These are for you." She was crying still. "Forgive me, Mallow," she said. "Please forgive me."

"I do," said Mallow. Lady Cindertallow's tears glistened on his face. "I have done you great wrong, Melisande. I ask for your forgiveness too."

"You have it, Mallow," said Lady Cindertallow, and Clovermead let the bear slip from her at last. She fell human to the ground, and she heard her mother shriek. All heat and light were gone from her, but she smiled, she knew she had done her best. The piper played her sweet welcome—

She gasped as heat flooded back into her. For a

moment the world was a red glow around her and she was on fire from her heart to her skin. All her blood pounded in her and the dust had vanished from her veins. She was wonderfully alive and tingling all over. She could see, and the world was full of moonlight and starlight, torchlight and color. She could feel, she could hurt, she could live, and it was the most glorious thing ever. *I didn't know how much I wanted my heart until I lost it,* she thought.

She tried to stir, but she was terribly weak and her mother held her in her arms. "Don't move yet," Lady Cindertallow said. Her face was more haggard than ever. "You—" She could not finish the sentence.

"You were on death's door," said Mallow. He was human again, a tall, thin man with curly red hair and pale skin. "I gave you back your heart just in time, Clo—Demoiselle."

"Clovermead is all right," she whispered. She could not speak any louder. "Thank you."

"Clovermead," said Mallow. "You are too kind." He turned to Lady Cindertallow. "Don't worry, Melisande. The dead I have summoned up will return to dust, and the venom in you will vanish when I go. You will be well again, with only a scar to show I wounded you."

"Where are you going, Mallow?" asked Lady Cindertallow.

"To the halls of the dead. They are my proper resting place." Mallow smiled lopsidedly. "I will ask Our Lady for a chance to see Ambrosius. If I do, I will tell him you are as beautiful as ever. And that you love him still."

"Thank you," said Lady Cindertallow. She reached

out her hand and beckoned Mallow. He knelt by her side, by Clovermead, and Melisande gently stroked his cheek. "Our Lady's blessings on your journey, Mallow."

"I will listen for her voice," said Mallow. He smiled at Clovermead. "It should be easy, now that I know what it sounds like." He stood up and stepped away from them. In the center of the room he bowed to Clovermead. "I will miss your kind heart, Clovermead." He turned to Lady Cindertallow. "You will always have my love."

"Lord Ursus!" he cried out. "I renounce Your Lordship! Take back this second life you have given me and never call on me again. I will not listen to you. I swear it in Our Lady's name." Mallow tore the leather cord with the bear-tooth from his neck and let it fall to the floor between his feet.

There was a howling of wind. It blew, stronger and stronger. A raging growl, hot and fetid, blew from the south. Then another growl, sorrowing and welcoming, sounded from all directions, and the first growl faded into silence. Dust whipped up around Mallow Kite. He gazed at Lady Cindertallow as the wind grew louder and tears, his own tears, fell from his cheeks. Outside Chandlefort came a sudden, grateful roar, silent no more, from a hundred dead bears as they fell apart, fell to dust. The dust grew thick and obscured Mallow from view. Then the wind died away utterly. The dust fell to the ground—and there was nothing there.

In the sudden silence Clovermead could hear ragged, jubilant shouts coming from the bedroom window. "What is that, Mother?" she whispered. She was a little stronger now, but she still couldn't move.

Lady Cindertallow put her comfortably to the floor and stood up. There was bloom in her cheeks again and color in her hair. The ugly yellow had vanished from her wounds. She went to the window, looked out, and smiled.

"The little man's servants and my Yellowjackets have held the gates against the bear-priests. The townsmen are cheering their victory."

"I'm glad," whispered Clovermead. Then she shivered with sudden cold and she was crying again. "Please hold me, Mother," she said.

Lady Cindertallow ran to her side and gently picked her daughter up. Clovermead could not stop shaking, and her mother held her tight, kissed her, and sang her lullabies. Her voice was hoarse and out of tune, but still she sang until late in the night. And only when the moon had set did Clovermead finally fall asleep, smiling in her mother's arms.

Chapter Eighteen

THE SPRUNG TRAP

THREE DAYS LATER THE FIRST REFUGEES FROM Queensmart came along the south road. They were the lucky ones, the cavalrymen who had cut their way through the armies of bear-priests as they broke through the Queensmart walls. They were wounded, they were exhausted, they were very few.

"There'll be more of us," said the cavalry commander who had brought away with him the flag of the last legion of Queensmart. He swayed with weariness as he stood in the Throne Room. "The foot soldiers should be along in a few days. The farmers with any brains will be on the move soon enough. They know they'll be safe from Ursus in Chandlefort for a while yet. If you'll let us take refuge here." He looked up at the throne, and his eyes were suddenly filled with doubt. Lady Cindertallow was still very thin, she held a cane in her hand, and her sword arm remained half-withered. The day was baking hot, but Clovermead sat next to her mother in a stuffed chair, with a goose-feather blanket wrapped around her and a hot compress on her head. "Or am I assuming too much? Are you still fighting against Lord Ursus, Milady?"

Lady Cindertallow laughed. "We must look worse than I imagined, Clovermead."

"We aren't as badly off as we look," Clovermead said to the soldier. Her teeth chattered and she pulled the blanket more tightly around her. It was taking a long time for her body to shake off the cold of the grave. "Well, maybe I am, but I'm getting better. We won't stop fighting."

Not ever, she swore silently. *Do you hear me, Ursus? You can destroy me, but I won't give in to you.*

"I'm glad to hear that," the cavalryman said to Clovermead with grave gratitude. Then he turned hesitantly to her mother. "Does the Demoiselle speak for you, Milady?"

"Always." Lady Cindertallow smiled at Clovermead and then at the cavalryman. "You are all welcome in Chandlefort. We have empty lands for your farmers and places in our army for your soldiers. We'll be in the fight against Lord Ursus until the end."

"Thank you, Milady," said the cavalryman. He cleared his throat, stood up, and held up the flag of the legion. "Would you be willing to fly this from one of your towers? It'll be a sign to the others that there's a place here for them."

"Put it above the south gate," said Lady Cindertallow.

And when the cavalryman had left the Throne Room, Lady Cindertallow sagged with relief. "Ursus will be busy down in the Thirty Towns for at least a year mopping up the garrisons of Queensmart. Hard luck for the Queensmarters, I suppose, but at least that gives us time to rebuild the gates."

"I love you, Mother," said Clovermead, "but sometimes you are awfully cold-blooded."

"I need to be to keep Chandlefort alive." She glanced at Clovermead. "So will you, when you become Lady Cindertallow."

"I'd like to find some other way."

Her mother grimaced. "I wish you success, Daughter. But I don't think you'll find it." Then she strode away to give directions to the Chancellor to find rooms for the exiles from Queensmart and to the Commander of the Yellowjackets to give them new weapons from the Armory.

The next morning Clovermead and her mother were waiting for breakfast in Lady Cindertallow's rooms when Waxmelt came through the door with a tray of orange juice, two omelets, and fresh baked rolls and placed it with a flourish on the table. He had changed out of his soldier's garb and back into his lordly clothing—but he wore an apron over his jacket and trousers.

"Your breakfast, Milady," he said. "Your breakfast, Clo."

Lady Cindertallow looked at him bemusedly. "Am I that short of cooks?"

"I have sent some to the hospice to help feed the wounded," said Waxmelt. "But I did ask for the privilege of cooking for you. You've employed me in ways I'm not at all suited for. I thought you should see what I'm best at."

"He's a really good cook, Mother," said Clovermead. She grabbed her plate and a fork from the tray and took a bite. "A tomato omelet! With, um, chives and something sweet thrown in. Right, Father?"

"A spoonful of honey," said Waxmelt. He took Lady Cindertallow's plate and put it in front of her. "Will you try it, Milady?"

Lady Cindertallow hesitated, looked at Waxmelt warily, and took a forkful of the omelet. She chewed it thoughtfully, then nodded approvingly. "Very good. I would ask you to cook for us more often if it were not below your station."

"Maybe he could have breakfast with us sometimes," said Clovermead, very casually. "He could come in with three omelets. Can a lord cook for pleasure?"

"It has been known." Lady Cindertallow looked at Waxmelt, sighed, and gestured to a third chair at the table. "Sit down, Lord Wickward. Shall I offer you half of this rather fine omelet?"

"I've already eaten." Waxmelt sat down gingerly. "If it's Milady's pleasure, I'd be glad to join the two of you for breakfast from time to time."

"I *will* need to consult with my new General," said Lady Cindertallow. "Why not make it a friendly matter?" She took a sip of orange juice, then another forkful of omelet. She smiled. "This really is quite good."

"I'm glad you like it, Milady." Waxmelt smiled in turn as he watched her eat. "I fear I'll make far more errors as a general than as a cook. You'll know I need your forgiveness when I bring you in a particularly fine meal."

"I'll try to be understanding." Lady Cindertallow looked out the window at the shattered gate of Chandlefort, which masons and blacksmiths were already struggling to rebuild. Her eyes went along the walls. There were some Yellowjackets left but not many. A motley assortment of servants, townsmen, and farmers were most of her army now. They had a somewhat more military bearing than they had had a few weeks ago, but they still had something of the air of a rabble in arms. "You have a victory to your credit, General—you and your servants have kept Chandlefort free from the bear-priests. I trust you'll do well enough."

"We held up against a few hundred cavalrymen," said Waxmelt. "I don't know how we'll manage when Lord Ursus' infantry comes north. We aren't real soldiers."

"You will be," said Clovermead. "And if anyone isn't shaping up, I'll come down and turn into a bear and growl at them. There won't be any slackers after that! I'll make a great drill sergeant."

"You see, Lord Wickward? You have no choice." Lady Cindertallow smiled at Waxmelt—then snapped her fingers. "I've been meaning to tell you: I had a talk with the Seneschal and the Chancellor. There'll be a pension for the wounded servants and for the widows and children of the ones who died. They even think we can find some more money for the servants' wages."

"And their hours?" asked Waxmelt.

Lady Cindertallow grimaced. "We're shorthanded as it is. That can't be fixed until the war is over." She laughed as she saw Waxmelt begin to protest. "Go talk with the Seneschal and the Chancellor! They can show you Chandlefort's accounts. If the three of you can find more blood to squeeze from my revenues, come back and talk to me. Go talk with them anyway. You'll need to haggle about the servants' wages. A lordly job indeed!" She shook her head in amusement, exasperation, and repulsion.

"It will be my pleasure, Milady," said Waxmelt. "I—we are grateful, Milady."

"I am too, Mother," said Clovermead. She put her hand in her mother's and squeezed it. "It's good of you."

"It's necessary," said Lady Cindertallow brusquely. Then she unbent a little. "I know what I owe your servants, Lord Wickward. When I am a little better"—she touched her healing arm—"I will go to my new soldiers and tell them that they have more than earned my gratitude and my respect."

"They'll be glad to know it," said Waxmelt. Then the conversation shifted to other matters, and Clovermead and Lady Cindertallow settled down to enjoy their breakfast properly. At the end of it Lady Cindertallow arranged that Waxmelt would breakfast with them at least twice a week.

Later that day Clovermead went walking through the Castle. She hadn't recovered all her strength yet, but she could walk as far as the parapets of the courtyards. She went out and sat on a bench in the sun. Happily she let the rays soak into her. *I want to feel the sunlight in my bones,* she thought. *I never want to feel cold again.*

Sorrel came and sat down by her side. "Hello, Clovermead," he said. "I am glad to see that you have come out of your sickbed at last."

"I thought I'd be up and bouncing around in no time, but I'm not healing as fast as I used to. I'm getting old."

"Then I am ancient." Sorrel smiled wryly. "Certainly

I must be getting white hairs. I think I spent a solid hour with the teeth of dead bears snapping at Brown Barley's heels, before they faded into dust. I hope there will be no more of the walking dead in our immediate future!"

"I don't think there will be," said Clovermead. Then she steeled herself to ask the inevitable question. "How's Saraband? I heard she was all right, but I haven't seen her since I left her in the chapel."

"She will be in good health soon," said Sorrel. "She is still recovering from a very sore neck in the hospice in the town. She said she would like to come see you when she is well."

"I'd be glad to see her," said Clovermead. *Would I really?* she asked herself, surprised. She thought of her cousin—thought of her kissing Sorrel. She felt a twinge of jealousy still. *But I can live with that,* she told herself firmly. *It doesn't matter that much. I'd like to be friends with her anyway.* "Please tell her to come on by whenever she likes."

"I think you should send her that message yourself," said Sorrel. His face had become very blank. "Lady Saraband and I are not on speaking terms right now."

"What? Why?"

"Lady Saraband finds that now that she has seen me at my business, she does not care for my profession as a soldier. She does not wish to conduct a romance with such as me." Sorrel's voice was growing more bitter. "I found this an unreasonable attitude on her part. We exchanged hard words on the matter before we parted, and we agreed we would not talk to each other again."

A dozen emotions jumbled all through Clovermead.

She was sorry for Sorrel, sorry for Saraband, but she couldn't help feeling happy, too. *It isn't at all nice of me,* she said to herself uncomfortably, *but there's some hope for me again. Sometime.* She thought of her scar and her missing tooth. *But I don't faint at the thought of Sorrel going into battle. It doesn't make me happy to think of him dying, but I wouldn't want him any different from the way he is. We're both fighters.* She smiled to herself. *Maybe he'll realize that too, someday.*

"I hope you don't stay too mad at Saraband," she said aloud. "I'd like to be friends with her, and I want the two of you at least to be civil to each other."

"Perhaps later," said Sorrel. "Not now." He gazed into the middle distance, then turned to Clovermead and shook his head. "You wish to be Lady Saraband's friend! How very strange. But can your friendship last? You will start dancing with her again, and you will be resentful of her in no time."

"Then I'd better learn to dance properly before I start her class again." Clovermead hesitated, then asked, "I don't suppose you'd be willing to dance with me? I know I crushed your toes last spring, but I promise I won't this time. I don't want Saraband and me to have any reason to get mad at each other. Would you? Please?"

Sorrel laughed. "It will be at least as much fun as exploring through cellars with you." He extended his hand to Clovermead. "Shall we shake on it? I will be your instructor and I will far outshine Lady Saraband in that skill! When you dance in her class, you will be the most fleet-footed young lady this side of the Harrow Moors."

"Shake and shooken," said Clovermead solemnly, and she squeezed his hand. *And the pleasure will be all mine,* she said to herself with satisfaction. *I will like dancing with you, Sorrel. And who knows? Maybe someday you'll start to think you like dancing with me.*

A few days more passed, and by then Clovermead was almost fully healed. Lady Cindertallow's spies confirmed that Lord Ursus' army was inside Queensmart, and the farmers left Chandlefort for their fields again. They would be safe at least until the next spring. Soon the sound of hammering filled Chandlefort as the farmers began to put up new barns and houses to replace the ones the bear-priests had burned.

When the full moon rose in the sky once more, Clovermead went out into the fields. She took broken Firefly and walked along a road at night. She didn't exactly think her father's sword would protect her from any danger, but it was still comforting to have it with her.

She smelled the sharp scent of bear-musk as she walked beneath an apple tree. She smiled and turned from the road. In a few minutes she came to a canal. Brookwade was swimming in it.

Hello. Clovermead sat down by the side of the canal. *How are you doing?*

I killed two bear-priests, said Brookwade happily. *I'm still free of Lord Ursus. Your farmers haven't all come back to their barns yet, and I've been gorging myself on the cattle feed they left in the troughs. All in all, Our Lady smiles on me.*

Clovermead laughed. *And the other bears?*

Those who lived? Gone to their old haunts. Brookwade grew more sober. *Many of us died attacking the bear-priests.*

It was worth it, but most have had their fill of bloodshed for a long time. And they are afraid Lord Ursus will come looking for revenge. He rumbled puzzledly. *I confess I find it strange that he has not sent his blood-net back into us. Your sword has more power than I thought.*

I'm surprised too, said Clovermead. She brought it out from the scabbard. *It's broken. I went looking for the tip outside the walls, but I couldn't find it anywhere. I don't think I'll be able to free any more bears.*

I'm glad you freed as many as you did, said Brookwade. He grinned. *I'm glad you freed me!* He paused a moment. *I will be going from Chandlefort soon. It's no place for an honest bear. But you can call on me if you need me. We bears have trouble thinking of wars and battles, but I know there's more fighting needed against Lord Ursus. Come to the Reliquaries, come back to Kite Hall. I'll be there when you need me.*

Thank you, said Clovermead. Brookwade came over to her and she hugged him.

Maybe we can have another bout? said Brookwade wistfully. *You didn't beat me fairly the last time. Best two out of three, Haybrawler?*

I beat you fair and square! said Clovermead, laughing. *I'm not quite up to strength yet, but I'll be glad to fight again the next time I see you.* She grinned. *If I bring friends, don't call them snacks!*

I won't, said Brookwade. He rubbed Clovermead's nose with his. *It's late and I should get to sleep. I think I'll be gone tomorrow. Farewell, Clovermead.*

Good-bye, said Clovermead. *Lady keep you.* Then Brookwade was jumping down the canal, splashing Clovermead as he went, and trotting out of sight.

Clovermead sat down by the edge of the canal and took off her shoes and socks. She lowered her feet into the cool water and let it trickle through her toes. It was a relief to know she was warmer inside than the water on her skin. She sighed happily and sleepily. It was a nice, warm summer night. A cool breeze trickling through the air brought a hint of autumn on the way, but it would be warm for a long time to come.

Clovermead glanced at the sword lying by her side, and she shook her head in puzzlement. "Where does that light in you come from, Firefly? I never heard that Ambrosius was any sort of magician. Are those medallions he carved what make you so powerful? Or is it something else?"

"Something else," she heard. A low, laughing voice was behind her, and a friendly hand touched her shoulder. In the moonlit water of the canal Clovermead saw an old woman's reflection. Clovermead looked up. Now the woman was young—and now she was middle-aged. Her appearance shimmered as much when Clovermead looked directly at her as it did in the water. Clovermead scrambled to kneel before her, but the woman laughed. "Don't bother yourself! Here, I'll join you." She sat down by Clovermead's side. She was barefoot too, and she let her feet fall comfortably into the canal and hang in the water by Clovermead's. "Isn't it a lovely night? I shouldn't confess to liking one season more than another, but I am fond of summer evenings. The first time I came walking through Linstock, fireflies glowed everywhere in the dusk. The way they lit up the darkness was lovely! I'm happy to see that you've named your sword Firefly. I was afraid you'd think it should be named Diamondflame or Bearbiter or something like that. Firefly is much nicer."

"I'm glad you like it, Lady," said Clovermead. She slid it from her scabbard and looked sadly at its broken tip. "I'm afraid it won't be much good anymore."

"Nonsense! This sort of thing is easily mended." Clovermead gasped, because the woman had the missing fragment of Firefly in her hand. The woman smiled. "I went to comfort the bears and men as they lay dying, and I saw this. I thought you'd want it. May I?" She reached out a hand, and Clovermead nodded. The woman fit the fragment into the broken blade, there was a shimmer of light, and then the blade was whole. Clovermead cried out in wonder and touched its smooth surface. The faintest crack bore witness that the two parts had ever been separated. "It will strike well," said the woman. "The line is so you remember it was broken. Wounds can heal, but they shouldn't be forgotten."

"Thank you," said Clovermead. She bowed her head to the woman. She hesitated a moment. "Will the bears stay free?"

"Yes," said the woman. The affirmation rang through the night air and echoed sweetly into the distance.

"I'm glad," said Clovermead. She paused a moment. "How did they get to be free, Lady?"

"It isn't a magic sword," said the woman, and Clovermead couldn't help but feel disappointed. The woman laughed. "It's your father's sword and a good remembrance of him, but it has no special powers. The light in the sword came from you."

"I've never given off sparks before," said Clovermead. "Why did the light come then?"

"Your powers are greatest in my service," said the woman.

"Where do they come from, Lady?" asked Clovermead. "I still don't know."

"From Ambrosius," said the woman, and Clovermead's heart leaped with joy. "Let me show you," said the woman. She pointed across the canal. "Look." A white bear came into view. She strolled along the edge of the canal, sniffing for fish.

"Boulderbash!" Clovermead cried, as she recognized Lord Ursus' enormous enslaved mother. "What are you doing here?"

"She can't hear you," said the woman softly. "This happened many years ago." And Clovermead realized that the land across the canal had changed. It was still summer, but there were pine trees everywhere, and Boulderbash was by the side of a lake, not a canal. Boulderbash herself was younger than she had been when Clovermead last saw her. Clovermead could see Lord Ursus' blood-net fixed in her mind, but it was slack. This summer he had let his mother wander free.

Boulderbash speared a trout with her paws, gulped it down, then scooped up a dozen minnows. The edge of her hunger dulled and she went in search of dessert. She bounded into the underbrush—and howled as something bit into her front paw. She reared up, and a steel trap came up from the concealing leaves, biting deep into her fur and flesh. *I hurt!* she cried in surprise and shock and anger. She tried to shake off the trap, but it was thick and strong. She pulled at it with all her strength and a length of chain came loose from the dirt, but she could not rid herself of the metal jaws. She bashed it against a tree, deeply scarring the trunk with her thrashings, but the iron didn't even bend. *I'll have to chew my paw off,* she roared angrily, fearfully. *Lady's curse on those two-legs who laid this trap.*

There was an indrawn breath above Boulderbash. She looked up and she saw a small boy crouched high on a tree branch. He looked down at her with fascination but no fear. He was towheaded, with twinkling blue eyes and a calm expression that overlaid a look of mischief on his face. He was terribly familiar, and it came to Clovermead that she was looking at her own father as a boy. It was Ambrosius Beechsplitter, half herself, up in the tree. He was no older than she was now.

Ambrosius said something, but all Boulderbash understood was the friendly tone of his voice. He gestured to her, but it didn't mean anything either. Boulderbash fell back from the tree, and she roared her sorrow and her pain again. Blood trickled from where the points of the trap dug into her paw.

Very cautiously Ambrosius crawled out of the tree. He said more words to Boulderbash, but they were still so much gibberish. He started to walk toward her. *I should bite him,* thought Boulderbash. *Then they'll know how much their trap hurt me.* But she was curious, too. *Most big humans aren't bold enough to come near me. How daring this small one is!* She looked at him curiously, but she didn't see any of the human knives on him. She sniffed, but there was no bad odor to him. She let him come closer.

He stayed away from her jaws, spoke reassuringly to her again, then bent down by the trap. *What's he doing?* Boulderbash cried out—and then she could feel the teeth coming loose from her leg. She roared with delight as she realized that he was freeing her. He trembled before her roar, but kept pulling open the jaws. It was an agonizingly long and wonderfully short time until he had pulled the trap enough apart for Boulderbash to withdraw her paw. Then he let it close with a snap that almost snipped his fingers away. He fell to the earth, breathing hard, and Boulderbash could tell he had tired himself out to free her.

How marvelous of you! growled Boulderbash. *How kind of you. I never knew a human to do such a thing.* Then, more sadly, she thought of Lord Ursus, and she told herself, *My own son doesn't care if I live or die.* She shook her paw, then padded over to Ambrosius and looked him in the face. Solemnly she licked his cheeks. His eyes went wide, but he stayed very still. *So brave!* Boulderbash marveled. *Lady, I wish you would reward him. I can't thank him properly for what he's done.*

What would you give him? The voice was terribly loud, marvelously beautiful, and the world shimmered in light.

Give him my tongue, said Boulderbash to Our Lady. *Give him my strength and my endurance. Give him*—she thought of Ursus when he had been a little cub and of everything she had tried to teach him. She thought of how much he had ignored and how much he had forgotten. She loved her child so much, she could see him bounding playfully through the forests, tiny and laughing.

She saw him grown, with blood on his jaws, and she knew he had done such evil. *Give him what my own cub has rejected, Lady,* she said, with a sorrowful roar. *Make him what a bear should be.*

He will be a proper bear, said Our Lady, and it was a roaring in the wood. *He and his children, and their children, for so long as they wish to keep your gift. And they will put to rights what your son has twisted.* The world was full of flaring light—and then the world was as it had been.

Thank you, little one, said Boulderbash, and Ambrosius' eyes went wide.

You're welcome, he thought, and then, *Did you speak to me?*

I did, said Boulderbash. She licked his cheeks again. *You've been kind to me. Don't ever stop, little one.* She thought of Ursus again and how the kindness had left him as he grew. She wanted to cry, but she blinked back her tears. *I'm grateful to you.* Then she turned from him.

Wait, she heard Ambrosius cry as she went into the woods. *Don't go away. Tell me how I can hear you speak!* But Boulderbash could not think of anything but Ursus, and she wanted to weep in privacy. She roared her misery to the world as she ran on her wounded paw.

The scene vanished, and there was only the summer evening in Chandlefort. Clovermead's mind whirled. "That's why I can turn into a bear? And speak to them and free them? It's a gift from you, Lady?" She smiled with wonder and joy. "I knew the power didn't come from Lord Ursus, but I'm so glad to know it comes from you and Father, to know the reason why I have it."

The woman looked soberly at Clovermead. "It is a

gift and a charge. You have it because Ambrosius freed one bear. You have it so that you may free all bears from their captivity to Ursus." She paused a moment and said softly, "It's a great burden, Clovermead. You may renounce it if ever you find it too heavy."

Clovermead thought about the vivid joy of turning into a bear. She thought of the sharp need of all the enslaved thousands of bears whom Lord Ursus held captive in the Lands of Lady Moon. The joy and the responsibility were both overwhelming.

"Did Ambrosius ever turn into a bear?" she asked.

The woman nodded. "Sometimes, before he came to Chandlefort. After that he stayed in human form so as not to frighten people. Not even your mother knew what he could do."

"I guess that makes sense. I sure have alarmed people by being a bear! Though it must have been awfully lonely, if he couldn't even talk about it with Mother." She thought a bit longer. "Can I just free all the bears now if I put my mind to it?"

The woman laughed. "You're still growing and learning, Clovermead. You couldn't shape-shift, either, until you were old enough to use that power properly. You'll have strength enough in good time."

"And the need for it too, I'll bet."

The woman nodded. "Soon enough everyone who stands against Ursus will have to fight with all their strength."

"Then I shan't give up your gift just yet." Clovermead shook her head. "Oh, Lady, I'm awfully scared."

"I'm always here for you, Clovermead," said the

woman. She leaned close to Clovermead and kissed her on the cheek. "Now be of good cheer! There's time yet before the final battle. Enjoy yourself for now." Suddenly smiling, she kicked a spray of water from the canal to spatter at Clovermead. Clovermead giggled, leaned down to scoop a handful of water back at the woman—

Her eyes flew open as her hands scooped at air. She had fallen asleep with her feet in the canal, but now she woke and there was no one by her side. There was only laughter in the air and the shimmer of moonlight.

"I must have dreamed it all," Clovermead said to herself. She sighed. "Was that a true dream, Lady? Did Ambrosius really free Boulderbash that way?"

Moonlight glinted on her father's sword beside her. Clovermead looked at it—and gasped. The blade was whole again. She ran a trembling finger along the barely perceptible scar in its metal.

"Thank you, Lady!" Clovermead cried out joyfully to the darkness. "And don't you worry. I'll be brave for you, no matter what happens." Then she let herself relax as the water of the canal wrinkled the flesh on her toes. The stars twinkled above, and the fireflies twinkled in the fields below.

Her toes were definitely cold. She drew her feet out of the water and let them dry a moment on the grass. "Brr! Time to get home and under covers, Clovermead." She picked up her shoes and sword and started to walk. "Home," she said to herself reflectively as she ambled along the canal. "I guess it is by now."

And whistling cheerfully, she made her way toward Chandlefort.